a s p e n

m a r o o n e y

Also by Levi S. Peterson

Canyons of Grace

Greening Wheat:
Fifteen Mormon Short Stories (ed.)

The Backslider

Night Soil: New Stories

aspen marooney

LEVI S. PETERSON

SIGNATURE BOOKS • SALT LAKE CITY

1 9 9 5

To Althea, Karrin, Mark, and Lars

COVER DESIGN BY RON STUCKI.

∞ *Aspen Marooney* was printed on acid-free paper
and was composed, printed and bound in the United States.

© 1995 Signature Books, Inc.
Signature Books is a registered trademark of Signature Books, Inc.

99   98   97   96   95   6   5   4   3   2   1

Library of Congress Cataloging-in-Publication Data
Peterson, Levi S.
Aspen Mulrooney : a novel / Levi S. Peterson.
p.   cm.
ISBN 1-56085-078-7 (pbk.)
1. Class reunions—Utah—Fiction. 2. Women—Utah—Fiction.
I. Title.
PS356.E7694A87   1995
813'.54—dc20   95-39846
                                                    CIP

Contents

1. The Greenshow

It was July, and mirages shimmered in the flats south of the freeway. Sometimes palm trees or buildings floated on the surface of these illusory lakes. At the wheel of their Buick, Durfey took the mirages as likely figures for the future, which never arrives but recedes with each new accession of the present.

They stopped for gas in Baker, a dusty little California desert town. Inside a mini-market, Durfey bought a red apple and washed it in the rest room. Back on the road, he offered Elaine a bite. She ate one side. When she returned it, he finished the other side and slipped the core under the bucket seat.

"I hate to think what else is under that seat," Elaine said.

"It'll feed the vermin," Durfey said. "Nothing goes to waste in the desert."

Across the Nevada border she said, without apparent provocation, "Nobody but you would spend his honeymoon at his sister's house."

"A mistake," he admitted.

"All I remember is we had a picnic at the Green River, which was brown and muddy."

He said, "People expect too much from honeymoons. For example, they expect the Green River to be green."

He mulled over the elusive reference to that old fiasco, their honeymoon, and concluded that she had Aspen Marooney on her mind. From a long time back, their honeymoon had served as a handy symbol for her dissatisfaction with their marriage, the substance of which lay with a person whom Durfey hadn't seen since high school. He hadn't attended earlier reunions precisely because Aspen Marooney might have been expected to be there.

To his astonishment, Elaine had said a few days after the announcement of the forty-year reunion had arrived, "It would be a shame for you not to see your old friends. None of us have many years left." She typed a letter in Durfey's name, enclosed a recent photo, and wrote a check to cover expenses.

In the middle of Las Vegas, where the freeway passed the gaudy Excalibur casino, Elaine said, "The best part of our honeymoon was when we called it off and went home to our little basement apartment."

"Yes," Durfey agreed, "that was the best part."

It was possible she was feeling guilty for having fallen back momentarily into her old jealousy. He couldn't be sure. During the early years, she would have slid across the bench seat of their car and snuggled close. Now belts and bucket seats kept them apart.

Elaine had found no reason to take exception to Aspen Marooney during the first ten or fifteen years of their marriage, Durfey having had the good sense not to talk about her. But about the time he realized he was approaching middle age, he began to reminisce more and more about his adolescence. He had developed an unthinking confidence in Elaine by then. It seemed he could lay his past to rest if she knew about it. It didn't occur to him that she might be threatened by it.

One Saturday morning while they were finishing breakfast and their sons Neal and Jimmy were in the family room watching cartoons, Durfey told Elaine that Aspen Marooney had helped him use a bed pan in the hospital after he broke a leg at a Richfield rodeo.

Elaine said, "Do you realize how often you talk about Aspen Marooney?"

"I haven't kept a count."

"Almost every day," she said. "And if it isn't Aspen, it's something else out of your high school days, as if that's the only good thing that ever happened to you."

"That's not true. I hated high school."

"Anyhow," she said, "I'd be grateful if you didn't talk about Aspen Marooney."

"Good enough," he said. "If it bothers you, I won't say another word about her. I'll keep a bridle on this unruly tongue."

During the following weeks he thought about this incident a good deal. With some astonishment, he admitted that Elaine was right. He had got in the habit of talking about his past almost any time he and she had a quiet moment together, and all too often the part of his past he brought up involved Aspen.

He decided, however, that he couldn't fall into total silence just yet. During the summer of 1951, following their graduation from high school, Durfey herded sheep in Fry Pan Canyon and Aspen worked as a waitress at the Fishlake lodge. Aspen got to driving over in the evening once or twice each week, and pretty soon she started staying all night and driving back to the lodge at dawn.

It was a terrible thing for them to have done, and Durfey made a clean breast of it with his bishop at the end of the summer. He knew he would eventually have to make a clean breast of it with the woman he married, because he had been raised to believe a man owed virginity to his bride. So even though Elaine asked him not to mention Aspen in her presence, he felt obliged to tell her about the summer in Fry Pan Canyon.

His confession brought them close to a broken marriage, and when they resumed their intimacy months later, it was a far cry from the relaxed affection of their earliest years together. Their emotional estrangement ended on a summer evening when she said, "It's nice to have the house to ourselves." The boys were staying the weekend with Elaine's parents in Altadena. "Are you interested in going to bed early?" she asked.

Within a year their daughter Sally was born, and they had gone a long way toward redefining one another. Elaine insisted that they give up certain pretensions in their old way of behaving. In particular, she asked him not to pay her extravagant compliments and not to tell her he loved her. She felt, properly so, as he esteemed, that words are cheap and often come easy and without forethought. She felt that love isn't love if it's intermittent. She thought of love as being steady as a pilot light in a furnace. So he agreed never to tell Elaine he loved her.

In the late afternoon, they pulled off the interstate at Cedar City and took a motel suite with two connecting rooms. An hour later their daughter Sally and her husband and their two little girls arrived from Riverside. The two couples planned to see a play that evening, and on the next two days Durfey and Elaine would drive to Richfield for Durfey's reunion while Sally and Steve and the girls visited Zion Park and other scenic places, and each evening they would reassemble in Cedar City for another play.

The arrangement was a concession to Elaine's reluctance to stay overnight in Richfield. Though it was a county seat and boasted a main street with curbs and gutters and a new commercial district south of town, Richfield suffered from the dilapidation of its central residential district, where backyards were full of disused barns and corrals and gardens overgrown with weeds.

On their rare visits to Richfield, while they drove up and down its elm-shaded, ditch-lined streets, Durfey tried to explain that he actually disliked the town. He had had very little to do with it until he entered Richfield High. His attachment was to the mountains that rimmed the wide valley, the sagebrush plains, and the farm he grew up on in Glenwood about ten miles east of Richfield.

That farm and the tiny scattered hamlet of which it was a part haunted him steadily. Forty years later he still woke up mornings feeling there was something he ought to go back and find on that farm. And sometimes it seemed that what he wanted to go back to find was the future because he had had one to look forward to while he lived on that farm.

Each of the motel rooms had two queen-sized beds, and Elaine and Sally stalked back and forth between the two rooms and finally decided that the girls would sleep in one of the beds in Elaine's and Durfey's room, ostensibly so Sally and Steve could go out with friends after the play, which looked to Durfey like a blatant declaration of passionate intent.

He peered into a dresser drawer. "It looks clean," he said. "No fleas." He began transferring socks and pajamas from his suitcase to the dresser. "Actually," he said, when Sally had left the room, "what those two have in mind is a good idea. We should have thought of it first."

"Hush your mouth," Elaine said.

The little girls, Sandra and Katie, were oblivious to their grandparents' exchange. They sprawled on one of the beds, leafing through picture books Elaine had brought along. Sandra murmured and pointed to something in her book, and Katie craned her neck to see.

While Durfey watched, Elaine hung blouses and slacks in a closet. What Sally and Steve or anybody else might do in private wasn't of interest to Elaine. A couple's sex life was none of her business. She didn't want to sully her mind with details. Elaine had a simple, straightforward view of moral volition. She believed if people wanted to they could always choose the right. For her, this was as simple as turning a radio on or off. Anybody had the ability to do it.

Sally, just out of the shower and in a robe, came to the door between the rooms and asked Durfey to bring Steve in from the parking lot for his shower. Durfey went out and found his son-in-law bent under the hood of his battered Mazda sedan.

"I turned off the air conditioner to make it over Cajon Pass," Steve

5

said. "When I turned it on again, it quit. It blows hot air. What a sizzler!"

"The ladies are calling us to prepare ourselves for high culture," Durfey said. "I'm under orders to bring you in. Time to shower and powder up, then we'll swing by the Chinese restaurant for dinner."

Durfey was tall, lean, and bald. Steve, a bit shorter, weighed twice as much and had a bushy head of hair. He tended to let his mouth gape and he wore thick glasses. Although he was intelligent, he didn't appear so. He was the manager of a feed lot in West San Bernardino, and his pay wasn't impressive.

"So where do you recommend we go for sightseeing the next couple of days?" Steve asked.

After mentioning the usual—Cedar Breaks, Zion, or the Grand Canyon if they wanted to start early in the morning—Durfey remembered the site of the Mountain Meadows Massacre. "It's out there only about forty miles," he said, waving southwestward. "There's a monument, a tiny creek, a lot of sagebrush—not much else to see."

Steve had never heard about the massacre so Durfey told him how militiamen from Cedar City and Parowan helped several hundred Indians slaughter about a hundred white men, women, and children emigrating by wagon train from Arkansas to California. Steve wanted to know why they had done it. That was a good question. Nobody really knew why they'd done it.

"I gotta go get my shower and you better go get yours," Durfey said. "Anybody who makes our ladies late for the greenshow will be dead meat."

He crossed the parking lot and retrieved the apple core from beneath the seat of the Buick. He went inside, congratulating himself for remembering the core and wondering how Steve could have gotten to almost thirty without hearing about the Mountain Meadows Massacre.

"In regard to automobiles," he said to Elaine while he took off his shirt, "that boy is indifferent to both safety and aesthetics. He

6

could afford a better car than that Mazda."

Elaine reminded him that Sally and Steve were saving money for a house. Acknowledging that, Durfey went into the bathroom. He noticed, with his usual distaste, the mirrored image of his sunken chest and the stringy muscles that sawed along his breast and arms. He called for clothes through a crack in the door, and Elaine's hand appeared with underwear, pants, and shirt.

A little later, at the greenshow that preceded the play, the shower proved a waste of time. While he sat on a grassy hillock watching the singers and dancers on a tiny outdoor stage, Durfey saw a large three-legged dog threading his way among the crowd. The dog got along nicely with a single hind leg. The other leg was amputated above the proverbial crook of the dog's hind leg. Durfey admired the animal's pluck and found himself feeling benevolent toward the canine family generally, being put in mind of his own little dog, Poot, which he and Elaine had deposited at a kennel in Irvine as they set out on their journey that morning.

Immediately beside Durfey rose a small sapling, which the dog paused to sniff. As Durfey's mind frantically grasped what was transpiring, the animal raised his stump slightly and spurted a stream of urine toward the thin trunk, splashing Durfey's arm and chest. A stranger behind Durfey laughed. The dog departed and Durfey went on watching the greenshow, supposing that if the dog wasn't part of the greenshow he should have been. He imagined dogs pissed on people regularly in Elizabethan times.

He was astonished by the Shakespearean festival at Cedar City. There was an immense incongruity in performing the bard of Stratford under the hot, dry stars of the Great Basin. The actors weren't hometown talent. They came from all over the U.S., and during their hour or two on the stage they made him regret his arrested development. They made him feel he should be something more than the owner, manager, and chief factotum of an insurance investigation agency.

Durfey knew all the alleys and insignificant streets of Greater Los

Angeles. He had knocked on every kind of door, seen every kind of scam. He couldn't get over the innate fraudulent nature of humankind. Every third person tried to cheat an insurance company. All the more reason why a man who had risen no higher than insurance investigator deserved to be pissed on by a three-legged dog.

Elaine and Sally stood in the crowd on the other side of the greenshow stage, each holding a little girl by the hand. They were tall, regal, handsome women, despite having, both of them, a bumpy nose and a big mouth full of white teeth. They were immaculately made up. Sally's hair was long and black; Elaine's was silver and ended in a page-boy curl. Elaine had got thick in the belly and hips, but no one noticed because she was so clever at dressing. She had grown up in Altadena and remained a pure and undeviating citizen of southern California, whose taste Durfey accepted without a murmur. She had picked out the yellow slacks and faint blue T-shirt he was wearing, and for the next day she had selected blue slacks and white T-shirt and a blue-gold golfing cap to cover his bald head. He didn't blame Elaine for transforming him. It was the drift of an entire civilization that turned him from a ranch hand into a freeway squirrel.

Nonetheless, he felt something of an impostor in color-coordinated, permanent-press casuals. In this context he thought of his father, a short, dirty man with exceptionally wide shoulders and scoop-shovel hands. Wearing soiled bib overalls, his father convoked his seven sons for Saturday farm tasks with an irascible bellow: "Richard, Lyle, Maury, Durfey, Curtis, Gilbert, Tilman!" One day when Durfey was only a freshman and already on the basketball team, Balis gazed up along his son's frail, ill-postured body and said, as if with great distaste, "Durfey, who in hell gave you permission to grow so tall?"

Durfey too was wearing overalls. They saved him the trouble of cinching a belt, and he liked the freedom they gave to his private parts. They had a large pocket centered over his breast, in which he carried string, carpet tacks, raisins, and sometimes a pencil and pad to satisfy his notions of being an author. His sophomore year he won a prize for the best Christmas story, a tale about an armadillo who decorated a mesquite bush with downy thistle balls. His mother said it was a cute story. His father said, "You never saw an armadillo in your whole damn life."

That was true. He'd read a book on the Texas Rangers which mentioned armadillos and mesquite. He fancied someday he'd go down to see for himself where the last outlaw died on the Rio Grande.

At the point where Durfey was considering whether to find a rest room and wash his arm and T-shirt, he was approached by a vendor, a woman near his own age bearing a basket of red apples. With a low curtsy, the vendor offered him the basket and with it, since she wore a peasant blouse and a tightly laced corselet, a generous view of her cleavage. He bought an apple, stuffing it into his pants pocket on the side not dirtied by dog urine, and was rewarded by another revealing curtsy from the vendor, who then went on across the lawn calling, "Apples 'ere, red apples 'ere."

He debated whether a woman of sixty was to be thought of as a wench. Feeling the uncomfortable bulge of the apple in his pocket, he fancied it must resemble a misaligned cod-piece. He again noted his wife, conspicuously pretty among the crowd on the opposite side of the stage, and his mind returned to the pillowy cleavage of the apple vendor, a pleasant sight for which he felt guilty, having long ago concluded that the generic interest of human beings in any attractive member of the opposite sex was a fated violation of the vows of marriage.

Admiring an apple vendor's cleavage was a petty crime indeed, easily repented of and forgotten. What was not so petty was the return of Aspen Marooney's memory. For obscure reasons these surroundings seemed natural to Aspen, so that he had an irrational expectation of her imminent appearance and, with that expectation, a subtle euphoria.

There was a pleasant campus prospect from where he sat on the grassy hillock: rolling acres of lawn, overhanging elms, and venerable academic buildings, to say nothing of the open air theater—a modern replica of Shakespeare's Globe—and the greenshow stage. It couldn't have been these that reminded him of Aspen Marooney. Perhaps it was the calm, silvered sky above the elms or the timbered wall of mountains darkening to the east. A dry, balmy evening in a Utah summer evoked a distinctive emotion. He couldn't imagine such an evening anywhere else.

He could first remember Aspen Marooney at a high school dance early in his freshman year, a time when he wouldn't have dared so much as to think about dating her. Everyone knew her and liked her, and everyone deferred to her opinions. During his junior year he took a typing class she had enrolled in. By chance the teacher assigned him a seat in front of her. They chatted while performing finger drills, and the teacher soon separated them. Dating her was still out of the question. However, when the annual girls' choice dance came along, Aspen asked him to be her partner.

That was a catalytic turn for Durfey. It was spring and he was seventeen and the furnace that heated the pit of his stomach answered all his prior questions as to the nature of love. As expected of those who were truly in love, he had little appetite and slept poorly. Although he recognized decades later how easy it is to sentimentalize juvenile affections and conceded that adults do well to treat those affections with ridicule, he was still forced to admit that he had never stopped loving Aspen Marooney, nor had he ever loved anyone else in the same way.

As it happened, he didn't go to the girls' choice dance with Aspen. Her parents learned of the date about a week before the dance, and her father put his foot down and said she'd have to break it.

"I can't take you to the dance," she told Durfey in a nearly deserted hall of the high school. "My family's going out of town. I have to go with them."

"Gosh," he said, "I'm sorry. But it's okay."

"It's not okay. But I have to go with them."

Durfey went home and talked it over with his mother, who set him straight. His mother said even if Aspen's parents were going out of town, it was only to give her an excuse for breaking the date, and it was wicked to offer such a mealy-mouthed excuse because it could leave Durfey with the idea that she might be glad to have him ask her out later on. That was the beginning of Durfey's understanding of the proper station of the Haslam family in Richfield.

Even a town like Richfield had its aristocrats, plebeians, and slaves. The stratification began the moment the pioneers settled the place, or it had already existed among them as they arrived in groups. No Haslam had lived in Richfield from within two years of its founding. Tiny villages were their acceptable purlieu. So it wasn't to be marveled at that the Marooneys of Richfield found the Haslams of Glenwood deficient in matters of civilization. As Durfey would later recognize, dwarfish, untidy men like Durfey's father ran in a genetic line. Haslam men attracted and married and sometimes abused women without ego or spunk. They had an instinct for achieving poverty on their small, ill-kept farms. In their estimation, water was for irrigating fields, not for bathing bodies or washing clothes.

In contrast, Aspen's father derived from Irish immigrants of mercantile background. Trained as an undertaker, Horatio Marooney had migrated from his native Boston to Denver, then on to Grand Junction, and finally to Richfield where he established a successful mortuary. He married a young woman of prime pioneer stock, Adelia Boran, and the two entered the society of the town's best couples. He became a voting partner in a bank with offices in southern Utah towns, and he was a co-founder of the Rotary Club of Richfield. Aspen's mother, a poet of local renown, served as president of the Richfield Art and Culture Club.

On rare occasions when Mr. and Mrs. Marooney met Durfey after

Aspen had broken the date, they greeted him with unexpected kindness. Afterward he could see that they didn't intend that he take their rejection personally. They expected him to understand that certain categories of men and women are ill suited for each other. Judging their vital interests to be secure, they could beam urbanity upon him with little condescension.

In the early summer following his junior year in high school, Durfey and his brothers Maury and Curtis built a corral of aspen poles at the family sheep camp in Fry Pan Canyon. White talcum adheres to aspen trunks, which transfers to the hands and clothing of those who cut and carry them, as Durfey observed during the week it took to prepare the poles and assemble the fence. Ever after, white powder of any sort—powdered sugar, foot talcum, chalk dust—reminded him of aspen trunks and a girl named Aspen Marooney.

That a couple named Horatio and Adelia Marooney, who christened their children Hope, Seamus, and Patrick, had arrived at Aspen for the name of their second child and last daughter struck Durfey, even at seventeen, as prophetic. The leaves of the quaking aspen are hinged to their stems in a sideways manner, allowing them to tremble and flutter in the slightest breeze and perform a mad dance in a wind of any strength. It wasn't that Durfey conceived of Aspen Marooney as trembling, fluttering, or dancing madly in any sense. It was that a mountainside of aspens, shimmering yellow in a September sun, gave substance to an intuition of her personality. The two were emotional equivalents: a mountainside of sun-torched trees, a girl with brown hair, high cheekbones, and a small, up-turned nose.

Later in the summer between his junior and senior years, a bronc tossed Durfey off at the Pioneer Day rodeo, and his leg broke in three places. Being a cowboy was just one of many romantic impossibilities he had learned from books. He had supposed an affinity existed between him and the Roman-nosed bronc that stood at malevolent ease while he slid onto its back in the chute. He fancied the ancient spirit of the centaur would weld equine and human nature into a chemical unity. It wasn't to be so. Free of the chute, the horse spiraled in wild, crazy loops, jolting to earth at a devious remove from where it had last taken footing, contriving all too soon to leave Durfey hanging in mid-air for a frozen second before he fell, with flailing arms, into the hardpan gravel of the country arena.

Durfey spent weeks in the Richfield hospital, a one-story war-surplus barracks painted battleship grey inside and out. One morning before dawn, Aspen appeared like a wraith in the shadowy door of his room and in the unexplained absence of the nurse administered a bedpan beneath his buttocks. She had been on her way to the drive-in where she worked, which opened early for the tourist trade, and on an impulse she had entered the hospital and searched its unwatched corridors till she found Durfey, whose injury had been spoken of around the town during the past two or three days. For the remainder of his stay, Aspen came by the hospital before dawn every morning except Sunday, without her parents' knowledge, bringing Durfey paperback books and odds and ends from the refrigerator at home wrapped in waxed paper. During the school year that followed they continued their surreptitious romance, meeting at dances and after ball games and in the shadows of the sycamores behind the drive-in where Aspen worked four nights a week during the winter.

Aspen Marooney was a girl of high ideals. She liked the word *standards* and used it constantly. She said standards were the cure of the world's ills and she loved them more than life itself. Nonetheless, she clung to Durfey while they danced, breast to breast and belly to belly, and she put energy into kissing, and it was she herself who first undid her blouse and guided his hand inside and later undid his pants and pulled up her skirt, and Durfey would get heated up till the pain was excruciating, but there was no relief because she'd suddenly stop and say they'd gone too far, and remind him how they were promised to standards and how standards would rehabilitate his life and how, after he'd served in the military and had come home from Korea and gone to the university and become a pharmacist (there being no pharmacist in Richfield at the time), then, he being duly rehabilitated by standards, she would marry him.

It didn't occur to him to question her vacillation between passion and standards any more than he questioned gravity or the rising of the sun. As far as he was concerned, she was one of the elements of the primitive world, the seed ground of all good things, and he respected her and was inclined to believe anything she told him. Her voice had a mesmerizing timbre and her body seemed in some manner radioactive. Later he doubted that other people sensed this charisma as he had and was willing to admit the possibility that she was no more than a mirror or a shield for deflecting and returning high energy particles which had their origin within himself.

Their romance culminated during the summer after they graduated from high school when Durfey was herding sheep and Aspen was working at the Fishlake lodge. On the second or third visit she paid to his camp, they took a stroll in the moonlight. Shadowy willows and ash trees stood along the rushing creek and aspens and firs on the canyon slopes. The bedded sheep were clearly visible in a steep, grassy clearing because the moon was so bright. The breeze carried a pungent scent from high up the canyon.

They stood on the creek bank, and he rhapsodized, as he had the capacity to do in those days. In this instance his ideas came from a novel he had read about Russian lovers exiled to Siberia, which had an exciting scene about an escape from wolves in a horse-drawn sleigh.

"Moonlight is a dye," he said. "It dissolves the night and tints everything Siberian white. A hundred years from now this moon will be shining over Siberia, and the Russian wolves will be howling mournfully. Five hundred years from now, somebody will look at the moon and will say, There used to be a girl named Aspen Marooney."

He was dirty and smelly from working, and he gently broke from her embrace, stripped, and waded into the rushing creek and bathed. She stripped too and waded in beside him and scooped handfuls of water and splashed them over his face and shoulders, letting her hands soothe his breasts and belly and back with wet, swirling strokes.

"I've washed away everything wicked that could possibly be," she said. "Do you promise, no matter what happens, to go to church and make something of yourself and repent and someday take me to the temple? If I let you, will you be steady and firm and true and never waver and be somebody I'll be proud of?"

He'd have done anything she asked. He'd have swum the Colorado from bottom to top. He'd have climbed Mount Nebo backward and blindfolded. He'd have filled the open pit copper mine at Bingham with a wheelbarrow and hand shovel.

They waded to the bank and went hand in hand to the camp wagon, which contained his bed, and she let him make love to her. He felt feverish and out of his mind, as he had felt following the operation that placed pins in his broken leg. From the fact of her yielding he abstracted a future of unending happiness. As for the deed itself, he was astonished that it had to be so voluptuous and carnal, that it had no other route to achievement than this inordinate, unauthorized animal connection of his and her flesh.

By the end of the summer of 1951, Aspen had spent the night in Durfey's sheep camp ten or twelve times. Sometimes they made love outdoors on a blanket, sometimes in the stale, dark confines of the camp wagon. They desired, expected, even prayed for her pregnancy, the condition that would leave them with no alternative except to confront her nay-saying parents with the announcement of their wedding. But that eventuality didn't occur, and at the end of the summer remorse seized her and she insisted they cease and desist from outlawish behavior and forthwith confess what they had been doing, each to a different bishop, of course, since his ward was in Glenwood, hers in Richfield.

15

The incident that provoked her change of heart occurred near dawn as they were finishing a breakfast of pancakes and coffee. They heard a vehicle laboring up the narrow dirt track in the bottom of the canyon, and she ran frantically to her car, only to sit there with the door open, her hands gripping the wheel in shame because Durfey's father had arrived in his old pickup.

His father got out and hauled a couple of boxes of groceries and a ten-gallon can of drinking water to the camp wagon. He listed and lurched while he walked because he was almost a dwarf and had truncated, malformed legs. He whistled to himself, oblivious to the tears glinting on Aspen's cheeks in the quaint, crepuscular light of dawn.

When he was through unloading, he patted Durfey's arm. "I don't plan to meddle," he said. "I'm going home to your mother and tell her as far as I can see there's nothing to the stories going around that the undertaker's daughter is spending nights in our boy's sheep camp." He nodded pleasantly to Aspen as he went back to his pickup. He started the engine and drove away. Durfey never heard another word about the matter from him.

Durfey's confession to his bishop was an anomalous event. Durfey hadn't been to church since he was nine or ten, and he had to identify himself to this shepherd of the Glenwood flock. None of the male descendants of his great-grandfather had gone to church after nine or ten. His bishop was floored. A large, bald-headed man, the bishop sat awhile in the overstuffed chair of his living room, still masticating his supper, eyeing Durfey with stunned surprise. "Would you repeat that?" he finally said.

Durfey said, "I've been shacking up with a girl all summer and I want to repent of it. I want to quit that kind of stuff and be decent."

The bishop didn't ask who the girl was. He simply said, "You're forgiven. Just put the matter behind you and forget about it. Why don't you start going to church?"

Durfey did start going to church and found it wasn't too bad. He discovered he could sometimes get off to sleep for fifteen or twenty minutes at a stretch during a meeting, and in any event sermons didn't seem as long as they had when he was a boy. One evening during the fall of 1951 when he'd come in late from chopping silage, his mother let him know how pleased she was about his going to church. While she set bread and milk and slices of homemade cheese in front of him, she said she hoped he'd keep it up for the rest of his life.

His father said, "Just don't pester me with it."

"You hush your wicked tongue," his mother said with unaccustomed fervor. "It'll be on your head if you talk this boy out of living right."

But he hadn't been talked out of it, and he went on living a churchly life. He did so partly because he needed the solace of believing that somewhere down the road the big plan of things included a little happiness for him. Aspen had gone away to college, saying her future didn't include him, and he dragged through autumn as a hired hand, grieving as much as any widower. It was during that autumn that his past became his future, and he got into the habit of thinking more about what might have happened than about what was actually going to happen.

Ironically, Elaine owed her marriage, whatever it was worth, to Aspen Marooney, because somehow or other Durfey managed to keep himself religious enough to pass muster with Elaine after he got back from the army and entered BYU. Elaine certainly wouldn't have married any man who didn't go to church.

Brass horns announced the main fare of the evening, the tragedy *Macbeth*. While the crowd filed obediently into the theater, Sally and Elaine deposited the girls at the baby sitting service in a nearby building. The perimeter of the theater was circled by a roofed balcony, and the center, where Sally and Elaine joined Steve and Durfey, was open to a sky in which stars already twinkled.

"Now, Mother, please remember it's just a play," Sally said to Elaine, who hated tragedies. "You're supposed to enjoy it."

The stage was sparsely set, and the costumes were of leather and metal and coarse spun wool—indicative, Durfey supposed, of the harsh society and barren wilds of medieval Scotland. The actors strode, sat, bent, turned, scowled, and gestured, enhancing their script through pantomime and motion. Their words, often incomprehensible, flowed in measured cadences.

The weird sisters prophesied that Macbeth would become king, pricking him with the wicked ambition to murder his sworn lord, the present king. While Duncan slept in Macbeth's castle, Macbeth wavered in his bloody design until the fierce Lady Macbeth goaded him on with taunts and derision.

"Why don't they come to their senses while there's still time," Elaine murmured in Durfey's ear.

"You wouldn't have a plot," Durfey said.

Fate would not grant the Macbeths a peaceful tenure in their usurped station, which they maintained by means of other murders. The ghost of Banquo, matted with gore, appeared at a feast, causing Macbeth to rave deliriously before his guests. Lady Macbeth, walking in her sleep, piteously tried to scrub Duncan's blood from her hands.

"I can hardly stand this," Elaine whispered.

"You don't have to watch it," Durfey replied. "Close your eyes."

"I can't waste my ticket," she said.

After the play Sally said, "Wasn't that good! It just sent chills down my spine."

"I'm glad it's *Love's Labors Lost* tomorrow night," Elaine said.

"You have to remember, Mama, it isn't real," Sally said.

"When you get a certain age," Durfey said, "it's real, even on a stage."

Sally and Steve went away with their friends, and Durfey and Elaine retrieved the sleeping girls from the baby sitting service and drove to the motel. Sandra woke and cried, and Elaine soothed her until she went back to sleep.

Remembering that a dog had pissed on him, Durfey took a

shower. While he soaped his body, he thought about Macbeth and his lady. He was thinking they were as much the victims of their own violent natures as the people they had murdered. He got to thinking then about the Mountain Meadows Massacre, which was a tragedy, too, not just for the people who were massacred but for the otherwise honest Christians who assisted the Indians in murdering them.

He put on his pajamas and joined Elaine on the side of their bed, where they gazed at their sleeping granddaughters. Elaine was mellow just now. She leaned against Durfey, encircling his shoulders with her long, fleshy arm. "I'm glad we took Poot to Halbert's kennel," she said. "It's a much better place than that Doggie Dell."

"Yes, Poot will be fine," Durfey said.

"You can't expect a dog to adjust any better than a little child," Elaine mused. "He certainly has a way of accusing you when you leave him—his big hurt eyes saying, 'Oh, dear, not again! Please take me with you.'"

Ordinarily, their pug-nosed Shih Tzu padded with cheerful aplomb about their condo, his combed yellow and white hair trailing on the carpet, concealing his stubby legs and even his abbreviated muzzle. The pet served, in Durfey's estimation, as a love fetish between his master and mistress. Each showered endearments upon the dog, especially when the other was present—a behavior whereby, so Durfey concluded, they expressed their speechless love for one another.

They kissed each other good night and got into the bed, and Elaine lapsed into a soft, reassuring sleep. To assist himself to do likewise, Durfey fell to recalling the names and personalities of the milk cows he had known as a boy: Pet, Pippin, Sally, Jerse, Blackie, and others whose names sometimes recurred to him in the night but slipped away by morning, causing him to mutter while he shaved, "Drat, what *was* her name?"

Perhaps a half hour later, when it occurred to Durfey that he wasn't to be blessed with sleep, he got out of bed, took a Gideon

Bible from the dresser drawer, and went to the bathroom where he could read without disturbing his wife and granddaughters. He read in Genesis, curious whether the fruit of the tree of the knowledge of good and evil was specifically named as an apple. He found no mention of any particular fruit. He pondered again Elaine's claim that people can always choose the right if they want to. The problem, as Durfey saw it, was with wanting to. If people want to choose the wrong badly enough, they aren't free to choose the right.

In time he went back to bed and lay listening not only to the sweet rhythmical breathing of Elaine and the girls but also to the wheeze of an air-conditioner beneath the window, which reminded him of his long dead father who, in the final throes of emphysema, had gasped so loudly he had been audible from another room.

Durfey had an impulse to awaken Elaine and reassure her the class reunion wouldn't be a big deal. It'd be over in a couple of days, and they'd be on their way back to Newport Beach and their little dog Poot. But it didn't make sense to wake her up and reassure her about something she was already reassured about. She already knew the reunion wasn't a big deal. Otherwise she wouldn't have made the decision that he and she were to attend.

2. Plummeting into a Pool

The night before the reunion, Roger wanted to make love. Aspen was bottling apricots and said it would be a bother. He said he meant later in the evening. She said she knew that's what he meant. He moped around, packing his bag, reading the newspaper, generally looking glum. So she said they'd make love after all. When she was through with the apricots, about ten o'clock, they tried, and, as she'd thought, it didn't work.

The next morning their neighbor Ted from next door wandered over to say goodbye. He helped put their bags in the trunk and offered to take in their mail. They said thanks, but no, because Robin and Julian, their youngest, now grown, would be at home. Ted noticed that the broken hood ornament on the front of the car dangled on a tiny cable instead of standing erect. After he had replaced it in its proper position and let it topple two or three times, he said, "That's a sign of impotence if I ever saw one!" He struck Roger on the shoulder and laughed in a pleasant way. Roger acknowledged the joke like a man with the flu, lips thin, almost blue, brittle as ice.

Aspen was of two minds about Roger's frequent failures. On the one hand, you might say she had had too many babies and it was her fault he couldn't get enough friction to finish the job. On the other hand, you shouldn't blame the site where a man digs for buried treasure if his shovel isn't so good anymore.

Down the road about a half hour they turned off at Alpine to call on their daughter Debra, who was at home with preschoolers as expected. The clothes washer and dryer were humming and a clean, moist scent filled the kitchen. The vacuum stood ready in the middle of the living room. Debra was suffering from morning sickness, which with her always went on until the day she went into labor. She looked terrible: black circles under her eyes, a listless stoop to her shoulders. Roger made her sit down and held her hand while they sorted through the highlights of the several weeks since they had been together.

"Now, sweetheart," he said after their chat, "you're going to feel better."

"Thank you, Daddy," she said. "I do feel better."

Roger soothed and encouraged people without arrogance or forethought. Just a word from him gave tired veins a fresh shot of blood sugar. A squeeze of his hand worked like an antibiotic.

Leaving Debra, they drove to Orem and stopped at the apartment of their daughter Loraine. They got the key from under the mat and went in and put several jars of apricots and a fifty dollar bill on the table. Loraine always needed money. A threadbare path crossed her carpet from door to door, and the drain in the kitchen sink was a gaping hole. Loraine worked days for a computer company and four evenings a week for a convenience store. Sherry, twelve, and Jason, nine, were in school all day. Anita, the youngest, came home at noon from kindergarten and went to the neighbor's. In the evenings Sherry was in charge at home.

One night Loraine discovered her husband fondling Anita in her crib. Later she found he had done things to Jason too. She divorced him, and the judge allowed Jim visiting rights in the presence of a responsible party. The problem was making sure someone else was present. Jim was out of work and lived with his father and mother, who kept threatening to hire another lawyer to reopen the case.

Loraine was cynical about men. She'd tell her friends, "Don't leave your husband alone. If he goes into your kids' bedroom at night, follow him in. See what he's up to!"

Nonetheless, she had plans to acquire a live-in boyfriend. One day when she and Aspen were alone, she pulled a packet of condoms from her purse. "You just as well know what direction I'm headed," she said.

Aspen read the fine print on the back of the packet, tore it open, and shook out the moist condom. She had never seen one before.

"Now you've ruined it," Loraine protested.

"I'll pay for it," Aspen said.

A condom was a latex parachute, ready to billow in the wind of a man's passion. A condom was Pandora's box, potent enough to afflict Loraine's life with unimagined tribulations, the least of which might be another, even more perverse and violent Jim. There was no use saying anything to Loraine. She thrived on ignored advice. At twelve she declared her allegiance to her eldest brother, Gerald, who had decamped from home and gone wild. She said she was going to drive trucks and ride bulls like Gerald. When she turned twenty-one, she was going to become an atheist.

"You can tell Daddy about the condoms if you want," she said. "I'm not going to be a hypocrite."

"You tell him yourself if you think it's so important," Aspen said. "It'll break his heart. You just as well face that."

Roger had silvery hair, a refined face, brightly polished gold spectacles. He was director of counseling for Deseret Industries, a chain of Mormon thrift stores in cities all over the West. He visited loading docks, workshops, and retail outlets, studying the handicapped and advising their advisors. He saw goodness in idiots, strength in cripples.

One night after a snowstorm Aspen went out with cap, gloves, and shovel to clear the driveway. Their country lot was fringed with willows and cottonwoods. Every shrub had a lovely unfamiliarity. Low clouds reflected the distant city lights. Aspen thought of Roger, who was at church conducting ward business. At this moment, the world was as Roger always saw it: mantled in white and suffused by a heavenly glow. Roger rooted for Loraine, sturdily predicting her victory over adverse circumstances and her own stubborn will. He said her tough talk didn't add up to anything. He said she was no more an atheist than he himself.

Aspen knew why two of her children had gone bad. They were God's tax on a recalcitrant mother. The other six were cut from Roger's template. They were predictable, mild-mannered, and reverent. That was no surprise. A father's rectitude ought to count for something in the subtle scheme of reward and retribution operating in the mortal world.

After they left Loraine's apartment, Aspen and Roger stopped by the Orem mall to pick up Evelyn Chancellor. Aspen and Evelyn had known each other since first grade in Richfield elementary school. Currently Evelyn ran her own business as a certified public accountant. She dyed her hair jet black and wore brash red lipstick.

Aspen went inside while Roger parked in a convenient no-parking zone. She and Evelyn emerged under a staggering load of pamphlets and programs for the reunion.

"You big yam," Evelyn shouted at Roger, "why didn't you come in and help carry this stuff out?"

Roger scrambled to heave boxes into the trunk, apologizing profusely.

Evelyn climbed into the rear seat and they headed for the freeway. "So what's going on in the Power Tower?" she said to Roger, meaning the church office building where he worked.

"Business as usual," he said. "Everything is absolutely routine."

"Oh, come off it!" she said. "Tell me the latest scuttlebutt. Careers are ruined every day in that building; throats are cut, bodies are sold."

"There's none of that where I work," he said. "People come at eight and go home at five. They write memos and make phone calls and have lunch in the cafeteria. That's all."

"What a bunch of wussies," she said.

She pulled lipstick from her purse and applied a fresh coat, peering into a tiny mirror. "Gotta keep up the Big Pretty," she said. "Don't want people thinking I'm plain."

She put away the lipstick. "When will this society get over its fixation with buns and breasts?" she said. "Butts are made to sit on, not show off. Tits are just a piece of anatomy, like shoulders or knees."

"Give us a break," Aspen said.

"What do you mean?"

"I mean talk nice around Roger."

"Lord, Aspen, you're so defensive!"

"I'm not offended," Roger assured them, though Aspen didn't believe him.

Roger knew Evelyn was putting him on, but he didn't know how to defend himself. He liked his language well cooked and mixed with delicate sauces. It was the same as seeing the world in a white mantle. He thought people shouldn't make flippant talk out of dire circumstances. He thought bad words were a kind of violence in and of themselves.

"Enough chatter," Evelyn said. "Let's talk about the reunion. Here, kid, look yourself up." She handed Aspen a copy of the pamphlet. It contained informative letters from about half the Class of '51. Apparently the other half couldn't be bothered. Of course, the other half included eight who were dead.

Aspen thumbed through the pamphlet and found her letter in the S section where it belonged. Evelyn had typed *Aspen Sheffield* at the top of the page. Nobody ever called her Aspen Marooney. She could go weeks at a time without remembering her real name was Aspen Marooney.

There were two photographs, one from the 1951 yearbook and a recent one she had sent in with her letter. The yearbook photo didn't look like anybody in particular—just a pretty girl on a ladder

25

helping decorate the gym, smiling broadly and waving a hand. The recent photo had her in a short brown jacket and skirt, looking experienced and matronly. Her body was angled so that her hips appeared narrow. She thought her snub nose, always ridiculous, could pass for an elevator button. The more she stared at herself the more her smile seemed made elsewhere and transported to the scene.

Some of her classmates had sent family photographs. It was hard to find them among spouses, children, grandchildren, and dogs. She saw their point in wanting to hide.

Roger glanced from the road once in a while. "You look good in that picture," he said. She patted his knee. You could count on Roger. He'd never let you down.

Evelyn wanted to know if she'd come to Durfey Haslam's letter. Aspen turned to the H's and there it was, along with the mandatory photos.

"He lives in Newport Beach," Aspen said. "His wife is named Elaine. They've raised three children and they've got a dog named Poot." The only new information for her was the dog. She'd followed Durfey for forty years. When she went back to Richfield, people told her what he'd been doing.

She knew the boy in the yearbook photo. He had let his long body slouch and had hooked his thumbs in the pockets of his jeans. His hair was thick, brown, and wooly and shingled high above his ears, a curly thatch on top of a crooked pole. She didn't know the man in the other photo. His head gleamed like the cover of a marble tureen with a fringe of bristle on either side. His eyelids drooped as if he were half asleep. His cheeks were furrowed, his nose beaked.

What had she expected? You can't reconstitute a memory like a box of potato flakes. You can't turn time in both directions like the pages of a book. A reunion is a staging, a recitation, but not a recovery of what used to be.

"She was like bigtime in love with that galoot," Evelyn told Roger.

"Yeah, bigtime," Aspen said. "Bigtime as in zero."

"I believe she's mentioned him," Roger said.

"She broke his heart," Evelyn said. "She walked out on him and married you."

"You're thinking of Trelawny Smith," Aspen said. "It nearly killed him when I got married."

"You never went out with Trelawny Smith," Evelyn cried.

"Dozens of times!"

"She's holding out on you," Evelyn said. "She and Durfey Haslam used to slip around after hours. You'd see them in his pickup down one of the lanes at one or two in the morning."

"Sure you would," Aspen said. "You could find us making out behind cattle barns and pigpens any old time."

Roger laughed. His hands remained steady on the steering wheel. They didn't seem like the hands of a man who had any particular thoughts in his mind. Roger loved to drive. He was never happier. He felt like he had power and was going somewhere.

As for Evelyn, she couldn't go ten minutes without making trouble for a friend. A lot of people have to betray their friends. Aspen didn't know why, but she'd seen it over and over. For the moment Evelyn had given up. Maybe it wasn't much fun trying to create suspicion in such a placid man. In any case, she didn't know as much as she thought she did about Durfey Haslam.

Roger asked about her business, and Evelyn launched into a discussion of the problems of being a CPA. Aspen wasn't interested in accounting. You add or subtract and find out whether your clients have made a profit or a loss, and you try to figure out how best to cheat the government out of the taxes you owe. That's all there is to it. So she mellowed into Mount Nebo's jagged face and its high bald peaks and the rolling valley through which they yachted like a sagebrush sea.

Sagebrush is a shrub with a small, woody, black trunk and lace-budded branches colored somewhere between kitchen sage and coarse-ground pepper. Sometimes after a summer rain, winds off the Wasatch brought the scent of wet sage into Aspen's suburban

27

home. She'd think then about Durfey Haslam. She'd remember a day when he and she took shelter from rain beneath a juniper. Their horses stood with rumps to the wind. Sagebrush was everywhere. Durfey saw a small purpling bottle in the muddy clay. It might have been a whiskey flask. He unscrewed the metal cap.

"I've let out a genie and now mischief is afoot," he said.

"What kind of mischief?" she asked.

"This bottle had happiness in it," he said. "Now the happiness has got away."

"I didn't see anything in it."

"Oh, it was there—the pure elixir of happiness," he said, screwing on the lid and throwing the bottle away.

Durfey read a lot and had a quaint vocabulary and his mind seemed muddled with possibilities. He fancied he would captain a schooner between Florida and the Bahamas. He would serve as a sergeant in a Scottish regiment. He would be a gamekeeper in the Black Forest of Bavaria. When he expounded on these fantasies, Aspen had a hard time not believing they might come true.

Years later, when the scent of moist sage came off the Wasatch during a summer storm, she wondered whether she could find the bottle again if she hunted for it. She wondered whether, if she found it and unscrewed the cap, there'd be a tiny drop of happiness shining in the bottom. With Durfey anything was possible.

They left I-15 at Nephi and drove south till they reached Salina where Gerald had his truck repair shop. They stopped and went in. Gerald was in his office, his feet on his desk, a phone in his lap. He motioned Evelyn to the only other chair and let his parents lean against the desk. A butt smoldered in an ashtray and a blue haze filled the room. Through a door they could see a couple of men working on the engine of a big truck.

"Didn't think you'd sucker in on a high school reunion," Gerald said to Evelyn. "Thought you'd have more sense. You're in for a couple of days of talking about how wonderful your typing teacher was. Hot dog!"

Half rising, Evelyn cuffed his knee. "If I was your mother, I'd teach you some respect."

"Sure you would," Aspen said. "You could staff a finishing school all by yourself."

"Nobody sends me any reunion notices," Gerald said, rubbing his ear. "I wouldn't go if they did. I don't say school isn't worthwhile, though it didn't do me any good. I told my boy Donnie, 'I'll kick your ass if you drop out.'"

Gerald was short, bald, beefy in the shoulders. He had a porous nose and florid complexion from too much drinking. Black grit rimmed his nails. He didn't clean them because they'd just get dirty again the next day.

"Me and Donnie are roping in the Richfield rodeo tomorrow night," he said. "You ought to drop by and watch."

Donnie lived in Price with his mother, who had divorced Gerald nearly ten years before. Gerald and Donnie did a lot of team roping in rodeos and sometimes took good money.

"I doubt we could make the rodeo," Roger said.

"We ought to do it," Aspen said. "It's been a while since we saw them rope."

"We're roping the next night too."

"One or the other, we'll make it," Aspen promised.

They had a little chat about the truck repair business, which Gerald said was booming because a new coal mine had opened in Salina Canyon. He was going to hire a couple of new mechanics and spend his time managing the business rather than repairing trucks.

As they left, he said, "You don't want to bother yourselves with no damn rodeo. Tell you what we'll do. Donnie and me will try to catch you over at Aunt Hope's house sometime over the weekend."

The travelers pulled onto the segment of I-70 that runs through Sevier County. They rolled across a wide valley full of alfalfa, corn,

29

and wheat. Mountains rimmed the valley all around. Long rows of sprinklers sparkled in the sun.

Aspen was thinking they ought to make one of the rodeos. She doubted Gerald would try to catch them at Hope's house. He drove through Salt Lake a dozen times a month and never stopped. He rarely phoned, and it was against his nature to write.

Gerald was a middle-aged man of dirty habits for whom Aspen would have performed the most menial of services. She would have cleaned his toilet, dug hair out of the drain in his bathroom basin, scraped the old wax off his kitchen linoleum, anything that would serve as an excuse for being near him. She never offered because he would have said, "For chrissake, Mom, don't be stupid."

Roger rocked the steering wheel with his delicate fingers. Aspen watched those long, tapered fingers and their clipped, clean nails. Roger trimmed them nearly every day at his desk in the church office building. They were entirely unlike Gerald's coarse, black-rimmed nails. They had to be. There was no genetic connection between them.

Sometimes when she had no satisfaction from a drink of water, Aspen knew it was confession she was thirsty for. She'd plan then on telling Roger very soon—next month, maybe. For a day or two she'd really believe she'd do it. Over the years she had evolved a litany of confessions. She knew half a dozen versions by heart, each an eloquent text. By now, of course, the original wrong was amplified by a thousand unseized opportunities. There was no logic to her silence. She *knew* Roger would forgive her, *knew* he wouldn't fail as Gerald's father.

They came to Richfield, and Roger exited. On Main Street they passed a patrol car that did a U-turn and came up behind with a red light flashing. It was John Izatt, Aspen's and Evelyn's former schoolmate and Richfield's chief of police. He wore cowboy boots, a Stetson, a large revolver, and a shiny star.

"Howdy, howdy, howdy!" he said, reaching in and shaking everybody's hand. "Shirley Sue is looking for you, Evelyn. She says

30

if you forgot the pamphlets she's going to send you back to get them."

"Tell her to quit fussing," Evelyn said. She handed John a pamphlet and he looked up his letter and photos.

"Real nice," he said. "Look there. I kind of like the air of authority in this photograph. In fact, I'd say it was law and order incarnate you are looking at, now ain't it?"

"You don't even know what incarnate means," Evelyn said.

"That's the truth. I'm a man of few words. Can't hardly read the comic strips without my wife's help. Still can't do long division. What's a policeman need of long division?"

"So how big is this police department you rule with such an iron hand?" Evelyn said.

"Me and three part-time officers, that's it. Four men in the division. One of the larger metropolitan departments, you might say."

Down the street a man with long hair came out of the Willow restaurant. John gave him a long stare. The fellow got into a battered Volkswagen van and drove away.

"Those damn hippies," John said. "I keep an eye on 'em. If they think they're stopping off in this town, they've got another thing coming."

As Aspen knew, the hippie era wasn't over as far as John was concerned. Any man with long hair or an earring qualified. John had a boxful of country/western tapes in his patrol car. In his opinion people who habitually listened to rock were bound to get into drugs and perverted sex. He couldn't understand the school district allowing strobe lights and rock music at school dances. Rock music fed the lawless impulse in young folks and was the prime cause of teen pregnancy.

John peered into the car again. "Can't stand here talking all day. Gotta go see why Mrs. Samuels is burning trash. She knows you can't burn trash in the city limits."

"You don't look happy," Aspen said. "Cheer up. Tomorrow's the

31

big reunion. It's like we were starting our senior year all over again."

"That Aspen!" he said. "She reads me like a book. Ain't no bluebird of happiness on my shoulder this morning. Trelawny Smith is in town for the reunion. I had a nice chat with him a few minutes ago. Haven't seen him in a long, long time. He's a vice president of that company up north of Ogden that makes solid fuel booster rockets for the space shuttle. Travels everywhere. Drives a Cadillac. Me? I've got four kids, nine dogs, and five horses. Plus one wife and eleven cars, every one of them used. I mean the cars, not the wife. Got her brand new. Of course she's depreciated down to about zero now. Like me."

"You've stayed out of jail and the state asylum," Aspen said. "That's more than a lot of people can say."

"That's a fact," John said. "Except I was in jail once. A little mistake that don't need expanding on. But I'll tell you what the real problem is. People don't like the present police force. People say I don't have enough tact. They say I come down too hard on these high school kids. They say I ought to retire. Hell, I'm not ready to retire. I'm only fifty-eight."

Aspen caught a final glimpse of him over her shoulder as he returned to the patrol car. His paunch hung over his belt like a sack of potatoes. It got bigger every year. She wished she had started measuring it when she first noticed how big it was. She thought about agreeing to trim some fat off her hips if he'd trim some off his belly. She loved him like a brother, and every time she made it to Richfield, she looked him up.

It was no surprise local people were out of sorts with John Izatt. In a city you don't know the cop who pulls you over and writes you a speeding ticket. You'll probably never see him again. In Richfield everybody knew John. They kept an eye on him. If he let the dandelions get out of hand on his lawn, somebody wrote a letter about it to the Richfield *Reaper*.

They drove to Shirley Sue's house, where Evelyn was going to stay. Shirley Sue gave Aspen a hug and made Roger promise to get her to the high school in time for the big parade the next morning. As they drove on, Aspen wondered how she'd measure up at the reunion. She pitied John, who had already decided he'd make a poor showing.

Expectations weren't so strenuous for a woman. Aspen had eight children and twenty-two beautiful grandchildren and a husband who stood high in the administration of Deseret Industries. By Richfield standards, she could have done a lot worse. There'd be no need to mention that two of her children had gone bad. There'd be no need to mention that three of the grandchildren were being raised in another church and three others in no church at all. It was too bad people had to worry about a report card at their forty-year reunion. But that's the way reunions were.

They found Hope's and Dan's house swarming with unexpected visitors who had come home to celebrate Pioneer Day. There were Hope's twin sons and their wives and children and Hope's and Aspen's cousin Esther and her husband and their daughter with a couple of their daughter's children—twenty-three bodies in all, counting Aspen and Roger and the aged Adelia, who was spending the summer with Hope and Dan.

Roger said, "We'll go get a motel room. We don't mind."

"You certainly will not!" Hope said. "There's bed space for every adult and the children can unroll their sleeping bags on the carpets."

It was a large, splendid house, partly financed, like Aspen's house, by a portion of their father's estate. It stood on the lot where Aspen, Hope, and their two brothers had been raised, replacing the incommodious old house of their childhood.

Adelia was seated in the living room in her favorite rocking chair. She crocheted with aplomb, lifting her eyes occasionally to gaze through an arched doorway at the ruckus of children in the family room and kitchen. Roger hugged her warmly and knelt beside the arm of her chair and began to talk. Her face beamed with pleasure.

Aspen sat on the piano bench, looking on. She grieved to see how her mother had wasted since their last visit, grieved also to see how relieved she felt that it wasn't yet her turn to take the aged woman into her house.

"Aspen, dear, how are you?"

"Just wonderful, Mamma."

Aspen replaced Roger at her mother's side. She caressed her frail hand and kissed the tips of its bluish nails. Adelia was made of porcelain. At any moment she might snap. Behind her brass-rimmed spectacles blinked alert, quizzical eyes. Her hair wasn't grey. It was predominantly black, interlaced by tiny threads of pure white.

"Have you finished the enclosure of your garden?" Adelia inquired.

"It's done," Aspen affirmed. "We hired a contractor. I'm not much on mixing cement."

"Can you imagine those neighbors letting their peafowl run at large?" Adelia said to those who looked on. "When I was there this spring, Aspen couldn't keep a thing in the soil. Lettuce, tomatoes, even onion transplants—those birds scratched them out and devoured them. Aspen threatened to shoot them. I said, I trust you don't mean that, Aspen; ladies don't shoot guns. She means it all right, Roger said; she's been known to shoot chickens. Be that as it may, Roger insisted they build an enclosure to protect the vegetables against marauding peacocks. Better that than bad blood between neighbors, he said. As patient as Job, that's Roger. Always a peacemaker."

"We ourselves have a rather unpleasant situation here," Dan said. "Our neighbor in the back has a pen full of young roosters that begin crowing about three in the morning."

"Aspen used to raise chickens and pigeons in our backyard," Adelia said. "I'm afraid it was a notion she brought home that summer she spent with Esther on Aunt Phyllis's and Uncle Isaac's farm. I have always contended that your father was no ordinary farmer, Esther. He was a horticulturalist of the first order. No one grew fruit and berries like him. He won prizes every year. In fact, the Utah Eperstein raspberry is named for him. Yet you allowed Aspen to come home to us at the end of that summer with—what shall I say?—with certain raw edges."

"I don't doubt that at all," Esther said. "We had raw edges by the bushel around our place."

From the arched doorway, Hope announced that dinner was ready. "I'm afraid Dan and I have arranged things like a couple of army cooks," she said. "Please forgive the informality. We'll put the little children and Mother at the table. The rest of us will have to find seats as best we can. Please wash your hands, everyone Mother, maybe Roger will help you to the table."

Hope and Dan had set a pot of beans and a giant salad and a couple of gallons of milk and a big pan of fresh baked rolls on the kitchen counter. The little children and Adelia were served; then the adults and older children paraded by cafeteria-style and loaded their plates and found a chair or sat on the floor.

Shawn and Shane, Hope's thirty-year-old twins, exchanged jokes. Sitting on the stepdown between the dining area and the family room, they ribbed everybody and fed off each other's exaggerations. Hope and Dan sat in the background beaming as if the happy old days when their children were young had come back again.

Soon a three-year-old at the table began to say, "Stupid!" over and over to no one in particular. He emphasized the word each time by banging his spoon on his plate.

"We don't say 'stupid' in this family," his mother said. This was Cindy, Shawn's wife.

"No," the child agreed, "and we don't say suck-ass either."

The other children exploded. Shawn stood up and said, "Well, then don't say it."

"Don't scold him," Cindy said. "It'll just make things worse."

"Where do they learn these words?" Hope said.

"Television! They learn everything on television," Esther said.

35

Aspen sat crosslegged with a napkin across her lap and a plate on the carpet. She was utterly happy. Nobody minded the uproar. Anybody was welcome here. Every new person added love instead of diluting it. She no longer felt unattached. She was a brick securely mortared in a wall. That's what a family was all about. An individual without a family was a drifting, sterile, pitiable thing.

After dinner the children went onto the front lawn, where there was a trampoline. The younger women sprawled on the lawn, keeping an eye on their bouncing children. Adelia returned to her rocking chair in the living room. Roger pulled a chair beside her and began to take notes on her early life. He planned to write her biography for the family.

In the kitchen Aspen and Esther rinsed the dishes and placed them in the dishwasher while Hope tidied up the leftovers. The three women chatted happily. They couldn't remember a time when they didn't know each other. Esther was a year older than Hope, three years older than Aspen. Esther had a sturdy frame, thick ankles, hips as wide as a doorway. She habitually wore pant suits of polyester knit. She was their first cousin, the daughter of Adelia's sister Phyllis. She and Norman lived in San Diego.

Hope was more formal. Even while doing housework she wore a skirt, dress flats, and hose. It was her custom to wear small elegant gold necklaces, which she removed only for very active labor like vacuuming or mopping. As for Aspen, she wore the cool flowered dress in which she had traveled. Aspen fancied her legs, struck high on the calf by a hem, were handsome. At home she was likely to be found in jeans. Her only jewelry, other than small earrings she put on when going out, were the rings she wore on the third finger of her left hand.

As they finished the dishes, Cindy came to the kitchen and asked whether there were tampons in the house. Hope said no and Cindy headed off to the store.

"It starts without much warning," Hope explained.

36

"You ought to talk her out of tampons," Esther said. "They cause cervical cancer."

"I'm glad I'm through with that business," Aspen said. "I hated periods."

"Well, you kind of feel like a dried-up pea pod when it quits," Esther said. "You feel like you've lost something even if you didn't want more kids."

"The Bible calls it the curse of Eve," Aspen said.

"It was for sanitary reasons," Hope said, "they used to send women out of the camp of Israel to have their periods."

"Reason I liked having periods," Esther said, "was that I got a week's vacation every month from old Mr. Horny in there." She nodded toward the family room where Norman sat before the television set.

Aspen said, "The day I started my first period, I said to Mother, 'Well, it's begun.' She took me into her bedroom and showed me a big box of Kotex hidden in her closet. I said I already knew the box was there. 'Yes,' she said, 'because Hope couldn't keep her mouth closed like I told her to. Now I don't want you buying these from a store till you're grown up. Do you understand that? Everybody in town can see what you're buying. You just take what you need from right here. And I don't see any need for you to discuss this with other girls. I have a book if you'd like to read about it though maybe not just yet.'"

"We come from a line of prudes," Esther said.

Hope said, "I think Mother handled it exactly right. At least you didn't feel embarrassed."

"How could you not talk about it with other girls?" Aspen said. "There was a machine in the high school rest room where you could buy a napkin for a nickel."

"My goodness! A napkin for a nickel!" Esther exclaimed. "Well, times have changed, haven't they?"

At ten Aspen and Roger said goodnight and retired to a bedroom at the back of the house, sequestered from the thumps and shouts of children having baths and settling down in sleeping bags. Aspen put on a light summer gown and got in bed. Roger sat on the side of the bed, methodically unlacing his shoes, pulling off his socks, unbuttoning his shirt.

"I run out of steam awfully early anymore," he said. "What's happened to me?"

He would be sixty-four at his next birthday—nearly six years older than Aspen. She expected to outlive him. Long before he died she would of course tell him about Gerald. She had to do that. The dead share in God's omniscience; they discern the deceptions, frauds, and infidelities of those they have left behind. He had to know from her own living mouth. He had to forgive her before he died.

Lying beside him on this hot July night, she repented of her indifference to his sexual need the night before. She promised herself she'd work harder at helping him succeed at the first opportunity after they got home. She caressed his hand with a penitential tenderness, as she had her mother's hand. He murmured sleepily, "I do love you, Aspen." She felt much better and went to sleep.

Long before dawn she was awakened by a crowing so unnatural she would not have identified it without Dan's prior mention of the cockerels in his neighbor's backyard. After that, she slept only fitfully, vexed by the raptures of the immature fowl.

At a moment of waking, she thought of the passion she had to feign in order to help Roger make love. Later, she remembered a rooster she had owned during her early high school years, a great green-grey speckled bird with a vigorous, blood-red comb, calculating yellow eyes, a sturdy black beak, and thick, scaly legs. Still later, she remembered from long ago a dream of the prophet Isaiah, who had appeared to her nude from the waist up, his nether parts obscured in darkness, his face annealed by misty light, his torso gleaming with sculpted lines of muscle. She had awakened with a pulsing joy in her pelvis—the first orgasm she had ever experienced.

When dawn showed dimly at the window pane, Aspen got out of bed and went down the hall to shower. She paused to peer into the living room, where little bodies slumbered on the sofa and carpet. Her eye fell on the silhouette of the rocking chair where her mother habitually sat. In the half light it might have been a judge's seat. An empty judge's seat seemed a sign of thwarted justice. It seemed a sign of flouted laws.

In the bathroom she slipped off her gown and stepped into the shower. While warm water slithered across her soapy arms and shoulders, she contemplated, for the thousandth time, the most startling and least explicable presumption of her entire life, which was that, hand in hand with Durfey Haslam, she would have had the courage to present herself pregnant before her parents.

She stepped from the shower, dried off, put on the gown, and returned to the bedroom where Roger still slept. The cockerels continued to crow but Aspen paid no heed. She put on light yellow slacks and blouse, attached tiny gold earrings, penciled her brows, and applied and blotted lipstick with the slightest tint of orange.

Fully dressed, she left the house by the front door and took a walk down the street. The early sun struck the white steeple of a nearby church. Robins chirruped in overhanging elms. An elderly householder was out irrigating his roses. She spoke to this man, whom she knew from long ago. She went on, thinking of the summer she had spent on Aunt Phyllis's and Uncle Isaac's farm. During that summer she first crossed over into the territories of the ungoverned. During that summer roving bands of brigands first appeared in the mountains of her mind.

"You mustn't come back saying, 'We was' and 'You was,'" Adelia had insisted before her departure. Aspen was not to eat mashed potatoes with a knife. "Uncle Isaac uses his fork to load the blade of his knife with potatoes and gravy before conveying it to his mouth," she said. "That's a perversion of nature."

39

Adelia and Phyllis had grown up in a school teacher's home, and for all her praise of Uncle Isaac as the foremost horticulturalist in Sevier County, Adelia believed her sister had come down seriously by marrying a tiller of the soil. On the farm Aspen learned to shoot a gun, catch carp and suckers, and poison gophers and ground squirrels. She loved feeding the chickens and pigs and taking the cows to the field in the morning and bringing them home in the evening. She picked peas and beans, hoed weeds, and tramped hay with good will if not with pleasure.

One morning she and Esther were hoeing corn. The sun was already hot, and the rows seemed interminable. Three girls of Esther's age rode by bareback and said they were going swimming. "Let's go with them," Esther said, dropping her hoe.

They threaded their way through a series of corn fields and a large willow patch and emerged on a high bank of the Sevier just as the riders arrived by another route. A bend in the river formed a deep pool at the base of the bank. Over the pool a rope dangled from the limb of a giant cottonwood.

Esther and her friends stripped off their clothes and ran shouting and splashing along a submerged sandbar and plunged into the pool with a headlong dive. Aspen stood paralyzed on the high bank without so much as unbuttoning her shirt. She had never before seen naked girls running under an open sky, never before taken off her clothes out of doors.

"Rip off your clothes, shorty, and come on in!" shouted one of Esther's friends. Aspen undressed and slid down to the sandbar and stood with muddy water flowing past her ankles. The girl who had invited her approached with an outstretched hand. Aspen grasped her hand, and the girl said, "Run!" They launched themselves into a sprint, churning the water with frantic feet. Suddenly the sandbar ended, and they sank with flailing arms into the deep, brown pool.

Aspen rose to the surface freed from an assumption. She'd thought her muscles might shear if forced into violent activity. She'd seen they wouldn't and was ecstatic. She swam the pool a dozen

40

times and dashed up the sandbar, wheeled, and returned, diving headlong into the pool as she had seen the others do. She followed the others in a mad, muddy scramble up the steep bank. She took her turn seizing the rope that hung from the giant branch and catapulting herself far out over the shining pool. "Look at that waterpup go!" one of the girls shouted.

The sight of brassy girls with breasts and pubic hair plummeting into a pool of shining water enticed Aspen into a civil war. By the time she came home to her mother and father, she had seceded from their Union. For a while she kept her insurgents in check, ordering them to stay hidden in the mountains. But when her parents forbade her to date Durfey Haslam, the rebels emerged and took over.

How would Aspen greet her accomplice in rebellion on this first day of their reunion? How was she to express her contrition for having sacrificed him to a foolish cause? Adelia often said, "You can't make a silk purse from a sow's ear." That meant her daughters and granddaughters weren't to marry farmers or truck drivers.

Aspen hadn't married a farmer or a truck driver. So the matter was settled. There was no need to think about it at this late date. She turned back to the house, supposing Hope would need some help putting breakfast on the table. She had decided to greet all her old friends with an affectionate hug and a kiss. If Durfey Haslam was present, that's the way she'd greet him too.

3. An Unrepentant Friend

As they left the motel, they opened the door between the rooms so Sally and Steve would hear the girls when they woke. Outside, Elaine told Durfey they were to take the Mazda and leave the Buick for Sally and Steve because the air conditioner on the Mazda wasn't working.

"You mean we gotta ride in this bucket of bolts?" Durfey said. He opened the Mazda's trunk and made sure it had a spare tire and a jack. "That Steve is an improvident boy," he said. "You never know what he'll keep in a car."

The Mazda handled well enough on the freeway though it amplified road noise like an echo chamber. Air rushed by the half open windows, and the little engine throbbed. Light traffic plied the parallel tracks of the freeway. An early sun stood over the high blue eastward line of mountains.

"You measure a man's importance by his car," Durfey said. "So I drive up in this Mazda."

Elaine said, "Nobody will notice."

"I should've brought my tax return. If they give me a name tag, I'll print my income on it."

"By all means," she said. "There isn't a chance they'll like you for your own sake."

Between Cedar City and Beaver they saw a taxidermy shop next to a village cemetery. A sign on the large new metal prefab building read: Summit Taxidermy.

"There has to be a connection between that shop and the cemetery," Durfey said. "That taxidermist probably competes with the local mortuaries. He probably stuffs dead people so their loved ones can stand them in a corner of the living room, or maybe he mounts their heads so they hang them over the fireplace."

"That's revolting," Elaine said.

About twenty miles past Beaver, they saw Mormon crickets on the shoulder of the road. Durfey pulled over and opened his door. The black, wingless insects were as large as mice. There were thousands of them milling slowly on the pavement's edge and in the yellow grass of the barrow pit.

"My gad," Durfey said, "they've come to celebrate Pioneer Day."

It was, in fact, Pioneer Day weekend, and these insects with hinged hind legs were of the species that had threatened pioneer crops in the Great Salt Lake Valley. Sea gulls from along the lake gorged on the crickets and saved a part of the crops, so the story went. Upon being admitted to the Union half a century later, landlocked Utah named the California gull its state bird.

"I knew a kid who was just as ugly as one of these crickets," Durfey said. "I wonder if he'll be at the reunion."

An hour later they pulled into Richfield and drove to the high school, where, as they expected, a Pioneer Day parade was staging. Someone had decided the Class of '51 would ride in the parade on a flatbed truck. Accordingly, a shiny red Ford truck awaited in the line of floats, festooned with bunting and a sign reading: "Welcome Home—Class of 1951." A row of back-to-back folding chairs occupied the center of the truck bed. A small crowd had gathered around the vehicle.

"I've never heard of anything like this in all my life," Elaine said. "It just blows my mind."

She had been speaking in a similar vein once or twice a week ever since the announcement of the reunion. Having watched the Rose Parade every New Year's Day while growing up, Elaine made some claim to a cultivated taste in parades. Actually, as Durfey knew, she looked forward to this bizarre exhibition in Richfield. It confirmed her prejudices about Utah, and she intended to take photos to show their friends in California.

Elaine drove away, and Durfey went down the line of floats to the truck. Twenty-five or thirty of his classmates milled about, hugging and kissing and talking excitedly. They patted bald pates and paunchy bellies, pinched one another's cheeks, and peered into one another's bleary eyes, as if to prove these strangers were utter frauds and impostors who could only pretend to a connection with the virile youths and nubile girls to whom they had said goodbye forty years before.

An obese woman with a triple chin and waddling gait accosted Durfey. She grasped his shoulders with strong fists and peered up into his face. "Who *are* you?" she said with exasperation.

That was exactly the question running through his mind. She turned out to be his cousin Rosalyn Bailey. He was stunned. She had been a majorette in the marching band—lithe, trim, and pretty. Now she hugged him with a vigorous grip, and his arms relented among her folds of flesh. He knew it was truly she and he was comforted.

He heard his name and turned. There stood Carrie Payne. She was tall and gaunt and had long, dangling arms. She looked remarkably like her former self despite grey hair and wrinkled cheeks. She lifted his golfing cap and said, "Gone! All that brown curly hair is gone!"

"It's true," he said. "After forty years of drought and overgrazing, the native herbage has given way to barren earth."

"These teeth are false," Carrie said, grimacing so he could see her dentures. "But people say you can't tell them from the real thing."

"That's right," he said. "They're veritable pearls."

"I'm just flabbergasted," she said. "Are you really that rowdy kid who used to wear boots and ride broncs at the rodeo and kicked in the Sanpete High School bass drum after a football game and bit off Bradford Higley's ear in a fight?"

"It's me," he said. "The same handsome, engaging ruffian whom you mention from days of yore. None other."

"You always were a blast," she said. "I never saw a guy try out so many crazy things as you did. But you better watch out. Bradford Higley hasn't got over you biting off his ear. He was in Albertson's the other day. He said, 'I'm going to break that Durfey Haslam's face.' I said, 'For heaven's sakes, grow up; if you hadn't been so belligerent, your ear wouldn't have got bit off in the first place.'"

Bruce Horrocks came up from behind just then and in a moment was telling Durfey he'd been a grade school principal in Granite School District in Salt Lake City for the past fifteen years and was getting close to retirement. Bruce wore a suit and tie, as if he couldn't stop being a principal even on his days off. Then Evelyn Chancellor came along and with a cry threw herself on Durfey. She turned up her face with pouted lips so he had no choice but to kiss her.

"If you aren't a sight for sore eyes," she said. "My God, I'd forgotten what a long drink of water you really are." She told him she had been divorced three times and was now doing okay as head of a small accounting firm in Orem and certainly didn't need another man with a big dingle to thwart and frustrate her at every turn. "So don't get any ideas around me," she said. "Just keep your hands to yourself."

"Aw, heck," he said. "I was just about to drag you behind one of those buildings."

Evelyn was quickly replaced by Janie Schuster, into whose plump, pretty face Durfey gazed with fond remembrance. In high school he had thought about getting serious with Janie and probably would have if he hadn't taken a typing class with Aspen Marooney. She was now Janie Higley, married to the very fellow whose ear Durfey had bitten off in the most famous fight Sevier County had known in over half a century.

Up to the fortunate moment when he got his teeth onto Bradford's ear, the fight had been going badly for Durfey. Afterward, only the fact that Bradford had been pummeling him savagely saved Durfey from jail for his equally barbaric offense. Biting off an ear was something Durfey had seen in a western movie. Being a romantic, he wanted to try it out. When the judge put him on probation, his father said, "By Jesus, Durfey, you are one lucky coyote. Now why don't you quit getting into fights? You can't fight worth shit."

Someone was shouting, "Time to get on the truck. The parade's started."

While the classmates were climbing aboard, an apparition rolled into view. On a wagon, which was draped with bunting and pulled by a farm tractor, was a barber's chair. Strapped in the chair was a ewe, and standing behind the chair with a pair of electric sheep shears in his hand was their classmate and longtime Richfield barber, Toby Jackson.

This was a parody, as Durfey instantly grasped. His sister had informed him of the event to which the float alluded. The previous fall, while driving a mountain road in Garfield County, Toby came upon a half dozen sheep lost from a herd that had been trucked out of the mountains to winter pasture. He drove to Panguitch, borrowed his cousin's trailer, drove back into the mountains, caught the sheep, and headed home to Richfield. Unfortunately, he encountered a deputy sheriff, who arrested him for rustling. A couple of months later a jury refused to believe his claim that he intended to search out the owner. He spent sixty days in the Garfield County jail, a disgrace to his family and friends.

Toby's best friend from school days, Henry Ross, had persuaded Toby to brazen out the scandal by making fun of it. Henry's grandson sat at the tractor's steering wheel, while Henry himself walked back and forth, guiding the float into the line immediately ahead of the flatbed and trying to get some of Toby's classmates to ride with him as a gesture of affirmation. Although Henry was afflicted with a speech impediment that caused him to pronounce most l's as r's, he had a genius for arranging things. He had been a master of ceremonies at almost every high school assembly and dance, and the class prophecy had predicted he would become president of the United States. He presently owned an auto dealership in Albuquerque.

When he saw Durfey, Henry shouted, "Durfey Hasram! Crimb on this wagon! The reputation of the Crass of '51 is at stake. Show some soridarity to your former chum and drinking buddy. Time to herp him cast off the ignominy and shame!"

"Ignominy" and "solidarity" were big words. Durfey assumed Henry hadn't learned them at Richfield High. Durfey couldn't remember learning any particular words at Richfield High. The words he knew came from reading at home for escape.

Durfey positioned himself on the rear of Toby's wagon and sat with dangling legs, awaiting the start of the parade. He couldn't account for complying with Henry's request. He hadn't been close to either Henry or Toby in high school. He certainly had no interest in Toby's rehabilitation in the local community. At any rate, Elaine was in for a shock. She couldn't have predicted this float. Not in a hundred years.

All this time he had watched for Aspen Marooney. Now he heard her name, and she appeared beside the flatbed truck. Classmates grasped for her hands and leaned out to kiss her cheeks. Someone said, "Hey, Aspen, do you remember me?"

There was nothing astonishing in this. She might have been a stranger whom Durfey saw every day while jogging along the estuary in Newport Beach. She wore slacks and blouse of a light yellow material, which seemed destined to gather wrinkles. Her hair was grey and her hips broad. Her facial skin sagged, especially along the rounding of her lower jaw. She wasn't as tall as he had remembered. All these years he had fancied she was about the same height as Elaine. As he could now see, she was actually a couple of inches shorter.

Trelawny Smith jumped from the truck and hugged her. Hands locked, Aspen and Trelawny stood back and gazed at each other. An old jealousy surfaced in Durfey. Aspen had told him her parents wanted her to marry Trelawny. Through no fault of his own, Trelawny had become a shadowy ally of the Marooneys. In his presence Durfey couldn't think well of himself. Ironically, about a year after Durfey went into the army, his sister Mora married Trelawny's brother. That's how Durfey had kept up with Trelawny over the years.

Trelawny was as slim and good-looking as ever. He wore tight blue jeans, grey snakeskin boots and a white pinstriped western shirt. Though Aspen hadn't married Trelawny, she should have. He was a vice president of Thiokol. No one else in the Class of '51 approached him by miles.

Aspen introduced Trelawny to a silvery-haired man who had been trailing her. This man, undoubtedly her husband, seemed fragile despite his height, which was a little less than Durfey's. He wore a white shirt, a tie without a coat, and sparkling gold-rimmed glasses. He appeared to be a man who didn't laugh freely—just enough to fulfill the requirements of congeniality. Certainly he was self-disciplined. Anybody who'd wear a tie to a parade in July had to be self-disciplined.

Trelawny was now kneeling on one knee and making a stirrup of his two hands and saying in a voice Durfey could hear, "Here you go, Aspen. I'll give you a boost. It looks like they're about ready to roll."

But just as she placed her foot in Trelawny's hands, Henry Ross seized her arm and cried, "Hord it, Aspen! Hord it! Come here with me!"

Henry pointed out Toby Jackson in his tunic behind the barber's chair. "You gotta sit on that froat," he insisted. "We need more bodies. It's for the honor of the crass. We've got to stand behind

Toby and herp rehabiritate him. Look there! Durfey Hasram is herping out. Come on! Lend a hand!"

Aspen raised Trelawny from his kneeling position, bussed his cheek, and, husband in tow, followed Henry to the back of Toby's wagon. While the tractor engine revved, she put her hands on the edge of the wagon and hoisted her body onto the float beside Durfey.

"I'll bet you've forgotten me," she said. "I used to be Aspen Marooney. Now I'm Aspen Sheffield. This is my husband, Roger."

Roger spoke politely to Durfey, then turned a pleading face toward his wife, wringing his hands like a man trying to get some feeling into frozen fingers. Durfey supposed the ribaldry of Toby's float had struck horror into his fastidious heart.

Aspen said, "If I don't give this float a little respectability, who will? Henry and Durfey don't carry any weight in this town."

"That's true," Henry said, seating himself on the edge of the wagon next to Aspen. "It's a rear froat with Aspen on it."

Aspen squeezed Roger's hand and told him to pick her up after the parade. While he walked away, Durfey considered his speedy surrender. Aspen had made Durfey knuckle under many a time during the brief months he'd had some claim on her attention. She wouldn't have married a man she couldn't dominate. That was for sure.

Toby Jackson squatted behind Durfey and Aspen and put an arm around each of them. "Thanks a lot for riding with me," he said. "Never know who your real friends are, do you? Darn that fool Henry for talking me into this. It makes it look like I'm guilty, which I'm not. The sheepman I was taking those sheep to lives in Antimony. If that deputy had arrested me after I passed the junction to Antimony, that'd be okay, because that'd show I was taking the sheep home. But that son of a bitch arrested me ten miles before I got to the junction."

"Don't lose your nerve, ord buddy," Henry said. "This is your big day. Barbering business is gonna pick up. People gonna say, Did

49

Toby Jackson ruster a few sheep? What a laugh! No skin off our nose. What's a few sheep!"

"How's Emma?" Durfey asked Toby.

"Oh, lord! You never heard about Emma? She did away with herself after our baby was born. She took strychnine, which she got from that government trapper who lived in Monroe, damn him. Man, she died hard! Crawled over the furniture, screaming. Then I married a girl named Janice from Scipio. Doubt you'd know her. I'll introduce you this afternoon. Got four children. One by Emma, three by Janice."

Toby resumed his standing position behind the barber's chair. He wasn't a bad looking man in his white tunic. His hair, freshly shingled, was parted in the middle. Toby made the tragic sound commonplace. With a few simple words under a bright sun, he tossed off whole planets of grief. Durfey wondered if he had a gene that produced brevity when he accounted for life's losses.

The wagon began to roll, and the flatbed truck growled along only a couple of yards behind the dangling legs of Henry, Aspen, and Durfey. Frequent stops interrupted their progress, as if the leaders suffered from fits of indecision or had lost their way. During this preliminary stage, the parade passed through a residential district where no onlookers lined the walks—where, in fact, there were no walks for onlookers to line. Instead, irrigation ditches and weedy borders paralleled the street.

"So you got married and moved to California," Aspen said to Durfey during one of the stops. "I should just as well have married you myself. I had no idea you'd be anything but a farmer."

She turned to Henry. "If Roger and I fly down to Albuquerque, will you give us a discount on a fancy Dodge?"

"Lord, you shourd've tord me in advance," Henry said. "I'd've driven one up for you. Herr, yes, I can give you a discount. Dodge pickups are what I serr most of. But I can get you any moder you want. Any moder!"

In the meantime, Durfey was puzzled—shocked, almost—by

her blunt allusion to the marriage that had never been. Banter on an eventuality so pointedly unachieved seemed a violation of common decency.

"Your wife is named Elaine," Aspen said, returning her attention to Durfey as the parade resumed its progress.

"That's right. Her name is Elaine."

"Did she come to the reunion?"

"Absolutely. She'll be somewhere along Main Street, taking pictures to show our friends."

"Her father was a barber, wasn't he?" she said.

"How did you know that?"

"Somebody told me, years ago. Maybe it was John who told me."

"Of course," Durfey said. "John Izatt—the central clearing house for the Class of '51."

"Is she wonderful?"

"Yes, very."

"And pretty?"

"I've always thought so."

"You have a dog named Poot. And three children and I forget how many grandchildren. I read that in your letter in the pamphlet Evelyn had printed."

"You have the advantage on me since I haven't seen the pamphlet."

"I have eight children and twenty-two beautiful grandchildren," Aspen said. "Next month it'll be twenty-three grandchildren and, by Christmas, twenty-four."

"Good lord!"

"Didn't you know I had eight children?" she asked.

"Well, yes, off and on I kept hearing you'd had a lot of babies. I just couldn't quite believe it was true."

"Do you think I shouldn't have had so many?"

"There's the environment to think of."

"Oh, brother! Are you an environmentalist?" she said. "Well,

51

don't come talking to me about population control. My line reproduces like mice."

With increasing clarity, he saw the girl of forty years ago—a tiny, upturned nose, high cheekbones, a mouth like Cupid's bow. Simple qualities magnetized her surroundings—light mirrored by moist eyes, sound struck from vocal chords of an alto range. Or maybe, like gamma rays, that untarnished charisma derived from sources deeper than the sensory.

The parade turned a corner into another side street and went steadily forward till it turned onto Main Street, where sidewalks were packed with onlookers. On the corners, looking both forward and back, Durfey saw that the parade consisted of a dozen floats, a couple of high school bands, three or four mounted posses, a bright red fire truck, an ambulance, six or seven shiny new semi-trucks, a couple of rodeo clowns pedaling old washing machines, and a straggling retinue of children on bicycles and skateboards.

One of the floats was a mountain made of crepe paper with a young woman in Austrian dress and four or five children in lederhosen. A sign said Climb Every Mountain, and songs from *The Sound of Music* came from a hidden loudspeaker. Another float presented a bespangled woman on a revolving pedestal. A sign declared her to be Mother, Queen of the Home. Another float, dedicated to Patriotism, was an American flag made of red, white, and blue napkins stuck into chicken wire backing. On top of this giant flag stood a man who looked like Abraham Lincoln.

The high school band ahead of Toby's wagon was led by a baton-twirling majorette with pretty, high-stepping legs. Already her white boots were spattered with manure from the posses that had gone before. Apparently no one had followed the posses with a scoop shovel and broom.

"I pity those poor kids in that band," Aspen said to Durfey as their wagon turned the corner.

"A wasted sentiment! A little fresh horse dung never hurt anyone. Damn, I miss that smell."

She said, "I'll mail you a box of it next Christmas."

"I wish you would."

"That reminds me, did you ever make it to Spain? You said you wanted to be a matador. In fact, one day you got into a corral with a dairy bull. Do you remember that?"

"Do I ever," he said. "What a day!"

"You used a saddle blanket for a cape, and that hornless bull tossed you clear over the fence!"

"No bull tossed me over a fence," Durfey said. "I climbed over."

"Climbed?"

"Well, jumped. I went over on my own power."

"You flew over by jet propulsion."

"Frew over by jet propursion!" said Henry, "That's darn funny."

Aspen lifted Durfey's cap and gazed at his bald pate. She turned to Henry and said, "I could cry for his poor lost hair. Look how his cheeks have gullied. He's shrunk while I've got fat."

Durfey ran a hand over his skull. "Note the handsome gabling. I have an attic in my upper story where clever ideas gestate and hatch for power, profit, and pleasure."

"Isn't he something?" she said to Henry. "He never lacked for words."

"No, sir!" Henry said. "Not Durfey Hasram. He never lacked for words."

Durfey stared into her earnest face, only inches from his own. She wore lipstick, perhaps a little eyebrow pencil—no other cosmetic that he could make out. Her earlobes held tiny gold earrings. Her cheeks were slightly pitted, as they had been forty years ago.

He was beginning to relax. He felt almost euphoric. He had been off balance at first, not knowing how to read her, but now he believed he was catching on. He discerned genius in her conversation. She wasn't trifling with him. She was showing him how to reconstruct their past, how to domesticate it to the present. They had only to retell the past with unassuming ease, had only to be candid. If he wanted to hug her, he could. They were old friends and shared a permissible affection.

About half way along Main Street, the parade came to another halt. A mounted deputy sheriff trotted up the street to investigate. Soon a city patrol car came for John Izatt, who had been riding on the flatbed. Henry Ross also climbed into the patrol car. When Henry returned, he reported that, after turning off Main Street at a corner ahead, the horses conveying the grand marshal of the parade and his wife had bolted across somebody's lawn and down a driveway and the carriage had overturned in a vegetable garden. No one was hurt and officials were holding the parade till they could get the carriage righted and back onto the street. The grand marshall was willing to return, though his lady had decided to ride in a limousine.

Ambitious for the public good, Henry walked forward a block or two along the shady side of Main, and then back along the sunny side, telling everybody what the trouble was. In the meantime Toby was summoned for a business conversation with a woman, for whom he had agreed to haul a load of flagstone from a quarry in Piute County.

Durfey and Aspen remained on the back of the wagon, unnoticed by the crowd on either sidewalk.

"We have a little time," Aspen said. "So tell me the nice things your children have accomplished."

Durfey told her about his grandson Alex, Jimmy's boy, who had undergone two operations for mending a cleft palate. "He's been very brave," Durfey said. "Not a word of complaint."

"I'm glad he's all right," Aspen said. "You can't be happy if your grandchildren aren't happy, can you?"

"That's true," he said.

"My children have done quite well," she said. "Not as well as I had hoped. But really quite well. Certainly they've done better than I deserve."

A boy on a small bicycle rode past. He wore a cowboy hat and scuffed boots and, over his shoulders, an empty newspaper bag. "That kid hasn't made it home yet from delivering papers," Durfey said.

"He reminds me of that boy from Texas we found fishing in a cow tank," she said.

"I haven't thought of him in forty years," Durfey said. They had driven out in Durfey's pickup when Aspen was supposed to be on a school bus headed for a music festival at Kanab. On a back road in Piute County they came upon a freckle-faced kid with a tamarisk pole and cork bobber fishing in the muddy water of a cow tank. Like other cow tanks, this one would have been dry eight or ten months out of twelve. Some years it would never have had water in it.

"Where you all from?" the boy asked.

"Richfield," Durfey said. "Yourself?"

"Huletsboro, Texas."

"You're a long way from home."

"Done come to live in Marysvale," the kid said. "Daddy's working in the uranium mine up there." He pointed at a dugway and derrick on a nearby ridge.

"What you fishing for?" Durfey asked.

"Mackerel."

"Mackerel's an ocean fish."

"Catfish maybe."

"No catfish here either. You might just as well quit."

"Might be something else then."

The nearby band began to blare again and marched in place, apparently to keep up its spirits. A few engines revved. The sun was high and hot. Toby finished his conversation with the woman and now joined Henry and a group of men across the street.

"You couldn't leave that kid from Texas in peace," Aspen said to Durfey. "You couldn't stand to see him fishing in a muddy pool with no fish in it."

"Little did I know then," Durfey said. "That's what we all do."

"Oh, dear, that's so depressing," she said. "You're not going to be gloomy, are you? Haven't you caught at least a few fish."

"Oh, more than a few. Yes, I've caught many a fish in life's muddy pool. I've not been unhappy. Not at all."

"I'm so glad," she said.

Just then the two rodeo clowns pedaled by with their washing machines mounted on tiny wheels. Each could disappear by sinking into the tub of his machine and pulling the lid shut over his head.

"We're in a circus," Durfey said. "I wonder whose idea it was to have us ride in this parade."

"It was John's."

"Why didn't Shirley Sue override him? I used to think she was rather sensible."

"We could climb on the truck," Aspen said. "I suppose there's still room for us there. But of course that would make us appear indifferent to Toby's plight, wouldn't it?"

"Yes, we mustn't abandon Toby."

"I'll admit I'm worried Roger will tell Mother I've been on Toby's float."

"Good lord! Is your mother still alive?"

"She stays with Roger and me in Cottonwood every spring. Now she's here in Richfield with Hope and Dan. And she takes turns with Seamus and Patrick."

"She's still a woman of standards, I trust."

"More so than ever."

"So what will she think of this float if Roger tells her about it?"

"That it's a scandal. That it invites laughter. That it scorns repentance."

"Well, it is rather good-humored, isn't it?"

"That poor sheep tied in the barber chair is panting fiercely," she said.

"It'll be all right."

"It's eerie," she said. "A ram in the thicket."

"It's a ewe."

"I think it's going to die."

"Nonsense," he said. "About another hour and it'll be back in the pasture."

"Didn't you tell me once that if a sheep got on its back in such a way that it couldn't get right side up again, it could die?"

"I may have told you that."

"Is it true?"

"Yes, but it takes a while. Like all night. This sheep will be okay."

"You were clever with sheep," she said. "In Fry Pan Canyon you always made the flock graze in a certain direction."

"I had dogs."

"And I remember you sliced potatoes and onions into a Dutch oven and added mutton. It was wonderful—the best food I ever ate."

"There were a lot better camp cooks than I was," he said.

She asked whether he remembered ice skating on Piute Reservoir on a December night. The ice had rumbled beneath their blades, and they returned breathless to a roaring fire and drank soda pop turned to slush by the twenty-below-zero temperature. The broad sky winked with uncountable stars, made brilliant by an atmosphere devoid of heat.

"I remember," he said. He would have preferred not to remember. The ice skating was a prelude to things that shouldn't have happened. He drove her home, and she invited him in because her family had gone to Santaquin for a holiday visit. That was the last night he spent with Aspen, and the next morning she said goodbye without his knowing it would be for forty years.

The parade began to move again, and as engines up and down the line sputtered and roared, Henry and Toby climbed aboard the wagon. Both were animated, as if their conversations on the street had led them to believe that Richfield approved of Toby and his float. There was, in fact, an increased uproar on the sidewalks as Toby's float progressed along Main Street. People clapped and whistled as the tractor and wagon calmly putted by, and those ahead craned their necks and stepped out to see what was pleasing the crowd down the street.

"Jeez, they love it!" Henry exulted. He crawled to a side of the wagon where, again seated with dangling legs, he waved at the crowd with happy gusto.

Men in boots and jeans and caps with feedstore insignias on them broke into hilarity, shouting through cupped hands, "Clip me a little wool, Toby," and, "Who's that good looking feller you got in that chair?" and, "Hey, Toby, do you clean them shears before you cut hair?"

Oblivious to this raucous pleasure, Durfey studied the manure-spattered pavement beneath his dangling legs. He felt off balance. All this candor on Aspen's part, this unassuming ease, was maybe too much. Maybe he hadn't caught on to how he should read her. She appeared to lack an essential sensitivity. There was shock in the simple naming of Fry Pan Canyon, shock in the memory of its shady groves and rushing water. There were certain things from the past that couldn't be adapted to the present. No one should mention them. They should remain as if they had never been.

During the autumn of 1951, Durfey attempted to resign himself to never marrying Aspen Marooney. She had gone away suddenly to BYU in September, violating a promise made only a night or two earlier. He didn't suppose she would look him up when she came home for the holidays, but she did. Then for several days under a bright, cold winter sun they had driven the back roads of central Utah in Durfey's pickup. She was confused and unhappy and talked often about a Roger Sheffield whom she had met, a young man from Salt Lake entering graduate school in sociology. It was obvious he wanted to marry her. Furthermore, he measured up as far as her parents were concerned. Yet she asked Durfey over and over, "Shall you and I elope to Las Vegas and get married?"

Each time Durfey replied, "You bet. No need to tell anybody. Let's head down there and do it!" But she wasn't asking Durfey. She was asking herself and her answer was no.

On the night before New Year's Eve, while the thermometer stood below zero, they skated on Piute Reservoir. Numb with cold, they drove to Richfield, and she asked Durfey inside the Marooney home for the first and only time of his life.

She pulled lunch meat and mayonnaise from the refrigerator, and they made sandwiches and hot chocolate and took them into the living room, where she lit the gas log. She turned out the overhead light, and they ate in the blue flicker of a butane fire. After they had finished, she said, "I've made up my mind. I'm going back to BYU the day after New Year's."

"I figured you would."

"You just can't know how much I've always respected you. We'll always be good friends. You've given me so much to treasure. There'll be nobody like you in my memories."

"I wish you hadn't come home," he said.

"I'm sorry I came. But I had to be sure."

"I imagine you'll go for that Sheffield fellow."

"No, right now I'm just going to concentrate on my studies. I just want to get my head on straight."

He pulled out a handkerchief and wiped his cheeks.

"Oh, dear, please don't cry!" she said.

"I can't help it," he said. "It's so damned depressing."

She sat beside him on the sofa and leaned her head against his shoulder. She too began to cry. They held each other tightly, and soon, amidst their sobs and sniffles, they began to kiss and fondle one another. She let him unbutton her shirt and slide a hand into her jeans, and soon she pulled him up and led him down the hall to the bedroom she shared with Hope.

They undressed and got onto Hope's bed because Aspen's bed was a tangle of dirty sheets and rumpled clothes. They made love and he went to sleep. She woke him and said she couldn't sleep. She wondered whether he wanted to make love again. So they did a second time and fell into another slumber. Toward morning she woke him and said she still couldn't sleep. He said he wasn't a sex fiend, but she fondled and kissed him till he made love to her a third time.

"It's good to find out a man can do it three times in one night," he said. "I wouldn't have believed it if I hadn't experienced it myself."

He didn't go back to sleep. Soon he got out of bed and peered out a window and said, "I'm heading out of here before your neighbors wake up and see my pickup in your driveway."

He dressed and she put on a robe. They went to the kitchen and she cooked cereal for breakfast. At the table she asked him to come back that night and take her to the New Year's Eve dance.

"I'm tired of slipping around," she said. "Daddy and Mamma will just have to make the best of it if they find out. Maybe I'll tell them myself. Maybe I'll tell them they might just as well get used to Durfey Haslam."

It was still dark when he left. He turned in the black doorway and she kissed him. "I love you," she said.

He was cheerful as he drove away. It was clear she had cancelled that terrible idea of just being friends, so they were back to where they had been during the summer, counting on getting married sooner or later.

However, when he returned that night, the house was dark except for the porch light, and there was a note taped to the door that said, "Gone back to BYU. Just friends, please. Aspen."

He rattled the door but no one answered. He tried the knob and found it locked. He sat in his pickup in front of the house for maybe an hour while the wind spit a hard snow against the windshield. He was beginning to believe that the note meant what it said. He felt duped of what little innocence he had managed to achieve during the autumn just past, and his anger and guilt amplified till he was afraid he might do harm to someone, probably himself, and he started the pickup and drove home to Glenwood and sat at the kitchen table twiddling his thumbs while his mother kneaded dough for rolls for New Year's Day dinner.

A couple of days later Durfey reported for basic training, and three months later he was in Germany with the U.S. Army. He had a letter from his mother saying that sometime in February Aspen Marooney had married somebody in the Salt Lake temple. There had been a reception in Richfield, but of course the Haslams weren't invited.

For forty years Durfey had wondered whether he should have returned to his bishop to confess that last night with Aspen. He wondered whether he should have told Elaine. He wasn't encouraged by his experience of telling Elaine about the summer in Fry Pan Canyon. From that experience he had learned that the injury confession rouses is a powerful corrosive. It pits the friction pads between a couple, leaving them rough and prone to gather heat. So his last night with Aspen went untold.

Henry was ecstatic over the applause coming from the onlookers along the sidewalks. Though it was uncertain whether he could be heard, Henry shouted between cupped hands, "You bet, forks, this is it, the froat you've been waiting for! This is your very own barber, Toby Jackson. Herr, yes, he store some sheep and he's sorry for it. Anybody can make a mistake. Now come on in and let him cut your hair. He's got a speciar on next week. Two bucks a head! Come on in and let him cut your hair."

Toby, for his part, seemed to have gone mad. He was dancing like a prize fighter behind the barber's chair, waving both arms wildly in the air and snapping the cord of the shears like a whip.

"This is getting out of hand," Aspen said to Durfey. "If I'd known we were signing on for a lunatic train, I wouldn't have been so agreeable."

Durfey scarcely noticed. He was trying to feel reasonable about past events. He was reminding himself that the exploratory love of teenagers is a species of venture capital, to be invested on speculation and lost without surprise. It was Aspen's right to experiment with whether she had wanted to marry him. She had tried him on for size and he didn't fit. Yet, remembering their last night together, he was outraged all over again. Even by craft and cunning she couldn't have contrived to humiliate him more than she had by her manner of saying goodbye.

"Couldn't you do something to calm him down?" Aspen said in reference to the madly dancing Toby.

At that moment, Toby heaved his arm violently, and the cord attached to the shears lashed across Aspen's face.

"He hit me!" she cried.

"Lay off!" Durfey shouted, and as the cord flew by on another wild journey he caught it and yanked the shears from Toby's hand.

Balanced against the barber's chair, Toby stared down on Aspen, who had clapped a hand across her mouth and cheek.

"Damn you," Durfey said. "You cut her across the face with this cord."

"I didn't mean to do that," Toby cried. He knelt beside her, his hands fluttering. "Jesus, Aspen, you're the last person I'd want to hurt."

"It's all right," she said. "Just a little sting."

"For gosh sake, get back into prace, Toby," Henry called. "You had 'em eating out of your hand. Start waving again."

Toby took the shears from Durfey and stood behind the chair. "This is so stupid," he said.

Aspen turned her cheek to Durfey. "How does it look?"

"There's a little white welt," he said. "Nothing to speak of."

Just ahead, the band had struck up another march, raising a new din. The crowd was thicker along this portion of Main Street. Sunlight glinted on dark glasses. Bald heads shone. The crowd's mood was passive. No one shouted, no one waved. Henry let his hands drop into his lap, and Toby leaned against the chair.

Aspen got onto her hands and knees and pulled herself up behind the barber's chair.

"Come back here!" Durfey demanded. "He won't do any more of that wild stuff. I guarantee it."

"Atta girl!" Toby cried. He began to wave to the crowd.

"We should have been standing by him all the while," Aspen called down to Durfey.

"What's got into you?" Durfey said.

"Do your duty," she said. "Get up here where you belong."

"Do my duty!" he exclaimed.

Through cupped hands he shouted toward the crowd, "Practice abstinence and take your vitamins, folks! Look at the census figures. Be mindful of war, famine, and disease. Practice abstinence and take your vitamins."

Aspen bent over him. "Don't be crazy."

"They can't make out what I'm saying."

"Stand by me, Durfey," she said.

"Why the hell not," he said, pulling himself up behind the chair.

"Hot dog!" Toby exulted. "Old Durfey's here too." He began to dance again.

4. Revisiting the Farm

When Elaine returned to the high school, Durfey was chatting with a half dozen male friends in the street. He introduced her, and they all shook her hand.

One of the friends, named Hans, had a forefinger missing above the first joint. "He tried to shave a little block in wood shop one day," Durfey explained. "The jointer pulled his finger in and whittled it off. You should have heard him holler."

"You better believe I hollered," Hans said.

Hans offered Elaine details about his career. He presently worked for a shoe factory in Alabama that shipped soles to Korea, which came back in finished shoes. His job was with the computers. Everything was robotized. Machines did everything, except maintain themselves, which is where Hans came in.

Trelawny Smith said he was intrigued how an obscure high school like Richfield prepared a man to robotize a shoe factory.

Durfey said high school had nothing whatsoever to do with Hans's success. "Do you know what I learned in high school? The function of a salad fork! When it was time for the Future Farmers of America banquet, the adviser instructed us all in table manners. I knew about hay forks and manure forks. But I'll be damned if I'd ever heard of salad forks before."

While the debate over a high school education continued, Elaine looked Trelawny over carefully. He wore expensive western clothes, and his abundant brown hair was nicely trimmed and parted. Though she had never seen him before, she knew a lot about him because his brother and Durfey's sister lived in the Imperial Valley only a couple of hundred miles from Durfey and Elaine. The brother, Tyler, was a much plainer, more corpulent man than Trelawny. Durfey's sister Mora wasn't much for looks either. She wore baggy slacks and loose blouses and gave herself cheap perms.

Durfey often claimed the wedding of a Haslam and a Smith was the most unprecedented union in the history of Sevier County. Once after Mora and Tyler had paid them a Christmas visit, Durfey said, "It's a case of the peasantry marrying into the nobility."

"They don't seem so mismatched to me," Elaine protested. "They're neither one tidy."

"That doesn't matter," he said. "The wedding defied all standards of propriety. A Smith is a Smith and a Haslam is a Haslam, and never the twain shall meet."

Soon Trelawny's wife Pamela came by in their Cadillac and the group of friends broke up. "Look at that Cadillac," Durfey said to Elaine as Trelawny and Pamela rolled away. "They didn't pay a penny more than we paid for our Buick. And here we are driving Steve's Mazda!"

While they crossed the street to the Mazda, he asked Elaine whether she wanted to attend the Pioneer Day program.

"I'll do whatever you want," she said. "This is your reunion."

"Shall we drive out to the farm?"

She agreed. It was an ordeal that couldn't be avoided. The sooner they got it over with the better. Durfey got into the driver's seat of the Mazda. That's the way it was with them. If they drove together, Durfey took the wheel. Elaine didn't resent it enough to make an issue of it. In general, his self-esteem was low. If driving a car made him feel important, she was all for it.

They drove east through the older residential part of Richfield.

Durfey paid no attention to the ruined backyards with derelict barns and patches of weeds. Elaine could easily believe he saw only prosperous lots with cows and chickens and gardens, as they had appeared to him when he began riding the bus to high school in 1947. His fascination with Richfield made no sense. Since he considered his family a clan of pariahs, he ought to have been happy to assume a new identity in California. But he never stopped fretting about California. He didn't like transplanted palm trees in new shopping centers; he didn't like braziers on public beaches; he didn't like the glossy finish on the stain-resistant sofa in their condo, which he associated with California. "I'd like to see a little soil on the dadgummed thing," he said of the sofa.

He was always wanting to go back and renegotiate some old transactions in Utah. He wanted to go back to Richfield and humbly beg for acceptance. He couldn't feel good about himself till this decayed little county seat had forgiven him for being a Haslam.

After they had got out of town, Durfey asked whether she had liked the parade.

"It was just fabulous—four mounted posses and a dozen shiny new semi-trucks. And a fire engine too. You'd think people here did nothing but ride horses and drive trucks."

"Don't forget the kids on bicycles and skateboards," he added.

"Oh, no, I can't forget them either. I took pictures of everything. I can hardly wait to get the slides so we can show them to Jenny and Wilbur." Jenny and Wilbur were friends from Laguna Beach. Jenny was media specialist at the middle school where Elaine taught English.

Durfey said, "I suppose you were surprised to see me on that little float of Toby Jackson's."

"Well, yes," she said, "that was a surprise."

"Toby Jackson went to jail last winter for stealing sheep. That float was Henry Ross's way of rehabilitating him."

"I understood that," she said. "People were talking about it on the sidewalk. I'll admit it struck a bad chord with me. My father being a barber and all—it seemed a desecration to tie a farm animal in a barber's chair."

"It was just a joke."

"Some people didn't think so. There was a man with only one ear behind me. I won't repeat what he said about the float."

"Gosh, a man with one ear!" Durfey said. "Well, you know who that was."

"And the woman in the yellow slacks—they said she was Aspen Marooney."

"Her married name is Sheffield," he said. "I met her husband—a very nice man."

The road to Glenwood proceeded east on a straight line, then turned a corner and went south. On either side lay fenced pastures and fields of alfalfa and corn. The road hadn't been paved during Durfey's boyhood, and he often spoke of the rattle of gravel on the fenders of the family cars.

They went by a farm house with a trellis of climbing red roses. Durfey seemed not to see it. There had been a trellis of red roses in the front of their house in Santa Ana. One day Durfey said it made him think of Aspen Marooney. Elaine asked why. He said because there had been a giant red rose bush in the Marooneys' front yard, as he noticed when he'd driven by, not being welcome to call at the Marooney home.

A few days after this discussion about roses, Elaine told Durfey she wanted him to stop saying he loved her. "Because you don't," she said. "You're still in love with Aspen Marooney."

He said, "I do love you. Honest, I do."

She said, "I want you to treat me with more dignity. Don't pat me on the butt in the kitchen and don't be touching my breasts all the time when we pass in the hallway or when we're driving in the car."

A week or so later, Durfey did something that struck her in the worst possible way. He confessed what he and Aspen had done in his sheep camp in a canyon near Fishlake lodge where she was working.

He said, "I need to get this off my chest. Aspen and I more or less lived like husband and wife that summer."

She said, "What do you mean, like husband and wife?"

"I mean we had sexual relations. But we stopped. We repented. I went to my bishop and told him what I'd been doing. I told him we'd quit. He said, 'Good. Now just stick with it and you're clean again. And you don't need to talk it over with anyone else. It'll just be our secret, mine and yours.' I didn't mean to be deceitful by not telling you about it before. I just thought we'd get along better if I took the bishop's advice and kept mum."

Long ago Elaine had been in a girls' class at church where the teacher gave each girl a stick of gum and said to chew it. Then the teacher asked the girls to exchange their chewed wads of gum. Of course they refused. The teacher said, "That's the way it is if you have sex before you're married. You're like a wad of used gum."

After Durfey confessed his summer in the mountains, he and Elaine didn't have sex for three or four months. She was too angry. Also, she felt inadequate as a sexual partner. How could she compete with Aspen Marooney?

At last she asked her mother and father whether she shouldn't file for a divorce. Her father was lying on the sofa in their house at Altadena because he was suffering from leukemia, and her mother sat in a chair nearby. She told them as far as she could tell Durfey had never truly loved her. She told them what he had done with Aspen Marooney. They were shocked because they loved Durfey, and all this didn't seem to fit with anything they knew about him.

Her father said, "Does he still keep up a connection with this woman?"

"No, he just talks about her all the time."

"Does he drink?"

"Of course not."

"Does he squander the pay check?"

"No, he turns it over to me. He doesn't even have pocket money if I don't give it to him."

"Is he unkind? Is he mean to the boys."

"You know he isn't unkind," she said.

Her father pulled the cover around his neck and stared at the ceiling. He seemed tired, and in fact, as things turned out, he had only about a year to live.

Her mother said, "The issue seems to be whether or not he loves you. But that probably isn't important. He treats you right. That's what counts."

Her father said, "People love each other in different ways."

She broke down and sobbed, and her father said, "I'm sorry you feel so bad."

At any rate, divorce was out of the question. Later Elaine talked all of this over with her sister Joanne, who advised her to be more slinky.

"After all is said and done," Joanne said, "bed is the ice rink where the hockey game of marriage is won or lost. Don't stand on your dignity. If he wants to pat your butt at the kitchen sink, let him."

So Elaine bought a marriage manual and read it, and a night or two later she went into the room Durfey used as a home office in the house in Santa Ana. He was making some telephone calls. She said, "Do you want to go to bed early tonight?"

He stopped with a finger in the dial. He hung up the receiver and swung in his swivel chair. "You bet," he said.

During the years that followed, Durfey would sometimes mutter while having his climax, "I really do love you." The next morning in the shower he'd apologize for saying those forbidden words.

Elaine believed Durfey was in love with half of her, or, to put it another way, half of Durfey loved her. He was a used wad of gum in a sense she could never have imagined earlier. But as her mother had said, a man who earns a steady living and comes home at night and takes pleasure in his children doesn't grow on every bush.

They stopped first at the Glenwood cemetery. Glenwood wasn't actually a village; rather it was a cluster of farms with a gas station, church, and cemetery. Circled entirely by sagebrush, the cemetery was planted in grass and fenced with barbed wire. In one corner a few elm trees shaded a picnic table and an outdoor toilet.

They got out of the car and found the graves of Durfey's parents, Balis Haslam and Dorothy Sathkin. Next to them were the graves of Durfey's brother and two sisters who died in childhood. Balis and Dorothy had been born and reared in Glenwood on farms only a half-mile apart. According to Durfey, they were second cousins though they had claimed to be more distantly related. Balis was five years older than Dorothy and got her pregnant when she was fourteen, and they had to get married.

With his pocket knife Durfey uprooted a couple of dandelions between the graves. "When I die," he said, "bury me in a blanket so I'll decay in a hurry."

Elaine said, "You better not bury me in a blanket. I want the full works, including a waterproof vault."

"Lord," he said, "the world can't afford to bury people in waterproof vaults. We need to recycle our own bodies just like soda pop cans."

"That doesn't matter," she said. "I want the full works."

Durfey got on his knees and flipped his knife so that it looped through a couple of turns and stuck upright in the grass, a game he called mumbledy-peg. Sometimes Elaine would say, "Why don't you get a smaller knife? You don't need a saber just to pare your fingernails." He'd reply, "You can't tell when I might want to prune a tree."

That had made sense when they lived in the house with a yard in Santa Ana, back before the Hispanic barrios grew up all around them. In the condo at Newport Beach he had no yard work of any sort. It seemed a man raised on a farm had to carry a big knife with blades for punching leather and castrating calves even if it gave him trouble getting through the electronic gate at an air terminal.

Durfey went on playing mumbledy-peg in a distracted way. He often claimed he could think better while flipping his knife into the grass. He said what he really needed was a cow to milk every night and morning. He could have clarified his insurance investigations while pulling on her teats.

Elaine wasn't surprised when he announced it was time to visit the grave of his great-grandfather. That's what he had been thinking about. That's what she had been thinking about too. Small as the cemetery was, Elaine couldn't remember the location of this grave from one visit to another. But Durfey knew, and he led her to it. It had no erect stone—merely a rough rock buried flat under the grass with a circle about the size of a dinner plate cleared to show the ancestor's initials, O.M.H.

"Look at that grass," he said. "It's almost entirely grown over the stone. Lucky we came along, isn't it? Why doesn't somebody pay a little attention to it?"

"You might get a regular stone for him," she said. As usual, Durfey didn't listen. He was kneeling by the grave, cutting away the turf with his knife, enlarging the circle around the initials.

This great-grandfather had sexual relations with two of his daughters for decades. He kept the second daughter at home till she was thirty. His wife was a classic case of the defeated spouse who consents to the substitution of a daughter in her marriage bed. It was his grown sons, Durfey's grandfather among them, who put an end to this arrangement. They arrived at their father's house together, confronted him with the truth, and forcibly took away their thirty-year-old sister. They informed church authorities, and their father was excommunicated. He didn't regard this as fair. During the rest of his life he was angry and uncontrite and cruel to his wife.

In a mood of vengeance the brothers agreed there would never be a finished stone over his grave, just a rough-hewn rock with his initials crudely rubbed in. Durfey's grandfather impressed this on Durfey's father, and Durfey's father impressed it on Durfey. All the cousins of whom Elaine had any knowledge felt as Durfey did. When the community planted grass in the cemetery, this stone was buried flat with only the great-grandfather's initials showing. As far as Durfey was concerned, there was nothing to be done but visit the grave every three or four years and clear the initials of encroaching turf.

For years Elaine had tried to remain detached from this wicked man, who was no relative of hers. Then one day it had come to her with shocking clarity that he was an ancestor of her children, and her blood and his had mingled in her sons and daughter. It wasn't civilized to leave an ancestor without a proper stone. After Sally was grown, Elaine confided the sordid story to her and, once Sally's shock subsided, secured her agreement to assist in seeing that a proper stone be erected after Durfey was dead and gone and could no longer raise an objection.

She instructed Sally not to be deterred by her distant cousins who might still bear malice in the matter. After all, Sally was as much a grandchild as any of them. She was to go to court if necessary, Elaine having set aside a little trust from her teaching salary to see to it. Nonetheless, she could see why Aspen Marooney's parents hadn't let her marry Durfey. He really did come from a decadent line.

Leaving the cemetery, they drove to the farm where Durfey had grown up, which had been amalgamated into a larger property presently operated by a hired resident farmer. No one of Haslam descent had owned this place for almost two decades. When Elaine first saw it in 1955, Balis and Dorothy and four of their children were still living on it.

Durfey entered by a cattle guard on the far side of the new property and followed a lane among fields and across a couple of ditches so that he wouldn't have to go by the farmer's house.

Elaine said, "Why don't you just stop and let him know you're coming onto the place. He's not going to object."

He said, "I can't ask somebody's permission to see my own home."

Durfey stopped first by the old mink sheds. Balis was one of the first in Sevier County to raise mink, and especially in the later years, after Durfey had left home, he made some good money doing it. There were ten long sheds, now deteriorated, with sheets of corrugated metal hanging loose and grey weathered boards sprung from their nails.

"We asphyxiated them," Durfey said. "Come skinning time in the fall, I'd drive a little tractor and trailer down the rows between the sheds and I'd reach in and grab the mink and throw them into a revolving cylinder that had exhaust from the tractor engine coming into it, cooled through a little tank of water. So they'd die fast, and I'd throw them out into a bin of sawdust where the skinners could get hold of them easy."

"Didn't it bother you," she asked, "to kill cute, furry little things?"

"Mink are mean sons of bitches," he said. "You can wear thick leather gloves and they'll still bite them." That explained why his hands were covered with tiny scars.

Oddly, although he liked the idea of being a mink farmer, he didn't like the idea of mink coats. During the most recent Christmas season they shopped in Neiman-Marcus in Newport Beach, where Durfey noticed a coat of clipped, green-dyed fur. "My gosh," he said, "I used to breed, feed, kill, and skin those things. And this is what it all comes to! A shaved, green-dyed nap! That's so damned ugly."

Neiman-Marcus was in Fashion Island Mall. In the center of the mall towered a seventy-five-foot white fir Christmas tree, cut, so a sign said, in the northern Sierra. The tree had perfect symmetry and was flocked and adorned by three thousand large glass balls and three thousand colored lights. The tree glittered in the sweet, warm winter dusk of southern California. Standing in front of it, Durfey said, "This is purely artificial. There's nothing natural about Christmas in Newport Beach."

They went into a boutique called Victoria's Secret to get a gift for Sally. It was stocked with blouses, scarves, perfumes, and dainty underthings. Durfey pointed to a lacy bikini bra on a rack. He said, "It isn't gift wrapping that makes a woman." Elaine understood this as a compliment. Truly he loved her, at least by half. They went into other shops looking for some running clothes, which would be their Christmas gift to one another.

There was an estuary in Newport Beach dedicated to aquatic wildlife. At its mouth sat the posh Newport Beach Marina, afloat with luxurious ocean-going pleasure craft. On the bluffs above the estuary were mansions worth four, six, or eight million dollars apiece. In the waters and mud of the estuary ducks, geese, and herons swam and waded. Along a one-way road adhering to the south bank of the estuary, joggers and cyclists relieved the tensions of their California lifestyle.

Durfey had been jogging there ever since they moved into their condo. He asked Elaine to join him. She said, "Okay, but not dressed the way you go jogging." She wanted real running clothes— matching shorts and T-shirt and a bright sweat suit for foggy mornings. She said Durfey needed some real running clothes too. He agreed if she'd pick them out.

So between Christmas and their trip to Utah for the reunion, she and Durfey had been jogging three or four times a week along the estuary. They enjoyed the water fowl and were especially glad to see a new species turn up from time to time. There were also cottontail rabbits in the reeds along the bank. All of this was within earshot of six-lane traffic on Jamboree Boulevard.

After looking over the mink sheds, Durfey drove another hundred yards to the farm house, which was in ruin, with doors and windows knocked out and plaster falling off the inside walls and floor boards broken through. The house had been used for an animal shelter for a while, and there were piles of dried cow manure in all the rooms. All this had happened since the place was sold out of the Haslam family after Dorothy's death of a stroke, which occurred less than six years following Balis's death.

Durfey got out of the car and circled the house slowly. He picked his way through tall dried weeds and a litter of barrels, cans, and old boards with nails in them. He peered through a door and looked back at Elaine in the car. If she had been there beside him, he would have pointed through the door and said, "Right about where that floorboard is busted is where the bed stood I was born in. Right there is where I was born. I imagine I was conceived there too."

He'd have said, "The mistake we made was not tearing down this old house before we sold the place. It's better not to see the exact spot where you were born. I wish I had the strength of character not to come out and see this old place every time I come to Richfield."

When Elaine first saw this house during the fall of 1955, she and Durfey had just become engaged. They were attending BYU and planning to marry when the quarter ended in December. Balis and Dorothy and even Durfey were proud of the renovations that had been made a couple of years earlier in celebration of Mora's wedding. Among the improvements were an indoor bathroom and a new bedroom created from a lean-to on the side of the house.

Far from being impressed, Elaine was alarmed to realize the family had not had use of an indoor toilet until after Durfey went into the army. It was almost as bad to realize that during his growing-up years Durfey had slept with three brothers in a room next to the harness shop in the barn. She looked into the room, which still contained two double bed frames and was wallpapered with newsprint. A naked bulb dangled from the ceiling. The room smelled like the barn it was a part of.

Durfey's mother was small and skinny, and her legs slanted in from her knees to her ankles like an inverted triangle. On week days she wore calico dresses and flour sack aprons. On Sundays she put an embroidered apron over a dress suitable for church.

Balis and their children ate her cooking with relish. She put lard in her bread and pastry and used it to fry eggs and meat, and, so Durfey told Elaine, even spread sandwiches with it during some of the hard early winters he could remember. Believing raw meat was infected with tape worms and trichinae, Dorothy fried steaks and chops till they were like leather. She kept an open slop pail for the pigs under the kitchen sink, and she washed dishes without soap so she could salvage the dishwater for the pigs. She used a washcloth for washing dishes until it became limp and grey and seemed to Elaine to be seething with bacteria. Even after being washed, her plates and cups were greasy. For Dorothy, a clean dish was one that didn't have food visibly adhering to it.

Elaine couldn't help contrasting Durfey's home with her own. She hadn't thought of her childhood as opulent. However, she could see it had been sufficient. She lived in a two-story white frame house with two bathrooms. She had a bedroom to herself, and radios were scattered throughout the house. Her father's favorite disk jockey was Tennessee Ernie Ford, who came on at breakfast time. Her mother listened to classical stations, so Beethoven was likely to be thundering on the cabinet radio in the living room while she did housework. Elaine remembered Louis Armstrong singing "Blueberry Hill" and "What a Wonderful World" while she went to sleep. She loved Satchmo, a happy, big-mouthed man with a husky voice and an incomparable trumpet. As for rock-n-roll, it hadn't been invented and nobody missed it, least of all Elaine.

Her neighborhood was thick with eucalyptus trees. In the summer, doves cooed in the trees all day. When she was small, she had dolls and a tricycle. A little later she had roller skates and a bicycle. In junior high school she wore a Cashmere sweater and bobby sox topped with angora wool. A Cashmere sweater cost forty or fifty dollars. That was a lot of money in those days. But every girl had to have one.

She took piano lessons while she was in grade school. Every Thursday afternoon her mother drove her to Pasadena for a lesson. If she practiced diligently, her mother gave her a nickel to go to Dampner's drug store for a lime phosphate or a cherry Coke. Mr. Dampner asked how her skills were progressing. "It's very important to play the piano well, young lady," he said. "Don't get lazy and quit."

When she said goodbye to Mr. Dampner, she crossed the street and went down a couple of blocks and sat in the barber shop and then rode home with her father after closing. If he was going to be late, her father often gave her another nickel and said it was all right to go back to Dampner's. "But don't tell your mother," he said.

Upon her reappearance Mr. Dampner would be surprised. "Very extravagant parents you have," he would say. He wouldn't let her buy another cherry Coke. "A sherbet cone would be proper now," he'd say. "That won't ruin your supper."

Durfey said Elaine wasn't an intense person because her appetites had all been satisfied. He said she had no reason to be anything but complacent. She resented his condescension. He should have known life wasn't easy for anybody.

It was incredible that a little girl could safely walk the streets of Pasadena alone as Elaine had in the 1940s. Now smog and congestion were killing the Golden State. The barrios and ghettos were bulging with minority populations that couldn't be assimilated. The rich were getting richer, the poor poorer, and it seemed everybody was sitting on a powder keg that would soon blow sky high.

In the meantime Elaine had to say this in favor of California. Millions and millions of ordinary people had good jobs and could buy a house and have a car and shop at the supermarket and still have a little money left over for frivolities.

Durfey had made fun of her for washing their jogging clothes after every use. "We're just going out and sweat in them all over again," he'd said.

"If we did things your way, dirt would accumulate on top of dirt and stink on top of stink," she replied. "No, thank you. As long as there's a shred of pride in my body, I intend to jog in freshly laundered clothes." She didn't want to live extravagantly—just decently. She didn't think that was too much to ask of life.

Before her first visit to the Haslam home was over, Elaine and Durfey had negotiated their wedding arrangements. Though she had a feeling the wedding ought to take place in a temple as far removed from Glenwood as possible, Durfey hoped it would be in the closest, which was Manti. Reluctantly she agreed. Both her parents would be present. Ironically, Durfey's mother would attend without his father because Balis smoked and smokers couldn't go into the temple.

Durfey said his family would hold a reception in the Glenwood church. Her parents would have to be there, of course, and nothing would do but that they should stay as guests in the Haslam home. Elaine swallowed hard on that one, but finally agreed, knowing that her father and mother were kind, adaptable people. She knew she'd have to prepare them in advance. She was afraid one of them would say, "Well, if you have to be so apologetic about his family, maybe you should reconsider marrying him." But they didn't say that.

As for formalities in Altadena, Elaine decided a simple open house would be best. She reasoned there wouldn't be any need for Durfey's parents to attend. She told him they shouldn't go to all the trouble and expense.

"Oh, gosh no," he said. "They'll want to do it right all the way down the line. They wouldn't think of not showing up in Altadena." That meant of course her mother and father hosted Dorothy and Balis for several nights in their home. It also meant her other California friends and relatives got a closer look at her new in-laws than she wanted them to have.

A week after the wedding Balis and Dorothy arrived in Altadena in an old pickup. Elaine had decided that they would have to get Balis into something classier than the threadbare western-style suit he had worn at the Glenwood reception on their wedding day. So the next morning she took him around to nearby department stores till they found a blue double-breasted suit that could in some remote manner be said to fit his bizarre, stubby body. The bones connecting Balis's knees and hips were so short as to seem non-existent; his shoulders were so brawny they made a person think of a bull; his arms dangled like an ape's and, as Durfey often said, his hands were scoop shovels.

Balis was game. He had that silent fortitude seen in pets being bathed, clipped, and manicured at a kennel. He knew he was out of his own element, and he was totally ready to accept any instruction Elaine gave him.

As they were driving between one store and another, he said, "Durfey's a fine fellow. I don't know anybody who don't love Durfey."

"That's true," she said. "Durfey's wonderful."

"I don't think we did very well by him. You'll have to rip a few seams out of him and sew them up right."

"No, really," she said, "Durfey's wonderful."

He said, "I've been holding my breath this fall for fear you might want to back out."

"I wouldn't have done that."

"I'm awfully glad. Dorothy and me, we've kind of fallen in love with you ourselves."

Right then she was feeling frightened how close she had come to telling Durfey that his father and mother *couldn't* come to Altadena for the open house. She was saying to herself: What if I'd missed this chance to hear Balis say he loves me? She swore, no matter what happened, she'd love him too. And she always did until he died of emphysema a couple of years before her own father's death.

After standing at the empty door of the old house for a long time, Durfey came back to the car and got behind the wheel. He didn't start the engine but began to talk in misty terms.

He said that his generation of farm kids stood on a stark border between subsistence farming and market-oriented agriculture. Most of those kids moved to cities and entered an industrial economy because it was no longer respectable to live in poverty. He said his own career proved the adaptability of the human species. He had changed from a farm boy into an insurance investigator because he had to, not because he wanted to.

He said, "I traded dawn and dusk under an open sky, rich brown water in the ditches, and bottled fruit in the cellar for plush carpets and a giant screen TV. I traded the slow rhythm of the seasons for the pulsing frenzy of the Los Angeles freeways."

Of course Elaine was feeling a part of the California package that had been forced upon him. Along with the plush carpet and giant screen TV, which he hated, he had her.

He started the car and they drove slowly back along the road to Richfield. "This road used to be graveled," he said. "I can remember the rocks banging against the fenders of the car."

They went by the house with the trellis of climbing red roses. "Look at those roses," he said.

She waited for something more. But he had swallowed whatever it was he wanted to say.

She was thinking about all the concessions she had made—about putting up with Balis and Dorothy and overlooking all of Durfey's country habits all these years and more or less violating her own integrity so that he could have a happy sex life. She was thinking she had done for him what Aspen Marooney wouldn't have done. And what thanks had she got for her effort? After all these years of haunting Elaine's domicile like a ghost, Aspen Marooney had turned up in flesh and blood at this reunion, and Elaine had no idea what was going to happen next.

Durfey had become cheerful again. He began telling her how Balis had bought an off-key piano for his mother after she had become deaf in her old age. The piano couldn't be tuned because the threads on the tuning screws were stripped. Balis's mother had been pleased with it and played it nearly every day. The happiest musicians, Durfey concluded, are the people who can't hear their own mistakes. He told the story as if he'd never told it before. But of course he had, dozens of times.

When they entered Richfield, Durfey said, "Day after tomorrow we'll go home. We'll get Poot out of the kennel, and things'll get back to normal."

Elaine felt childish and petty and wondered why she had to keep breaking down from her resolve to entertain only pleasant and tolerant feelings throughout this reunion. She reminded herself how improbable, how absolutely coincidental, it was that after forty years Durfey and Aspen Marooncy would meet on a makeshift float dedicated to the rehabilitation of a felonious barber. Back in California, their friends Jenny and Wilbur would get the biggest kick out of that float. She was glad she'd taken a photo of it.

5. The Girl Most Likely

After the parade, Roger said he'd like to attend the Pioneer Day program and Aspen said okay. They gave a classmate, Sandra Faustlich, a lift to the stake center. The three went inside, where it was cool. The rows were still half empty and an organist practiced traditional pioneer hymns.

Roger asked how Aspen had gotten the welt on her face.

"Do I look pretty bad?" she said.

"It's quite a mark," he said. "Does it sting?"

"Toby hit me with the cord of his sheep shears," she said. "It was an accident. He went bonkers when people began to clap and shout. He was popping the cord like it was bullwhip."

"Sheer tomfoolery," Roger said.

"That's right," Aspen said. "I guess that's what a reunion is all about."

"That Toby has got a lot of nerve," Sandra said.

"You can grant him that," Roger agreed.

"Of all the dumb things," Aspen said, tracing the welt with a feathery touch. "Getting my face cut up before the reunion's begun. I'll stand out like a sore thumb."

While the organist rehearsed, Sandra brought them up to date on her life. She and her first husband ran a pizza parlor in Spokane.

He got horny with one of the help, and she divorced him and married a sailor in Bremerton. This fellow was soon transferred to Pensacola, and he got to drinking hard and knocked her around and broke her nose. "See how crooked it is," she said.

So she divorced him and married number three and moved to Wickenburg, Arizona, where they ran a TV repair shop. They had three kids, who grew up and left home the way kids are supposed to. But one of the boys wasn't much at making a living, so she had to tell him over and over, "Larry, I'm not a bank. Go somewhere else to borrow money."

Four or five years ago she got bummed out on husband number three. She left him and moved to Phoenix to be near her daughter, who had two of the nicest little girls. She was presently living with a generous, respectful man who wanted to get married. However, she hadn't divorced number three. She wasn't sure if she wanted to risk marrying number four.

"Good thinking," Aspen said.

"Though he seems like the nicest kind of man."

"You never can tell," Aspen said. "With some men it takes a while before their bad traits come out."

"Why not give him the benefit of the doubt?" Roger said.

Aspen scrutinized Sandra's nose. She couldn't see where it had been broken. It looked like the large, angular nose of Sandra's father. It seemed, now that Aspen thought of it, that a lot of her former classmates had their parents' less desirable features. That was what aging did: it exaggerated the enormities of a genetic line.

The Faustliches lived across the street from a small slaughter house at the south end of Richfield and weren't much higher on the social ladder than the Haslams of Glenwood. Mrs. Faustlich was a Mormon of sorts. It wasn't known what persuasion, if any, Mr. Faustlich followed. He frequented a cafe that served beer and he had other bad habits, too. He smoked cigars and swapped stories about the local Mormons with town loafers at the post office.

It was said that Sandra's mother had been the girl most likely to get pregnant in her generation. The same thing was said of Sandra during her high school years. The town seemed to take it upon itself to define such a creature among each generation of the young. The best that could be hoped was that the boy who got her pregnant could be persuaded to marry her.

Aspen's brother Patrick had an older friend who claimed he'd often got under Sandra's skirt in the balcony of the Richfield movie house. On one occasion, the friend had taken possession of Sandra's panties. Patrick had seen these panties with his own eyes. Aspen doubted the story. Rotten boys could steal panties off a clothes line and tell outrageous lies about getting a finger inside a girl while sitting beside her in a crowded theater.

It was a terrible breach of family ethics for Aspen and Patrick to discuss this matter. Brothers and sisters were supposed to pretend the entire world was neutered. They weren't to notice the existence of the private organs of either sex.

In a hurry one evening before going out, Aspen dashed for the bathroom in her panties and bra and ran into Patrick in the hall. Patrick cried, "Hey, buffalo butt!" and slapped her across the rump. Unluckily, Hope observed the incident through an open door and felt obliged to inform their mother.

"Your father intends to say a word to Patrick about his part in this," Adelia admonished Aspen after entering her bedroom early the next morning. "But you need to practice discretion. How's he to learn delicacy if his sister doesn't help him?"

About a month later Aspen and Patrick were at home alone on a Sunday evening. Patrick called Sandra Faustlich the girl most likely. Aspen denounced this title. "You don't know anything about her," she insisted. "She's a very nice person."

That's when Patrick told her about his older friend getting under Sandra's skirt on repeated occasions. Aspen was embarrassed and disgusted. Apparently Patrick was, too. With a belligerent scowl, he retreated from the living room, where Aspen lounged crosswise in an overstuffed chair, reading her civics text.

She was especially embarrassed because during this period she was secretly meeting Durfey Haslam one or two nights a week, and Durfey sometimes did to her what Patrick said his friend had done to Sandra. A few days later she asked Durfey point blank whether he talked about what they did under the sycamores behind Jacobson's drive-in after she got off work.

He said, "Hell, no."

"Some guys talk a lot about what they do with girls," she said.

They stood in a corridor of the high school, and Aspen's question made Durfey miss the numbers on his locker. He looked at her with disdain. "I wouldn't tell that kind of thing to anybody," he said. "That's between you and me." She had been worried that Patrick was trying to tell her he knew who was truly the girl most likely in town. Reassured by Durfey, she relaxed.

The president of the Richfield stake called the Pioneer Day program to order. There was a long prayer and a choir sang "O Ye Mountains High" and "Come, Come, Ye Saints," those haunting old hymns that broke Aspen down no matter where she heard them. Then came orations on the nobility and heroism of the pioneers, whom God had tested with tragedy after tragedy simply because they were strong enough to bear them.

A fierce, grieving thing had come alive inside the Mormon pioneers on the plains and in frontier Utah. A girl inherited it by growing up a Utah Mormon. No matter where she might wander, she wouldn't be able to forget or put away that fierce, grieving thing.

Aspen descended from pioneers on her mother's side. Her great-great-grandfather Armistice Chokling crossed the plains with his wife and two daughters in a wagon in 1849. Later he moved to Farmington and took a plural wife and sired a total of eleven children. One of his sons, Thomas Chokling, migrated south to Richfield and after the death of his first wife married two sisters at the same time. The youngest of these, Caroline Lorimer, was Aspen's great-grandmother.

On her father's side, Aspen descended from Irish immigrants of a mercantile background. "Your father's parents were forced to emigrate for religious reasons, being Protestants in a Catholic land," Aspen's mother said. "It wasn't poverty. They certainly weren't of common stock. Your ancestors were barristers, officers, educators, and merchants."

Horatio Marooney attributed great dignity to the mortician's profession. "We help people in their darkest hour," he often said. Aspen wandered through the mortuary hundreds of times and wasn't afraid of corpses. She knew her father's assistants weren't as reverent as he. Sam Binney stuck a cigar into the mouth of Bishop Orion T. Carpenter after he was in his casket and nearly ready for viewing. Bishop Carpenter boasted in his sermons that tobacco had never touched his lips.

Sometimes mistakes occurred. Once they had the wrong body in the coffin when relatives arrived for the funeral. Another time Horatio hung his new coat in the cloak closet and later saw it on a corpse just as the coffin was being closed and wheeled into the funeral. It was too late to salvage his coat.

Horatio was strong on Adelia's pioneer ancestry. He studied the family diaries and histories and consulted aged uncles and aunts about their progenitors. While on Sunday drives he narrated family stories to the children. His special heroine was their great-grandmother Caroline Lorimer Chokling. He told the story of her wedding day so many times that they knew it as well as he did. It was no surprise he applied the story to Aspen when she had asked Durfey Haslam to the Sadie Hawkins Day Ball.

The girl's choice dance held each spring was named after Sadie Hawkins Day in the comic strip "Li'l Abner." On that day the unmarried women of Dogpatch had the right to pursue unmarried men and, if they caught them, wed them. Aspen told her mother she had asked a boy named Durfey Haslam to the dance. Her mother, addressing envelopes to members of the poetry league, asked whether Durfey was Balis Haslam's son. Aspen said he was.

Adelia said she had been in the Haslam home on a Relief Society visit during the Depression. She said the home was unnecessarily squalid—floors soiled, windows without curtains, children in tattered clothes. From what she understood lately, nothing had changed.

"When the Haslams marry," she said, "their wives sink to their level. I've never known of a case where it was the other way around." When Aspen turned to leave, her mother called her back. "I'd like you to cancel your date."

"Okay," Aspen said, "I won't go out with him any more. I doubt he'd want to anyhow."

"No," her mother insisted, "I mean I want you to ask someone else to go to the Sadie Hawkins Day dance with you."

"It's too late. I've already asked him. He's already said he'd go."

"I want you ask someone else," her mother said.

Near evening Aspen cleaned the large pen where she kept her pigeons. She raked manure and other refuse into a pile and shoveled it into a wheelbarrow. A few pigeons watched. The rest had flown away through the open transom at the top. In good weather they foraged all over the countryside.

Her father came to the pen. He said, "Mother tells me you feel embarrassed to have to break your date with Durfey Haslam."

"I can't ask anybody else. He'd know. Somebody would tell him."

"Maybe you shouldn't go this year," Father said. "We could come up with a good reason."

"I don't see any harm to come from going out with him once," she said.

She trundled the wheelbarrow from the pen and dumped its load on the nearby garden. When she returned, her father said, "Your great-grandmother Caroline Lorimer Chokling was a sweet little lady living down in Elsinore when I married into the family. I remember her distinctly."

He didn't have to repeat Caroline's story. Aspen already knew it by heart. She loved the story. It seemed sacred, a parable for the benefit of the descendants of that heroic pioneer woman.

After Thomas Chokling's first wife died, he asked Cyrus Lorimer's permission to marry his young daughters Harriet and Caroline. The wedding party drove to Manti in four or five buggies. In Gunnison Caroline got out of the buggy and set off afoot for Richfield. She said she didn't love Thomas Chokling and wasn't going to marry him. Everyone knew she was in love with a gentile freighter attached to a government surveying party wintering near Marysvale. Cyrus Lorimer, who was at the head of the procession, turned his buggy around and caught up with his daughter and heaved her bodily into his buggy, and the party went on to Manti and the double wedding took place as scheduled.

Caroline bore testimony that for months after the wedding she was afflicted with nightmares of being bound with cords and chains. One night an angel appeared and cut the cords and broke the chains. She saw how foolish a thing love is and how glorious it is to be sealed by the priesthood to a righteous man.

"Will you break your date with this Haslam boy?" Horatio pleaded. "Will you believe just for once your mother has your best interest at heart?"

Her back to her father, Aspen went on scooping manure into the wheelbarrow.

"What has become of my little Aspen?" Horatio said. "I loved to carry you in my arms. And now you're grown up, and I can't do it anymore."

Yes, what had become of little Aspen, who loved her father passionately? She dropped the shovel and turned, sobbing, "Just tell me what to tell him. Just tell me."

With some disgust, Aspen noted Sandra Faustlich's beefy legs, tightly encased in nylons with a sheen. Why would a woman with such enormous thighs wear a short skirt? But Sandra wasn't stupid. At least she had managed not to get pregnant when she was a girl.

As she often did, Aspen had come around to thinking about arranged marriages. People said an arranged marriage was as likely to be happy as any other. Certainly that had been true in the case of Caroline Lorimer Chokling. Aspen took Roger's hand for a moment, then laid it back upon his lap. He smiled at her, then returned his rapt gaze to the orator in the pulpit. She did love Roger. Everybody loved Roger. He was so kind and supportive.

Her parents hadn't negotiated her wedding to Roger. She had negotiated it for them. She knew their specifications without error. They couldn't have done a better job.

After the Pioneer Day program they drove to a new church on the other side of town for the class luncheon. There was a noisy crowd inside the recreation hall—all the people who had been on the float and six or seven who hadn't, with spouses and companions.

Durfey and Elaine stood in a corner near the door. Durfey seemed perplexed. Aspen introduced Roger and herself to Elaine, who smiled pleasantly. She was very attractive, just as Durfey had said.

"What do you think of a float with a sheep tied in a barber's chair?" Elaine asked Roger.

"A wonderful bit of theater," Roger replied.

"The sheep died at the end of the parade," Aspen said. "I hold Durfey responsible. He assured me it wouldn't die."

"I was abysmally wrong," Durfey said.

Henry Ross was banging the bottom of a waste basket and shouting that it was time to find a table. Aspen said, "Let's sit together," and led the way to a table. She waited till Elaine selected a chair and took one beside her. Sandra Faustlich and Amy Gilder also sat at their table. Amy said her husband was home in Fresno working.

"It's wonderful to have you ladies sit with us," Durfey said to Amy and Sandra. "In high school your presence was always edifying and elevating."

"You big bag of wind!" Amy said.

Aspen explained her welt to Amy. "I was trying to be nice to Toby, and look what he did!"

"It sort of becomes you," Amy said of the welt. "I thought maybe you'd done it with make-up."

Henry Ross called on John Izatt to offer grace.

"That's a mistake," Durfey said. "John Izatt couldn't say a short prayer if his life depended on it."

After his lengthy blessing on the food, they crowded into two lines and served themselves at the Mexican buffet—tacos, enchiladas, Spanish rice, and so on. There were pitchers of pink punch on the tables but no coffee, tea, or cola. Shirley Sue, who had planned the menu, wasn't Mormon, but in Utah even gentiles picked up Mormon inhibitions.

They conversed aimlessly while they ate. Sandra said someone in Greeley, Colorado, had barbecued his neighbor's cat and eaten it. He was charged with cruelty to animals.

Durfey said, "I agree with the general principle of eating cats and dogs."

Roger looked askance.

"He's joking," Aspen said.

"I'm not joking," Durfey insisted. "Keeping pets in a pampered condition is a violation of sound ecology."

Aspen asked Amy what her husband did for a living. She said he worked for the IRS. Aspen said, rather proudly, that Roger was director of counseling for Deseret Industries from Phoenix to Seattle.

"You make it sound grandiose," Roger said.

Aspen asked Durfey what he did for a living.

"I make my living on fraud," Durfey said. "I'm an insurance investigator. I check out suspicious claims. You can't imagine how many there are to check out."

"You used to say you were going to be captain of a Caribbean cruise ship," Aspen said.

For the first time all day Durfey smiled his old sweet, warm, good-natured smile. "No cruise ship for me," he said. "It isn't waves lapping against a hull I long to hear. What I want to hear is a cow belching up a cud."

Everybody laughed, Roger most heartily of all. Aspen watched Roger's hands at work with his knife and fork. They seemed happy hands. She felt a headache, which seemed to have something to do with Durfey's warm, good-natured smile.

Durfey spoke of the problem posed by wetbacks crossing from Mexico into California. "They are lured by the smell of affluence. Do you want to know the future of Peru, Ghana, or Sumatra? Watch California. As California goes, so goes the world."

"He hates California," Elaine said.

"I will not bite the hand that feeds me," Durfey said. "Where else could a man of such mediocre abilities make so good a living?"

Roger and Durfey got into a conversation about psychometrics. Durfey wanted to know how a person would measure the potential in a given population for cheating on insurance claims. Brightening up, Roger said there were a number of ways of going about it. Durfey seemed impressed by Roger's explanations, and for a few minutes there was no other talk at the table. Across forty years Aspen remembered Durfey bathing in a rushing creek at dawn. She remembered pillars of muscle in the small of his back. Her head throbbed. After the luncheon she'd go to the drugstore and buy a pain reliever.

The conversation about psychometrics went on. Roger's silver hair was combed back with a flourish. From the side his gold spectacles seemed luminous. There had been many good times for Aspen and Roger, many unfeigned satisfactions. Once in a while there had been passion.

On their tour of Europe they had arrived in Nice in time to secure a reasonably priced room. A little before noon Aspen stood on a sunny balcony and said, "Let's go to the beach."

"Which beach?" Roger asked.

"Is there more than one?"

"I'm not sure."

"The topless beach is the one I want."

"I would prefer not to," he said.

91

She went into the room and placed a towel, thongs, and a one-piece swimming suit into a tote bag. "I'm walking to the beach," she said. "They said at the desk it's not far."

On the sidewalk she heard him shout. He waved from the balcony and said, "Wait for me. I'm coming too." When he caught up with her, satchel in hand, he said, "It's not much of a husband who won't go to the beach with his wife."

The streets were wide and clean, and palm fronds stirred in a breeze. They saw two young men in short-sleeved white shirts, ties, and name-badges, sedately riding their bicycles.

"Missionaries," Aspen said. "I wonder if they're allowed to go to the beach."

"I would think not," Roger said. "I can't think of anything more demoralizing to a missionary."

They put on their swimming suits and thongs in a beach house and went onto the sand. Gulls hovered on unsteady wings over the slow, sparkling surf. Though it was barely afternoon, a crowd of swimmers and sunbathers had gathered. Aspen and Roger spread towels, took off their sandals, and strolled into the water. They waded till the sea came to their hips, then swam back and forth parallel to the shore for perhaps a quarter hour. Emerging, they returned to their towels and lay on their backs, absorbing the sun.

Through half-squinted eyes Aspen watched a girl in her teens playing beach ball with a boy who might have been her younger brother. Neither paid the slightest attention to the girl's bare heaving breasts. Near Aspen, half reclining in a beach chair, was an emaciated woman of middle age. Her long, thin, coppery breasts lolled across her ribs like nippled stockings.

Roger lay with a cap over his eyes. "I'm exceedingly uncomfortable," he said. "I'll be grateful when you've had enough of this."

"You're still a missionary," she said.

"I suppose so," he said. "I'm not a hardy spirit, that's certain."

In time they dressed and returned along palm-lined walks to the hotel. In the evening they had dinner in a nicer restaurant than usual. Roger ordered apple juice in what looked like a wine bottle. Strolling to their hotel, he expounded upon the romance of a balmy night and the sweet scent of small white flowers blooming on ivy-covered walls. While she unbuttoned her blouse, he asked whether she would consider making love.

She wasn't eager. They had traveled a night train from Barcelona and the clatter of rails had kept her awake. But she said, "Of course."

The truth was, for all her fatigue, those passionate moments with the doors of the balcony open to a half moon were among the most satisfying they ever had.

Henry Ross went to the microphone and began the program. First he thanked John, Shirley Sue, and Evelyn for organizing the reunion. These stalwarts stood, and everyone applauded. Next Henry named the eight classmates who had died since graduation and asked for a minute of silence in their memory. Then Shirley Sue distributed prizes for those having the most children, the least hair, and the greatest distance to travel. Three classmates had nine children each, so they split the prize. Durfey was runner-up for baldest head.

Audrey Gilbert read predictions from the yearbook of '51. According to these prophecies, Richard Hunter would become a poet, Janie Schuster a counter-espionage agent, Jim Foreman a prison warden. They stood and told what they'd become—a grocery wholesaler, a housewife, and a baker.

Henry directed others to take a turn at telling their occupation and life story. Durfey groaned and said in a low voice, "Lord, we'll be here till midnight."

The program went on for almost two more hours. Aspen doodled on her napkin, sometimes glancing at Durfey. His downcast eyes gave the appearance of sleep. Sometimes she watched Roger's hands, which, as usual, were in repose. She also watched Elaine's hands, tipped with glossy red nails. Aspen's nails were short and plain. She never painted them. Elaine's engagement ring was more expensive than Aspen's. She wondered what her mother would say about that. What would she say if Aspen said, "You see he did all right after all. He went to California and he makes seventy-five thousand a year."

It was certain Durfey had told Elaine about his early fornications. Aspen didn't need to hear this fact confirmed. He couldn't have helped telling his wife. Aspen admired him for that. She hated a person with dark secrets.

Having covered her own napkin with doodles, she reached for Roger's. Her classmates droned on, one after another recounting what had happened these forty years. Durfey's face twitched, so she knew he wasn't asleep. Roger's hands now toyed with a fork. Elaine's hands, with those resplendent nails, lay folded in her lap. Durfey was lucky. Elaine was so placid, so serene. And, yes, she would have forgiven Aspen for her part in her husband's early derelictions.

When all the class had taken a turn, Henry reminded them of the Richfield rodeo that evening and gave directions for getting to Dennis Gundersen's summer home in Koosharem Canyon for the continuation of the reunion the next morning. In closing they sang the school anthem: "All hail to thee, our high school, the fairest in the land; we'll work for you, we'll cheer for you, with head and heart and hand."

On their way out, Aspen and Roger halted every few steps so Aspen could hug a classmate whom she had not yet greeted. Each time she had to explain again how she had gotten the welt.

In the car she said, "Please drive me to the drugstore. I have a terrible headache."

"Now why would you have a headache?"

"It's this welt," she said.

"Of course," Roger said with satisfaction. "Well, cheer up. I think it's fading."

6. A Renewed Interest in Rodeo

Durfey and Elaine chatted with Audrey Turner in the parking lot. Audrey, who never married, grieved over the children she had not been privileged to bear. Durfey said she was to be congratulated, considering the overpopulation of the earth.

"That's just a posture he takes," Elaine assured Audrey. "He loves children."

Durfey and Elaine got into the Mazda. "It's been snobbish of me to look down on your country high school all these years," Elaine said. "I envy how much like brothers and sisters you all seem to feel."

Just then Bradford Higley appeared at Durfey's side. He hadn't been at the luncheon, and Durfey was shocked to see that he would have easily won the prize for the baldest head. His maimed half-ear projected below his hairless scalp like a ruined weather vane.

Bradford jerked open the car door and shouted, "Out of there, Durfey Haslam, you son of a bitch! I'm going to kick your butt."

He was drunk, and his wife, Janie Schuster, was clutching his arm and repeating, "Brad, sweetheart, please come home, Brad, sweetheart, please come home!"

Durfey got out and Bradford instantly hit him in the mouth and knocked him against the car. Durfey slid down and rolled out flat on the pavement. He was conscious but had a curious sensation of being completely without energy. He couldn't do anything but lie there, gazing at a puffy white cloud high in the sky. Bradford seized his arm and tried to pull him up, undoubtedly for the pleasure of knocking him down again. But Durfey remained limp and Bradford couldn't manage to get him up. He stood back and gave him a sharp kick in the ribs. Henry and Toby pulled him away, while Elaine and Janie helped Durfey to his feet. Blood oozed from his mouth. He could feel a big gash in his upper lip.

"You're in trouble," he said to Bradford. "This is assault and battery, and don't think I won't press charges."

Bradford lunged against the grip of his captors and shouted, "That bastard went out with Janie when he knew she was my girl."

"You dumb fart," Durfey said. "She and me weren't anything but friends. She married you, didn't she?"

"You bit off my ear," he said. "I hollered uncle but you didn't stop biting. You chewed it up and spit it out and it couldn't be sewed back on."

A crowd had gathered, among them John Izatt, wearing his dark brown pants, poplin shirt, and high-crowned Stetson. He had a shiny gold badge but no gun. John was an affectionate fellow who deliberated before acting, and at present he was simply wringing his hands.

Elaine confronted John ferociously and insisted he arrest Bradford. She knew all about the fight between Durfey and Bradford. "He had it coming, getting his ear bit off," she insisted. "He was pounding Durfey to a pulp."

"No, don't arrest him," Durfey said. "I've changed my mind. Let's just forget it. I'm truly sorry I bit off his ear."

Tears were streaming down Bradford's seamed cheeks. "Thanks to you, I'm nothing but an ugly asshole. Every day I look in the mirror and see I ain't worth a pile of shit."

John became authoritative. "Break it up!" he shouted to the crowd, waving his Stetson. "This is just a little altercation between friends. Time to go home. See you at the rodeo tonight. Anybody who needs a place to rest up or use a bathroom, come on over to my house."

Durfey got behind the wheel of the Mazda. Elaine stood at the door and said, "You'd better let me drive."

"Hell, no," he said. "I can drive okay." He drove to Main Street and parked in front of the drugstore.

"Where are you going?" Elaine said abruptly.

"I need something for this lip."

"No, you don't," she ordered. "You're driving straight to the emergency ward."

"Gosh, no," he said, "I'm not hurt anywhere near that bad."

Elaine sat seething on her side of the car. He'd never seen her so angry. That made him angry, and he had a notion to slam the door. It was a strange business, this getting angry with each other when it was Bradford Higley they should be mad at.

The Sheffields' big Mercury sat in the next parking stall. Durfey noticed Roger at the wheel. The hood ornament dangled, and Durfey paused to set it upright but it refused to stay. He gave Roger a limp wave and tried to smile. Pain chopped through his lip and gum.

Durfey walked around to Roger's open window. "Bradford Higley just knocked me down," he explained. "This is what I get for biting off his ear forty years ago."

"My goodness!" Roger said.

"I'm going in and buy a little something to make it feel better," Durfey said.

He started to go, then came back. "That Mazda isn't mine, in case you're wondering. It belongs to my son-in-law, Steve. We let him and Sally borrow our Buick so they could take their little girls sight seeing in comfort."

Durfey went inside and found Aspen paying for something at the counter. As he approached, she gasped and clapped a hand to her mouth.

"You missed a good scrap," he said. "Bradford Higley just knocked me down in the parking lot for biting off his ear." He pointed to his swollen, bloody lip, which he could see in the mirror behind the cashier.

"You'd better go to the emergency ward," Aspen said.

"I'll find something that'll take care of me," he said. He went down an aisle and soon came back with a bottle of Tylenol tablets.

"Your lip is split," Aspen said while he paid for the tablets. "It'll have to be sutured."

"It isn't that bad, is it?" he said, leaning across the counter to catch a better view. He could see bloody saliva drooling from his mouth, and when he stood upright he felt dizzy. He took out his handkerchief and tried to wipe his chin. Aspen completed the task and crumpled the bloody cloth into his shirt pocket.

"You're in shock," she said. "I'm afraid you're going to faint."

It might as well have been Elaine who said that. At this moment he could think of no difference between the two women. Truly there was an interchangeability within human personality—the generic factor, the tendency of one person to be like any other person. It seemed he ought to dwell on this thought with the intent of transcribing it in his diary. In the meantime, Aspen steadied him by a tight grip on his arm. He swayed like a pine in a wind storm, and for a moment they were both unbalanced. She took a backward step to brace herself and dug her fingernails into his muscles—a wonderful sensation, he was thinking, after these forty years of famine.

"That Bradford Higley is still possessed by those old raw animal feelings," she said. "He's missed the whole point of living, which is to get the better of himself."

"I had it coming. I shouldn't have bit off his ear. That was a terrible thing to do."

The cashier had been taking all this in from just across the counter. "You can see he's hurt," Aspen said to the girl. "I used to know him. We used to be friends."

"It was something more than friends," he said to the girl. "We were experimenting, you might say. We were testing whether we could spend our lives together. As you see, we didn't."

His words were thick and ill formed, his swollen lip refusing to perform its usual modulations. "My advice to you, young lady, is that you not test relationships that way. Make up your mind early and let the poor fellow know. Don't lead him on so he doesn't know from one day to another whether he has a chance."

Aspen said, "That's not fair, Durfey."

"Oh, lord, I know it. I'm sorry."

"I was terribly confused," Aspen said. "I was paralyzed. It's horrible to feel that way."

Durfey steadied himself against the counter with a hand, and she released her grip on his arm. With his free hand he adjusted her collar and touched the hollow at the base of her throat.

She said to the cashier, "Please excuse us. This is the only chance we'll have to talk." She led him down an aisle where a stack of goods hid them from the cashier. She whispered urgently, with starts and stops and inexplicable alterations of pitch and tone.

"You have a son you don't know about. He'll be thirty-nine in the fall. He owns a diesel shop in Salina. He's not a good man. He smokes, he boozes, he runs with women, he makes fun of sacred things. He's broken my heart a thousand times."

He looked around as if she had asked him to help her find a certain brand of shampoo.

"Have you got it straight?" she said. "You have a son you don't know about. His name is Gerald. You fathered him. He couldn't belong to anybody else. He's short and big-shouldered exactly like your father."

"My father's been dead for a long, long time," he said. "I thought you might be at the funeral. But no Marooney ever went to a funeral in Glenwood."

"Can't you get what I'm saying? Please try harder. Oh, dear, your face is so grey. I think you're in shock."

"This will fix me up," he said, shaking the bottle of tablets. "Three or four of these and I'll be on my way to Cedar City. We'll see another play tonight, a frivolous thing that delights Elaine. Deep things aren't for her. Let your entertainment be cheery, she says. Take a broom and sweep reality out the door. Let mirth and merriment reign!"

He noted the welt slanting across Aspen's left cheek, making an obtuse angle with her lips, which were thin yet curved like an archer's bow. "You've been injured, too," he said, touching her cheek near the welt.

"Please be sensible," she protested. "There's something you have to understand. You have a son. His name is Gerald. If you went to the rodeo tonight, you could see him. He'll be a contestant in the team roping. He ropes with his boy Donnie. Gerald is good at heeling—the technical part."

"So your son is a cowboy," he said. If the truth were known, he had only the most perfunctory interest in her children.

She said, more urgently, "He's your son. He'll be thirty-nine in September. You fathered him. He'll be at the rodeo tonight."

A fact perched at last upon a ledge of Durfey's mind. He could see it clearly now, preening itself like a bird. He started to make a big, surprised O with his mouth, then grimaced because of his gashed lip.

"You wouldn't tell me something terrible that wasn't true, would you?" he muttered.

"But it is true," she insisted.

"When did I father him? Just tell me that. When?"

"That night."

"Which night?"

"The night we skated."

"Oh, Jesus!"

His mind wasn't a cliff now but a table, a kitchen counter maybe, and his ideas scattered like cockroaches except for one that he had put his thumb down on so it couldn't get away. The idea was that

100

Aspen had been five or six or seven weeks pregnant when she married Roger Sheffield in the Salt Lake temple, and he was suddenly filled with disgust for a man would go along with that kind of unholy deception. Then that idea wriggled from under his thumb, and he didn't feel disgust or anger or anything except a blank, dumb misery.

"Your poor furrowed cheeks!" she said. "You've got old, Durfey! All these years, I haven't thought of you as getting old."

"Oh, I'm old, Aspen, very old."

He saw goosebumps on her arms. He took her wrist and stroked her forearm, trying to rub away the goosebumps. "Damned air conditioning," he said. "When we were kids, nobody needed air conditioning. Now you can't survive without it."

"I've gone a little crazy," she said. "I have no idea why I blurted out all that about Gerald."

"Tell me it isn't true," he said. "Tell me you're trying to give me a good scare. My God, what'll I tell Elaine?"

"Oh, gracious," she said, "do you have to tell Elaine?"

"Well, don't I? How could I not tell her?"

"Well, if you must, at least wait till after the reunion. I couldn't face her tomorrow. She is so admirable. I'm so glad you've had her all these years."

"What I want to know is why you didn't tell me when you first knew about it? Just why didn't you? Wasn't that the time you should have told me?"

"Don't scold me, Durfey. I can't stand it."

"Don't scold you! You tell me forty years later, and I'm not supposed to scold you!"

"You're drooling blood," she said. She took the handkerchief and wiped his chin. "You have to go see a doctor. Like it or not, you've got to."

"Will you kindly stop giving me instructions about my lip?"

"We'd better go out," she said. "Please don't tell Elaine till after the reunion is over. That's all I ask."

101

"But is it really true?"

"Of course it's true. Now get hold of yourself. Go out and get in the car with Elaine and drive away. Then I'll come out. I couldn't face her now. And please, Durfey, go to the emergency ward. You look far worse than you have any idea."

She took his hand and led him down the aisle toward the door. "Please hug me," she said. So he hugged her and she kissed his cheek on the side opposite his battered lip.

"She's such a good woman, Durfey, and I'm so ashamed. Please don't tell her anything at all."

He went out of the drugstore, got into the Mazda, waved again at Roger, and started the engine.

"I had a good talk with Aspen," he told Elaine.

"What did she buy?"

"I don't have the slightest idea," he said. "Maybe some bobby pins."

"Women don't use bobby pins anymore," she said. "Don't you know that?"

He drove to John's house because John had said anyone was welcome who needed to rest or use the bathroom. His wife, Sharmane, gave Durfey a glass of water and he took a double dosage of Tylenol. He asked to use the bathroom. Seated on the toilet, he believed his thoughts were becoming more orderly and rational.

Certainly he felt more secure behind a locked door. He had the odd feeling that someone might assault him again. It didn't have to be Bradford Higley. It could be almost anybody. Kooks with semi-automatic rifles went into grade schools these days and wasted kids for no good reason. Gangs inculcated loyalty to no one but the gang. All the rest of the world was legal game, even old ladies and little children. A person could get shot standing in the serving line at McDonald's.

Maybe he should learn how to fight and then go find Bradford Higley and beat him within an inch of his life. He wondered whether he could enroll in a boxing course at the community college in Orange. He'd never heard of anybody learning to box at sixty. He had a .357 Magnum revolver, duly licensed, which he kept beneath the seat of the '81 Ford station wagon he drove when investigating insurance claims. He had a momentary fantasy of returning from California with the revolver and shooting Bradford. He'd blow his other ear off just by way of making his head a little more symmetrical.

He let that fantasy go by. He didn't want a life sentence though there was no question the old macho code still had a place among his feelings. In high school he'd made many a kid eat crow. He'd eaten a lot of crow himself, and he'd hated the sons of bitches that fed it to him.

He flushed the toilet and while washing his hands examined his lip in the mirror. Though it hurt terribly, he probed the wound with his tongue. It felt enormous. He was chilling some, a bad sign on a hot summer afternoon.

In the kitchen Elaine had just hung up the phone. "I left a message for Sally at the motel that we'd probably get there too late for the greenshow. We just have to go over to the emergency ward at the hospital and let a doctor look at you."

With that he gave in and let her drive him to the hospital, which was an impressive brick building of recent construction. They sat on a padded bench for forty-five minutes before a doctor could attend to him. The doctor was reluctant to attempt a patch job on the lip. "I can do it," he said, "but there's a real chance when it heals your lip will skew to one side or the other. It's only a three-hour drive to Salt Lake. I could phone ahead and have a plastic surgeon on hand to fix you up."

"For hell's sake, sew it up," Durfey ordered. "I want to get out of here in time to make that rodeo. At my age who cares about a skewed lip? I've got a grandson with a scarred lip anyhow. Now he won't have to feel so different."

He lay on a table and the doctor gave him a shot of anesthetic under the lip on each side of the wound and went to work, sighing and grunting and cursing under his breath. Durfey kept his eyes closed and could feel only the odd sensation of something like a round, raspy toothpick passing through his numbed flesh.

For the moment he felt that it was imperative that he go to the rodeo and see whether there really was a roper named Gerald Sheffield and, if there was, whether he really did look like he might belong to Durfey. He expected the resemblance would fail to be convincing. Aspen had told him a lie, pure and simple. They'd always agreed when she got pregnant they'd get married and then show up at home and tell their parents. That was one reason to think she wasn't pregnant when she married Roger. Another was Roger seemed too sincere and decent to marry a woman who had got pregnant by another man. He especially wouldn't marry her in the temple. But of course all this didn't explain Aspen's motives for telling Durfey a lie. She couldn't be malicious enough to ruin his peace of mind for no good reason.

A few tears trickled down his temples. "Gee," the doctor said, "I hope I'm not hurting you." He dabbed the tears dry with a tissue.

"Get on with your business," Durfey said with a thick tongue. "It isn't hurting. Get the thing over with."

The doctor was in fact about through, and as he snipped the ends of the final knot, he said, "Pretty darned good, if I do say so myself."

While the doctor was putting away his tray, Elaine asked Durfey what he had meant by saying he wanted to go to the rodeo.

"Haven't been to a rodeo in years," Durfey said. "Got a passion to go see one tonight."

"Sally and Steve expect us in Cedar City," Elaine said. "We've had tickets for months."

"I think he ought to go home and go to bed," the doctor said. "He'll be okay in the morning."

They came out of the hospital at 6:30, and Elaine got behind the wheel. She asked if he wanted something to eat. He said no. She said they could still make the play if they drove hard, but she was of the opinion that Durfey should go to bed instead of going to the play. She offered to stay with him. She didn't mind missing the play but was very strong on getting back and letting Sally and Steve know things were okay.

"I want awful bad to go to that rodeo," he said.

"I don't understand," she protested. "You never said anything about going to a rodeo before. Not once!"

"I know," he said, "but something has come up."

"What's come up? That's what I'd like to know!"

"Just something."

"You're out of your head."

"I'm not out of my head. I know perfectly well what I want. I want to go to the rodeo."

They were still in the hospital parking lot. She said, "I know it's your reunion. I know I ought to be mature and allow for some changes of plan. But there's a rodeo tomorrow night too. Couldn't we go to that one?"

"I'm sorry," he said again. "I've just got to go to this one."

"I hate rodeos," she said.

"I know you do."

"It isn't right for you to change plans all of a sudden like this. You have to give people some warning. You have to give them a chance to say no."

"You don't have to go to the rodeo. Just leave me here and take off for Cedar City. You can make the play if you hurry."

"No," she said, "I'll go to the rodeo if that's what you want. Just tell me why."

He was thinking that, on the one hand, candor was not only moral but efficient. Once said, truth remained steady, whereas a lie had to be amended over and over. On the other hand, if Gerald Sheffield proved to be his son—well, that would end a long, stable marriage. "I hope you will continue to comfort and visit your father," Elaine would explain to their children. "As for me, this half brother of yours living in Salina, Utah, is the straw that broke the

105

camel's back. You don't know your father as well as I do. In an emotional sense he has always been a bigamist. You can't imagine how desperately he has pined for this Aspen Marooney, and I don't doubt it's a matter of satisfaction to him to discover the embodiment of his yearning in this unknown son."

At this point, Elaine said she'd drive back to John's and Sharmane's. Maybe they'd let Durfey lie on their sofa for a while, and she could use their phone and let Sally know they wouldn't be in till late. However, by the time she pulled up in front of the Izatt house, she had changed her mind.

"I hoped things would turn out all right at this reunion," she said. "You might say it's a mistake for me to go back to Cedar City. But, considering everything, I can't stay here. Whatever has to happen will just have to happen. I hope you can get along without the car because I can't get back to Cedar City without it."

"You bet," he said. "You take the car."

"And please don't be foolish, Durfey. You really are in a state of shock. Take care of yourself. Lie down as much as you can. If you chill or get a fever, tell Sharmane."

"I'll be careful."

"So what am I to do then? Come back and get you at midnight?"

"I'll just sleep on their sofa. They'll let me. I'll borrow John's razor. You come back in the morning. Bring me a fresh shirt and some clean underwear."

He got out of the car and got as far as the bridge over the irrigation ditch. "Durfey!" she called. He went to her side of the car, leaned through the window, and pressed a cheek against hers.

"Everything has got so sinister," she said.

"No, not sinister," he said. "I promise you things will turn out okay."

Nobody was home at John's and Sharmane's, but the door was open, and he went in and lay on the sofa and covered himself with an afghan. Sharmane was startled when she came in the front door but said he was certainly welcome to spend the night. She fixed him an eggnog, which he sipped with a straw. John said he could ride with him out to the rodeo arena where he was due to patrol all evening.

Durfey went back to the sofa and was huddled there under the afghan when John's and Sharmane's daughter Anne, recently married, came in with her violin to rehearse for the family's performance the next day at the reunion in Koosharem Canyon. They sang some mournful old western songs, Sharmane playing an electronic keyboard, Anne her violin, and John a guitar. John took the vocal lead and the two women harmonized.

They sang a song Aspen used to sing. The lyrics said the saddest words were words of parting and the sweetest days were those that used to be, and the refrain pleaded for remembrance when the candle lights were gleaming at the end of the long, long day. In Fry Pan Canyon a gasoline lantern had hung on a limb outside the camp wagon. Inside the wagon Durfey burned candles. Candle light sharpened the shadows on Aspen's face while they ate or played checkers. Durfey turned his face to the back of the sofa and tried not to weep. Oddly, he couldn't distinguish whether he wanted to cry for Aspen or for Elaine. It broke his heart to think how devastated Elaine had been as she drove away.

At dusk Durfey accompanied John to the rodeo grounds in the patrol car. On the way, John mentioned that Aspen's son Gerald would be one of the contestants.

"Him and his boy Donnie do pretty darn well in team roping," John said. "That Gerald, he's a regular powder keg. Got a fierce temper. I arrested him a time or two a long time back. You wouldn't believe it, would you? Just shows you the best of families can have a black sheep. The rest of Aspen's kids, so far as I know, stick to the straight and narrow, go on missions, get married in the temple, don't screw around, never touch a drop of liquor."

John parked the patrol car and strolled around the grounds with

107

Durfey in tow. They passed through the bottom aisle of the grandstand, pausing frequently so John could shake hands and talk with people. It seemed his purpose was to provide atmosphere. With his Stetson and boots and frontier-style revolver, John looked like a western sheriff. However, his badge read: Chief of Police, City of Richfield.

Durfey wondered where all these people had come from. Some were dressed in boots, jeans, and high-crowned straw hats. He took them to be local. There were four or five tour buses in the parking lot, so a lot of these strangers had to be tourists on the national park loop. An entire busload appeared to be Japanese, dressed the way middle-class Californians dress—tumble-dry, wrinkle-free, permanent-press casual. Obviously there was a sartorial conspiracy between California fashion makers and the tourist industry of the Pacific Rim.

On the other side of the grandstand John and Durfey ran into a hot dog vendor who turned out to be one of their classmates, Jordan Seegmueller. Jordan hadn't attended the reunion during the day, and Durfey hadn't seen him in twenty or thirty years. He was of course startled to see Durfey's bandaged lip.

"I got hit by Bradford Higley out in the parking lot," Durfey explained. "He's still mad that I bit off his ear. With good reason too. I shouldn't have mangled it up before I spit it out. Then the doctors might have sewed it back on."

"That Bradford is a mean bastard," Jordan said. "He wanted to fight me last winter. I said, I ain't fighting you so just go ahead and knock me down. He decided against it and went away."

"How come you aren't attending the reunion?" John demanded of Jordan. "Here's folks like Durfey who've driven hundreds of miles, and you won't even cross town to see your old friends."

"Oh, hell, nobody wants to see me," Jordan said. "Here, you fellers have one of these hot dogs on the house."

Durfey said, "No, thanks. I can't do much with solid food right now."

John accepted with pleasure. "I had some supper," he apologized. "But, golly, I gotta keep up my flesh."

Jordan Seegmueller had a colorful history. One night fifteen years earlier he and his two sons had seen an alien spaceship hovering in the air about fifty yards off a forest road. According to their description, it was a big, disk-shaped spaceship, something like the one in the movie *Close Encounters of the Third Kind.* Jordan got out of the car and an electronic beam swept him up into the spacecraft. His frightened sons drove away, and the next day a sheriff's posse combed the area without finding a trace of Jordan. Days later he showed up on the roadside near Sigurd, still a little out of his head and able to recall only snatches of what had happened to him in the spacecraft. He and his sons took lie detector tests and were declared to be telling the truth.

"I saw you in that TV documentary last year," Durfey said to Jordan. "I guess nobody else in the whole class is as famous as you."

"Oh, dadgum," he said, "you can't imagine how hellish it's been! That incident ruined my life. Everybody thinks I'm a liar. But, honest, I ain't. It really happened."

"So what did those space aliens want of you?"

Jordan said it was hard to tell. He couldn't even begin to understand the language, which was something like Navajo—guttural with a lot of spitting sounds.

"Why'd they let you go?"

"I think they figured I was going to up and die on them. I had something like hypothermia. Shock, maybe. So they probably thought they'd just as well let a chicken's behind like me die on the ground."

A great fanfare of drums and trumpets sounded over the loudspeakers. Jordan said goodbye and went on hawking hot dogs and Cokes.

"What do you think about all that?" Durfey asked John. "Was he really captured by space aliens?"

"Plenty of people believe he was. Town's pretty divided over the question."

"So which side do you come down on?"

"Like the old Danishman said, it might be true, but I don't seenk so."

Durfey laughed without moving his lips, a sound something like a cough. John was going back to the patrol car so people could find him if an emergency came up. Durfey said goodbye and found a seat in the grandstand.

It was starting to get dark, and the arena was a brightly lit oval of soft, damp sand. A grand procession, led by a rider carrying Old Glory, circled the arena. Once all the horses and riders and carriages and Coca-Cola trucks and three-wheeled motorcycles were inside the arena, the spectators in the bleachers and grandstand stood at attention and the loudspeakers boomed with the national anthem.

Then the rodeo proceeded. There were the usual bronc riding, steer wrestling, calf tying, and bull riding, interspersed with entertainments by a clown and his trick donkey and a troupe of trained white horses and European riders dressed in leotards and sequins. Durfey didn't get much pleasure from the show. The pill he'd taken with his eggnog was wearing off and his lip throbbed. He saw Jordan Seegmueller pass along the bottom aisle of the grandstand a couple of times, having good luck selling his wares. Durfey concluded he didn't believe in visitors from outer space. He couldn't give a reason for not believing in them. He simply didn't. That didn't necessarily mean Jordan was lying. In fact, Durfey had decided Jordan wasn't lying. He was too sincere. As Durfey knew, people believe in a lot of things that aren't real. They experience a lot of things that never happen.

He remembered an insurance case in which an eighteen-wheel semi-truck loaded with baby grand pianos had supposedly been stolen. A witness, an aging woman, claimed to have seen the truck roll under a low railroad overpass. Citing measurements he and an assistant had made, Durfey pointed out the impossibility of the truck in question passing under the overpass.

"Maybe they let some air out of the tires," the woman said.

"It wouldn't go under even if the tires were flat," Durfey said.

"I know what I saw, mister," she said. "Take it or leave it. It don't make no difference to me what you write down in that report of yours."

It occurred to Durfey that, even though this Gerald Sheffield whose roping he was about to witness wasn't his son, Aspen might not necessarily be lying by claiming he was. Maybe she simply wanted him to be Durfey's son. Now there was something to chew on. Maybe she was still in love with Durfey. Maybe she'd got a little demented from fantasies over what might have been. Sometimes Durfey himself felt demented from things that might have been.

At last the loud speakers announced the team roping. Durfey made his way to the bottom of the grandstand and crowded in at the railing, getting as close as possible to the action. The third team of ropers were announced as Gerald and Donald Sheffield, father and son from Salina and Price. They came out of the chute and the steer veered in Durfey's direction. The lead roper, a boy of maybe sixteen or seventeen, threw a skilled loop over the steer's horns, and with a sudden flip the rear roper skipped a loop across the ground which miraculously encompassed both the animal's hind feet. The steer fell and the trained horses stopped short and backed up, tethering the steer out so it couldn't rise. The rear roper dismounted and helped the judge release the fallen steer. He took off his hat, and Durfey could see him clearly. He was bald, short, broad shouldered, and possessed of enormous biceps, very much like Durfey's father. His face didn't particularly resemble the face of anyone Durfey had ever known—bushy eyebrows, flaring jaws, a small, surly mouth. He looked every bit of the thirty-nine years he had to be.

The roper remounted and he and the young roper jogged

nonchalantly toward the chutes. The announcer said their time was fastest so far. Durfey left the grandstand and headed to the staging area, where they'd probably be loading their mounts in a trailer. The staging area was a jumble of pickups, trailers, lounging cowboys, and nervously pacing horses. It was illuminated by slats of light coming through the openings in a long, high bleacher. The straw-littered sand beneath Durfey's feet was rich with the aroma of horse manure and diesel fuel.

As Durfey expected, the short, bald, muscular roper and his willowy, downy-cheeked companion dragged saddles from their horses and hung them in the hutch of a trailer. Durfey stood a couple of yards away, obscure in a slat of darkness, and listened while they curried their sweating mounts.

"Well, goddamn, Donnie," the man said, "that was one fine performance you put on."

"I can't believe it," the boy said. "Sometimes everything goes just right."

"We got a chance for top money if we can just hold up tomorrow night. Three thousand bucks, believe it or not! You can have every damn penny of it."

"Oh, gee. What if we do!"

"Then maybe your ma will get off my back. I keep trying to tell her this ain't no idle sport. By Jesus, we're going to pay your way through college."

The currying finished, the ropers loaded their mounts into the trailer. The boy got into the cab. The man clanged shut the trailer door and strolled toward the front of the truck. Passing Durfey, he raised a casual hand and said, "Howdy." He climbed in and started the engine. The vehicle and trailer slowly pulled away.

Durfey followed. The sand was deep and he quickly fell behind. Gerald Sheffield had lifted a hand and said, "Howdy"—no more, no less. The truck and trailer disappeared through the outer gate. Plodding on, Durfey reminded himself that the cowboy is the noblest of American folk heroes, and risk and valor are the currency of his trade. He heard someone sobbing. Surprised, he realized it was himself.

A pretty cowgirl in tight jeans and a pearl-buttoned shirt stopped him and said, "What's the matter, darlin'?"

"I don't have any idea why I'm crying," Durfey said. "I had sutures done on my lip two or three hours ago. The medication the doctor gave me must have unhinged me."

"If you need a drink, honey, I'll share my liquor."

"No, thanks. But that's kind."

Durfey sat on a bale of hay until he regained his composure. Then he searched the crowd back of the grandstand till he found John and the patrol car. He climbed gratefully in and listened unobtrusively to John's conversation with a rodeo official who stood at the window. Soon the radio crackled. Though its message was unintelligible to Durfey, John appeared to understand there was a problem in town, and they roared out of the rodeo grounds. At the south end of town, just past a big new motel, they saw a pickup sitting with lights on in the turn lane of Highway 89. Investigating, they found a man passed out clutching the top of the steering wheel, his forehead resting on his hands. The engine purred softly and the turn signal ticked steadily.

"Drunk bugger," John said while he pried a wallet from the man's pocket. "I know this fellow. This isn't the first time. He's got some jail time coming now."

John pulled the man from the pickup and let him thump on the pavement. Seizing his two hands, he dragged him across the highway like a sack of potatoes. Durfey helped him deposit the dead weight upright in the rear seat of the patrol car. After John parked the pickup on the side of the highway, they drove to the county court complex. Soon the accused's wife arrived—a short, obese Goshute Indian from Skull Valley who spoke broken English. She was frightened and distressed, and John and the jail keeper said nothing to make her feel better.

Durfey saw that tiny Richfield, like vast Los Angeles, harbored police brutality. Richfield's chief of police had processed this man like so much baggage. As an insurance investigator, Durfey had some sympathy for John, who considered himself sorely tried. He didn't drink and couldn't understand why anyone else needed to. He couldn't understand why husbands and wives attacked each other with kitchen knives and scalding water. He couldn't understand why Richfield kids messed around with marijuana and cocaine and carried guns to school and practiced sodomy. As far as he was concerned, the whole world was in a fast lane to hell.

By the time John and Durfey got home, Durfey was reeling with fatigue and pain. He took another pain pill, which worked with merciful speed. He went to bed in a room with a bobcat skin and a rack of giant deer antlers on a wall. As he drifted into sleep, he saw a sack of potatoes, which someone was dragging across a highway. Soon it seemed he himself had been sewn inside and those lumps weren't potatoes at all but his elbows and knees and head and feet. It was clear he'd never escape without help. He couldn't imagine why he had allowed himself to be stitched into a sack in the first place.

He awoke at dawn to the sounds of someone splashing in water in the back yard. He went to the bathroom and took another pain pill. His lip was so sore he could scarcely swallow. Returning to the bedroom, he peered out the window and saw Sharmane with rubber boots and a shovel, irrigating lawns, garden, and orchard. Sharmane was a sturdy, square-jawed Salt Lake girl who had obviously adapted well to small town life.

Lying abed Durfey tried to revive his old fantasy about buying a farm in Sevier County when he retired. If Sharmane had adapted, why couldn't Elaine? But the old fantasy wouldn't come up on his screen. Maybe it had been deleted in the big power surge of the previous day. There was nothing like finding out you had a middle-aged son to mess up your data base.

7. The Lemonade Springs

Aspen filled a glass at the sink and swallowed a couple of Anacin tablets. "Got a big headache," she explained to Hope, who was taking lasagna from the oven.

Choppy music came from the living room, where Adelia sat at the piano with Shane's eldest daughter, giving an impromptu lesson. An old metronome ticked a solemn, familiar cadence. Hope asked how the reunion was going. Aspen said there had been unexpected events. She showed Hope the welt on her cheek. Telling how she had got it, she left out the fact that Durfey Haslam had been her companion on Toby's float. She also failed to mention the assault in the parking lot.

She peered from the window above the sink. A sparrow that had clung to a vine just outside the window flew away. In the street a tiny whirlwind spiraled grit, tumbleweeds, and paper high into the air. The whirlwind wobbled an erratic path along the graveled street, seemingly uncertain whether to continue or die.

"Do you remember the time you told Mother on me for getting into a dust devil?" Aspen said.

Hope looked from the window. "I remember you letting the dust devil catch you. I don't remember telling Mother."

They had been hiking in the hills in search of horned toads and

June bugs. One of the tiny tornados that stir in western valleys during summer afternoons whirled its way toward them. Its show of energy attracted Aspen, making her heart beat faster. She angled toward it and it enveloped her. Grit pelted her face; powdery dust penetrated her clothes, hair, ears, nostrils, even the pores of her skin.

Hope returned to getting dinner. Aspen stayed at the window. By now the dust devil had lost its momentum and collapsed in a shower of debris. A soda can tumbled from nowhere in the sky. A sheet of newspaper slipped obliquely from one plane of air to another till it came to rest on the street.

At this moment Aspen's field of vision included Durfey's face with its lacerated lip. She had memorized the ragged wound, had studied it from only inches away. She pitied Durfey, and pity had unanchored her good sense. She had begun to talk about Gerald. Now her secret was gone. She felt lonely without it. She felt deprived and violated. She turned from the window and began to set places for the children at the table, remembering that it was pity that made her fall in love with Durfey in the first place.

On the evening of the day a bronc pitched Durfey off at the rodeo, the Marooney family discussed the incident at their dinner table. His leg had a multiple fracture and he would have to stay in the hospital for an indefinite period. Her parents were of the opinion that, given his daredevil ways, even worse things lay in his future. All that summer Aspen had walked to work before dawn at the drive-in on Main Street. For several days following Durfey's accident she went out of her way to pass by the hospital. One morning she pushed through the double swinging doors, and found nobody at the front desk. She went down one corridor and then another, and she found Durfey with his bed light on.

"I need that goddamned nurse," he said. "I gotta shit. Oh, Jesus, I hate a bedpan. I've held it a couple of days. I'd hold it a hundred if I could. Go find her. Tell her I gotta shit."

Aspen went looking for the night nurse. Her car wasn't in the lot. Aspen returned and told Durfey she'd have to put the pan under him.

"Like hell you will," he said. "Give me the pan and get out of here."

"Lift your butt onto this thing," she ordered.

He wept and she pitied him, and that was her undoing. He got on the pan, and she went into the corridor until he called. She took the pan and went down the corridor toward a bathroom, meeting the night nurse, Wanda Hammersheid, on the way.

"Lordy," Wanda said, "my niece called and I dashed home for just a second. Don't tell anybody, Aspen, or I'm done for." She took the bedpan and went into the bathroom.

Durfey was in the hospital about three weeks. On the days Aspen went to work, she came by at the same early hour and stayed awhile. Sometimes she brought a book or something to eat.

On the day before he was scheduled to go home, his father came while she was there. Balis Haslam turned on the overhead light and looked her over while he scratched his stubbly chin. She had been seated in a chair close to Durfey's bed. She pulled the chair away and stood behind it, as if admitting she had no right to be present.

"I'm on my way to Pioche," Balis said to Durfey. "I'll be back tomorrow noon and I'll take you home. You're going to have to stay on that sofa in the living room. There's nowhere else to put you in that house. Lord, you're an inconvenience. You never told me you intended to take up bronc riding. When you get an idea like that, you ought to tell your old dad so he can talk you out of it."

He turned to Aspen. "What are you doing in this room before dawn?"

"I'm Aspen Marooney," she said. "I go to high school with Durfey."

"I know who you are," he said. "You go home to your daddy and mamma, young lady, and don't get something started with Durfey.

This boy of mine will have to move somewhere like Detroit and work in a factory. He'll have to go somewhere you won't want to follow."

Aspen left the hospital and walked on toward the drive-in. The morning star was bright in the east. She remembered the first day when she had carried Durfey's excrement in a bedpan and he had wept in humiliation. Nothing could be more astonishing, nothing more sacred. From that moment she was in love with him.

Aspen sliced French bread, brushed it with garlic butter, and put it under the broiler. Then Hope called the crowd to dinner. They needed to finish quickly so the twins and their wives and Norman and Billie and all the older kids could go to the rodeo. Roger, who sat at the table with Adelia and the smaller children, reminded the rodeo goers to watch for Gerald and Donnie in the team roping.

Roger cheerfully reported on the reunion. He said he envied the happy, homey spirit which prevailed so far. What he had noticed about a rural high school was that everyone knew everyone else. However, a vestige of adolescent conflict had marred the proceedings when, following the luncheon, a fellow named Bradford Higley had assaulted Durfey Haslam in the parking lot. Roger said he and Aspen had met Durfey at the drugstore and had seen that his lip was badly split.

"I imagine he's over at the emergency ward this very instant having it sewn up," Roger said.

"So once again we hear of the infamous Mr. Bradford Higley, whom I've never had the privilege of meeting," Adelia said.

"And the infamous Durfey Haslam," said Hope. "He bit off Bradford's ear the year after I graduated from high school."

Adelia said, "You'd think the youth of Richfield when my children were growing up were nothing but a pack of Scythians. And apparently little has changed among some of them."

"I don't think you should categorize Durfey Haslam with this

Bradford Higley," Roger said. "Aspen and I sat with Durfey and his wife at the luncheon, and they both seem to be sound, intelligent people."

"Well, that's a mercy," Adelia said, turning her attention to serving lasagna to a child sitting beside her.

"On the lighter side of things," Roger said, "a few of the class got up a comic float for the parade. They tied a sheep into a barber's chair with that reformed renegade the town barber standing behind with his tunic and shears."

Adelia required him to repeat the story of the float in greater detail. "That Toby Jackson!" she said when he had finished. "He's been nothing but a scandal all his life."

"He does seem something out of the ordinary," Roger granted. "I'm afraid he got carried away by the enthusiasm of the crowd and went to waving his shears about and struck poor Aspen across the face with the cord. Look. You can still see the welt."

"Aspen! Was she on the float?"

"Oh, yes," Roger said. "She and Durfey Haslam too, both recruited by that irresistible entrepreneur, Henry Ross, the one who had the idea for the float in the first place."

Adelia turned in her chair and peered at her daughter, who, as on the previous evening, sat on the carpet with her back to a wall. Adelia began to eat again, taking dainty bites and chewing demurely. Her hair was bunched about her head in Victorian fashion, with a bun above her crown. An annoying wisp fell over her left ear, and she repeatedly attempted to brush it upward into place.

Aspen was grateful Roger had interpreted the events of the day so cheerfully. Only the fact that he was the teller of the story had saved her a scolding. Adelia trusted his judgment. In her eyes he was Aspen's better half.

After dinner Aspen helped Hope and Esther clean up the mess in the kitchen. Fortunately, her headache was much better. When the table was cleared, the children who remained at home began to work in coloring books with crayons. At their request, Aspen made play dough from flour, salt, and food coloring. Roger and Adelia were in the den going over Adelia's papers for the biography Roger intended to write. Dan sat in the family room taking in a loud sitcom on TV.

Hope said, "I'd ten thousand times rather help these children than watch that boob tube."

For a while the women discussed the display of wealth, sex, and violence on TV. They drifted on to other topics, and Aspen was soon telling her sister and cousin how worried she was about her daughter Elizabeth, who lived in Manhattan.

"Heavenly Father wouldn't let anything happen to a girl as good as Elizabeth," Hope said. "So you can just quit worrying."

There was in fact no special reason to worry about Elizabeth, who was a solid, sensible, obedient, spiritual young woman, except that, of course, she did live in New York. Elizabeth and a friend paid a thousand dollars a month for a tiny apartment that had three deadbolts on the door. Every day dozens of people were mugged, raped, and murdered in New York. However, Elizabeth walked to work and claimed the extra deadbolts on her door weren't necessary because the Mafia ruled her neighborhood and weren't interested in molesting ordinary people.

At bedtime the women bathed the children and put them into their beds and sleeping bags, and Dan and Roger agreed to keep an eye on them while the women set out in Hope's car for a late visit with Esther's sister Maurine in Marysvale, where Esther would remain while Hope and Aspen returned to Richfield. They took the freeway south for fifteen miles, exited onto Highway 89, and entered Sevier Canyon. The car swayed on the tight curves of the canyon, its headlights falling on the roiling waters of the river. Near the end of the canyon they passed by the dark bulk of Big Rock Candy Mountain.

"There it is, the mountain made of sugar," Esther said, and she began to sing the old hobo song.

Oh, the buzzin' of the bees in the cigarette trees
Near the soda water fountain,
At the lemonade springs where the bluebird sings,
On the big rock candy mountain.

Big Rock Candy Mountain is a small peak on the flank of Sevier Canyon. Its sides are eroded into gullies and gulches, and its soil is a ripple of amber, brown, and caramel. The song existed before the peak got its name. However, it had carried the name for as long as Aspen could remember.

When she was a little girl, she asked her father to stop and let her taste it. Horatio said, "It's just dirt, honey."

Eventually she did taste it. As her father had said, it was just dirt. There was a seep of water at the base of the mountain called the Lemonade Springs. She tasted that, too—brackish water. She imagined, though these lemonade springs were phony, there had to be real lemonade springs somewhere. It stood to reason.

Later she came to believe that life always looks better than it tastes. Her eyes deceived her, but her taste buds told the truth. She knew kids were like hobos. She knew that kids *were* hobos of a non-transient sort. They had no jobs and they lived off handouts. They dreamed happiness into existence; their entire energy went into wish fulfillment.

She was still a kid when at seventeen she fell in love with Durfey Haslam. Durfey knew the trail to the Lemonade Springs. He knew the customs and accoutrements, the promises and pleasures, of Big Rock Candy Mountain. He had a loose, willing tongue and told her about them. In the trace of his footsteps she hunted for hobo heaven.

Beyond the canyon were fields and pastures with livestock sometimes visible in the lights of the car. Marysvale appeared—twenty or thirty houses set in the middle of a gulch. A street light burned at either end of town. Esther said, "No one knows why this town hasn't been washed away by a flash flood. Someday it will be."

Maurine greeted them with cries of affection and offered a drink made of pineapple and coconut. She was overjoyed that Esther would be staying. Maurine was a widow, and she lived alone with an autistic grandson whom her daughter had despaired of raising.

At the moment the boy lay asleep in a bedroom. He was of school age and had such anti-social habits that other children wouldn't associate with him. Maurine took him to a therapist in Provo. The boy had never been able to cry. He simply couldn't produce sobs and tears. On one occasion the therapist decided it was best to confront him with the fact that his mother didn't love him so that he'd recognize that she was never coming back and he could settle down and turn his need for affection to Maurine and maybe a few others who really did love him.

"So she doesn't love me?" the boy said.

"No, she doesn't love you."

He laid his head on the table for fifteen minutes. No sobs, no tears, just a vast mute misery.

When Maurine had finished this story, Aspen said, "That therapist ought to be shot. There was no good to come from rubbing that boy's face in the fact his mother doesn't love him."

"Well, golly," Esther said, "let's talk about something cheerful. Let's shake men and kids for a while. Let's howl at the moon."

"You hussy!" Aspen said.

"Yeah, mudmouth, that's me!" Esther said. "Last month our bishop preached against bad words like heck, darn, and golly. Didn't say a word about hell and damn and son of a bitch. What I wanted to do after church was say, 'Bishop, I couldn't agree more with you about putting down words like gosh, heck, and darn. Once words like that get loose, a community for shitsure goes to the dogs.'"

"Oh, lordy, that Esther!" Maurine exploded.

Aspen said, "Tell us about the time your dad dosed his hemorrhoids with turpentine."

Hope said, "Oh, dear, not that old story."

"I want to hear it again."

Aspen felt young and wicked. She needed escape, she needed oblivion. She felt ready to start another Boston Tea Party. She hated the way men run the world, the way they won't listen to what a woman says. She hated having to use nice words and not laugh out loud.

"This is how Mom told the story," Esther said. "Pop said to her, 'This fellow out at the dam says turpentine is good for piles.' Mom said, 'I wouldn't think so.' A day or two later Pop said, 'I don't mind a little pain if it would do some good.' Mom said, 'I wouldn't if I were you.' But he went ahead one night. He squatted naked on the bedroom floor and dosed himself with a rag soaked in turpentine. He hollered and screamed and tore around the bedroom knocking over furniture. He rolled across the bed, and when he came down on the floor on the other side he ran on all fours barking like a dog."

Maurine roared. Aspen laughed till she cried. Hope bit her lip and ducked her head.

"Reminds me of when my Herbert got circumcised," Maurine said. "He was thirty-five. His thing swole way up after the operation and he couldn't pee. The pain nearly killed him."

"I wish we could talk about something a little more edifying," Hope said.

"They don't circumcise baby boys so much anymore," Esther said. "They say a penis that's been circumcised gets calloused. It's like going barefooted for a long time. Your soles toughen up. So sex isn't nearly as much fun. I've heard of doctors who think they can make the prepuce grow back. They have a man stretch the skin that's left little by little until it makes a new prepuce."

"Maybe men who donate their organs could include their foreskins," Aspen said.

"That would be wonderful," Esther said. "If the surgeons can transplant a liver, they ought to be able to transplant a foreskin."

"Maybe they could invent a silicon prepuce and implant it," Aspen said. "Maybe they could sew it on like a celluloid collar."

"My word, I'm glad I'm not a man," Maurine shouted.

Around one o'clock Maurine said, "I feel so rotten saying all those bad things about Herbert. He used to annoy me the way he'd break wind in the car. But he was honest and everybody respected him and he was home every night. I can't get over him dying. I just can't stop crying."

She had brought them back to reality, and it was time for Hope and Aspen to go home. They knew they were just four aging women with wide hips, bulging legs, round bellies, and double chins. They felt like the leftovers of summer, dried up and bereft of seed.

On the porch Aspen and Hope hugged and kissed Esther and Maurine and said goodbye. They were all thinking of that poor autistic boy who lay slumbering inside. They pitied him for having no other happiness than sleep.

As she got into the car, Aspen noted the clean, powdery glow of the rural sky. "The lights from Salt Lake ruin the sky where I live," she said.

Hope said, "I don't think the skies anywhere are as bright as they used to be."

"Maybe our eyes have got filmed over with soil."

"Well, maybe they have."

"I apologize for all that loose talk. I don't know what gets into me."

"Oh, don't apologize," Hope said.

"Roger never talks like that."

"I know he doesn't. He's a wonderful man."

Aspen granted she wasn't herself tonight, hadn't been since meeting Durfey in the drugstore, perhaps wouldn't be ever again. At last she had told. Someone else knew. She mustn't lose her momentum, mustn't collapse like a whirlwind. Maybe tomorrow she could tell Roger. Adelia too. Anybody who had the right to

124

know. Maybe tomorrow would be the day.

Soon they passed by the hulking silhouette of Big Rock Candy Mountain. Just north of the mountain, in a widening of the canyon, they passed a modern motel with a glowing neon sign.

"Do you remember the old lodge that used to be here," Aspen said. "There was a store and a cafe and seven or eight little log cabins. That's where Roger and I spent our wedding night—in one of the log cabins."

"Well, yes, I guess I knew you stayed at Big Rock Candy Mountain on your wedding night. I think you told me." The red glow of the motel's neon sign receded. Headlights showed oak, ash, and cottonwood along the Sevier.

All wedding nights were hallowed for Hope. She could speak of love ignited and long, happy unions initiated on wedding nights. But around the topic of broken hymens, of orgasms unachieved, of babies conceived before they were desired she drew a circle of silence.

Gerald was conceived on the next to last night of 1951, not in Aspen's but in Hope's bed. Hope's bed stood neatly made. Aspen's was a mess. Aspen pulled back the cover on Hope's bed, took off her shirt and jeans, slid the bra straps off her shoulders, and motioned Durfey to turn out the light.

A week later in Provo Aspen waited for her period. She felt bloated but not in the usual way. It should have started on a Tuesday. On Wednesday she panicked. Her roommates were back from vacation and the university was in session. For a couple of days she waited, thinking maybe the stress of walking out on Durfey had thrown her schedule off. On Saturday she said to herself, "Face up to it. You're pregnant."

Euphoria came over her. "You can have him now," she said to herself. "You don't have any choice. This was what you were waiting for."

It was midday when she was in that mood. By night she was

hysterical. She wondered where she had ever got the idea she could go through with marrying Durfey if only she were pregnant and had to. She ironed clothes till midnight and then lay on her bed without sleeping till dawn. She thought about having an abortion. She didn't know where to go to get one. She thought about suicide. It occurred to her everyone would have to know why she had died.

Early in the afternoon she phoned Roger. She asked him to come over in the evening and he said he would. She gave him home-baked cookies and milk and showed interest in his experiences and ambitions. The next night he picked her up at the library and took her for a drive up Provo Canyon.

He told her a former bishop had told him a man should marry before he's twenty-five.

"Will you make it?" she said.

"I don't know," he said. "Maybe I need a little help."

He wanted to know whether she thought they ought to pray about whether they were the right ones for each other. When she didn't object, he parked the car and said a prayer.

"How do you feel?" he said when he had finished praying.

"I'm tired of being single," she said. "I wouldn't mind getting started with a family."

He said, "My goodness!"

"There's nobody in the world I respect more than you," she said. "But if we're going to get married, I don't feel up to a lot of folderol. I'd just like to get married and settle down."

Though it took a good deal of insistence on Aspen's part, they were married in the Salt Lake temple five weeks and three days from the night she got pregnant.

Their wedding day was cold. Clouds were low, dreary, and furrows of dirty snow lined the sidewalks. On the highest spire of the temple stood Moroni, facing east with his long-stemmed trumpet. Aspen took Moroni's trumpet as a warning. It told the world God wouldn't be trifled with. Leaving the car, she walked mechanically at Roger's side. She could just as well have been handcuffed and on the way to her execution. It could have been her own hanging that Moroni announced.

First, they had to get Aspen's endowments. She came up from the washing and anointing room and sat between Roger and Adelia in a large hall. Everybody wore a white robe. On the high walls an artist had painted planets and stars and cloudy blue spaces. Aspen drifted in those spaces, having no sense of gravity, no sense that she had anything solid to push against.

Adelia's face was radiant. She had promoted this marriage from the earliest moment of hearing of it, defending Aspen's haste against Horatio's reasoning that a wedding in March, between quarters at BYU, would allow the newlyweds a more leisurely honeymoon.

"Since they've found one another, let them get married now," Adelia had said. "A honeymoon's a silly thing anyhow."

After the endowment session, they went to a sealing room, crowded with white-clad relatives and friends. Bride and groom knelt on either side of a padded altar, holding hands and looking into each other's eyes, and the temple president married them for time and all eternity. When they had kissed and risen to their feet, the temple president gave each a hug. His eyes were bland, unsuspecting.

Roger believed he had just acquired an eternal mate but he hadn't. Aspen hoped she would die in childbirth or a car accident so Roger could marry a proper wife. That failing, she hoped God would let him choose a better wife in the Millennium. She hoped it wouldn't be utterly dark where God sent her following Judgment. She hoped it wouldn't be like a closet or a cellar or a coffin.

From the temple they went to a wedding luncheon in the Hotel Utah. Afterwards they gathered in the hotel foyer while a photographer took pictures of Aspen and Roger and their retinue. Then they drove the hundred sixty miles to Richfield for an evening reception at the church where the Marooneys attended meetings. After the reception everyone wanted to watch the newlyweds open their gifts. Outside they discovered Roger's car decorated with white shoe polish and Oreo cookies. Also, someone had hidden the keys. It was two in the morning before they checked into a cabin at Big Rock Candy Mountain on the road toward St. George, where they would spend the weekend.

"You can't go without a honeymoon of some kind or other," Horatio had insisted. "And don't take your school books with you, for heaven's sake!"

The cabin had thin plank walls and an iron bedstead and a small attached bathroom. The room was cold and depressing, and Roger put down their bags and sat on the edge of the bed. He scratched the back of his neck and stared at something on the floor. Aspen turned on the wall furnace. A hot dusty odor filled the room. Roger unlaced his shoes, then absent-mindedly retied them. It appeared he would prefer to wait till morning before proceeding with his nuptial duty.

Aspen knelt and took off his shoes and socks and massaged his ankles. She took his hands and brushed his palms against her hair, which hung to her shoulders. She turned out the light and stood in the gleam from the bathroom door and slipped off her shoes and nylons and dropped her clothes around her feet.

The next day, on a snowy overlook at Bryce National Park, Roger apologized for having been so passionate. Even now, if they were alone when driving by the motel at Big Rock Candy Mountain, he would say very quietly, "That's where Gerald got his start."

Driving through Elsinore, the sisters discussed their mother's retarded aunt who lived there. Aunt Brenda had never married but had sometimes held a job. Presently, another niece lived across the street from her and supervised the women and girls who were hired to help take care of her.

"Mother and I visit her every two or three weeks," Hope said. "She's senile as well as retarded. You can't make heads or tails of anything she says."

Their mother grieved for Brenda's unrealized life. They were

128

nearly the same age. When Adelia entered first grade, Brenda was starting her third year in that grade. Thereafter, year by year, school officials advanced Brenda with Adelia. Adelia was always careful to explain to all listeners that Brenda's retardation was owing not to genes but to her premature birth.

"There was no hospital, no incubator," Adelia would remind her listeners. "They kept Brenda in a shoe box on the open oven door of a wood-burning stove. Premature births run in our line. Roger's and Aspen's first child was premature, you know. That's why his legs have never developed properly. They were deformed right from the beginning."

Beyond Elsinore, Hope accelerated the car till the road rumbled beneath them. The scent of a dairy barn and drying alfalfa wafted through the vents. A white horse and a sheep were picketed on a grassy ditch bank. They appeared suddenly in the headlights and as suddenly disappeared.

"Durfey Haslam longs for the odor of horse manure," Aspen said. "Or so he told me on Toby's float this morning."

"How informative," Hope said. "Did he share other sentiments?"

"He was just being whimsical."

"Yes, he was always famous for that."

"The summer after I graduated from high school, Durfey herded sheep in Fry Pan Canyon," Aspen said. "I was working at Fishlake lodge. One day when I had the afternoon off I found his camp. Nobody told me where it was. I kept driving up and down first one canyon, then another. Once I had found his camp, I went back fifteen or twenty times."

The boughs of a giant cottonwood ballooned in the rush of the headlights. In their instant of visibility, the leaves appeared to flutter.

"Don't you have anything to say about my going to his camp so often?"

"That's nothing new," Hope said. "I already knew you visited his sheep camp. Everybody knew that."

"Everybody?"

"Certainly. It was common knowledge. I was working in Phoenix. Mother phoned me every week. She said, 'There's a wicked rumor going around. It can't be true though people who wish ill for our family have seized on it. No child of Horatio and Adelia Marooney could possibly be unchaste. We must close ranks as a family and keep our heads high until this vile rumor blows over.' That's what she said."

"I just don't believe that," Aspen said.

"Father and Mother knew perfectly well you were slipping around with Durfey Haslam all through your senior year. They knew you were visiting him in his sheep camp during the summer."

They entered Richfield and drove along the bright swath of Main Street. They took a side street and pulled into Hope's driveway. The garage door rose like a creature possessed of a mysterious will and clanked shut behind them.

"I didn't know they knew," Aspen said.

"Of course you didn't."

"Why did Mother tell you and not me?"

"If you were in Mother's place, what would you do with a strong-willed eighteen-year-old? Arrest her and put her in jail?"

"It might have made a difference if she had told me."

"Mother said, 'If we can just get her off to BYU this fall, everything will be all right.' And her confidence paid off, didn't it? You met Roger and he had been in the army and was going to college on the G.I. Bill and all in a rush to get married, and you had the good sense to say yes."

They got out of the car and went in through the kitchen door. A night light in the hall faintly illuminated the dining area and living room, where tiny forms lay in sleeping bags. A child awakened and wanted to go to the bathroom. Aspen helped the little girl find her way and got her back into her sleeping bag. Kneeling beside the child, she took note of her mother's empty rocking chair. Catching light from the hallway, the rocker cast a faint trapezoidal shadow on a wall.

In September 1951 Aspen had promised Durfey she wouldn't go to BYU. She said, "Just hang on till Christmas. Maybe we'll get married then."

A few days later she went on a picnic to Puffer Lake with Horatio and Adelia and friends from out of town. The canyons were afire with yellow aspens and scarlet maples. As they approached the last high switchbacks, Adelia ordered Horatio to stop. She was having an attack of vertigo.

Adelia circled the car, muttering, "My poor palpitating heart! Altitude makes me ill."

They decided she and Aspen would wait at this broad, level, beautifully forested spot while Horatio and their guests ascended the final heights to Puffer Lake. Then they'd return and have their picnic here.

Adelia was invigorated by her escape from the jolting automobile. She spread a blanket and sat crosslegged on it. She flung her arms and declared, "My emotions become so eager when I go out into nature! I could spend days in such a place, doing nothing but writing poems."

She might have gone on in this vein if she hadn't caught sight of a red and white bovine grazing at the far end of the clearing in which they sat.

"That isn't a bull, is it?" she asked.

"It's a cow," Aspen said.

Soon a second animal appeared behind the first. "Oh, dear," Adelia said. "They might both be bulls."

"They're cows," Aspen said. "But even if they weren't, range bulls don't pay any attention to people. They're not dangerous."

"There's a third!" Adelia said. "I think, Aspen, we must take shelter in a tree."

She found a pine and insisted that Aspen accompany her. At the base of the tree she said, "You help me up first, and then I'll pull you up beside me."

"Not on your life," Aspen said.

"Oh, dear. So we perish when security stands so close before us."

"You get in the tree," Aspen said. "If something comes along I need to worry about, I can climb up quick."

"That's true," Adelia said. "I'm the cumbersome one."

Aspen helped Adelia onto a horizontal limb about six feet above the ground. She sat with an arm about the trunk, her feet dangling a little above the level of Aspen's elbows.

"Much higher and I'll faint," she said. "Is this high enough? Is there room for you to scramble up?"

"Plenty of room," Aspen said.

"Well, then, make yourself comfortable on the blanket, and we'll go on with our conversation. We might just as well make the best of our situation."

Soon, at a moment when Adelia renewed her embrace of the trunk, an overhanging bough brushed off her glasses, which fell to the blanket and lay with opened struts, as if Adelia had set them down intentionally.

"Hand me my spectacles, dear, will you please?" her mother said.

Silent forces seemed to be working in Aspen's favor. There couldn't have been a better, a more providential, moment for confessing her sordid doings with Durfey Haslam, blindness having diminished her mother's capacity for disapproval. Aspen hesitated, and that was that. The moment vanished.

Her glasses restored, Adelia took up a familiar discussion of the reasons why Aspen should go to college. "It isn't that I think you should prepare for any but the highest of all callings, motherhood, but it's a proven fact your children will be more likely to take up honorable professions, or marry men in honorable professions, if you yourself have been to college. As you know too well, it's one of the keenest disappointments of my life that I never went to college."

A grey California jay teetered in a nearby aspen. It seemingly couldn't make up its mind whether its head or tail should be uppermost.

"So will you go to BYU?" Adelia asked. She looked down steadily upon Aspen, her eyes magnified by her glasses.

"Though it's too late to get into a dormitory," she went on, "we could drive you to Provo next week and get you registered and help you find an apartment."

The jay flitted away with a screech. Flies buzzed in the heat of late morning. The crushed grass beneath the blanket gave off a fresh herbal scent. Aspen took note of all this, then studied the progress of a solitary ant up an arching stem of grass. Any diversion was preferable to returning her mother's gaze.

Her mother began to plead. "Please, Aspen. Say you'll go. I beg of you, Aspen. Please say you'll go."

Aspen hated a hard-hearted person. She hated a girl who would say no to her mother.

"Please, Aspen. I beg of you."

"I'll go," she said. "If you really want me to, I'll go."

"Oh, thank God!" Adelia said. "Do I really want you to? In the worst possible way! But not for my sake, sweetheart. For your own, your very own. You'll live to thank me, I promise you."

After she had quieted the child, Aspen went to the bathroom and brushed her teeth. She examined her welt, a thin, slightly red line, pointing toward her ear as if it signified an obligation to listen carefully.

Leaving the bathroom, she met Hope in the hall. Hope, wearing a robe, murmured good night and went into the kitchen. In a wild panic, Aspen followed, joining her at the sink. Hope drew a glass of water and swallowed a couple of pills. Aspen slipped an arm around her sister's waist. Hope leaned her head against Aspen's head for a moment.

"You're a wonderful sister," Aspen murmured. "I've always looked up to you."

"Oh, posh. I'm as ordinary as oatmeal."

"You are so kind to Mother."

"So are you."

"You have a way with her that I don't. That's a fact. There's something I wish you'd help me tell her. I really don't know how to go about it. It would be a great blessing if you'd do it for me."

"Well, of course I'll help you."

"That ugly rumor Mother told you about—it wasn't just a rumor." Her arm was still around Hope's waist—an ample, soft, comfortable waist, which so far expressed neither resistance nor disbelief. She went on. "It simply isn't true that no Marooney child could possibly be unchaste."

Now came resistance—a stiffened body, a tangible anger. Hope said, "You used to tease me. You used to say, 'When I grow up, I'm going to be a cocktail waitress' or 'I'm going to marry a polygamist.' Don't make fun of me now. This isn't the way to make a joke."

"I'm not teasing you," Aspen said. "I slept with Durfey in his sheep camp. I've wanted to tell you for forty years. I've wanted to tell Mother. Please help me."

"No, I'll certainly not do that. Tell Mother! Have you gone insane? It'd kill her. That's exactly what it would do. It'd kill her."

Hope removed Aspen's arm from her waist. She gripped her hand, then dropped it.

"It happened often," Aspen said. "Maybe ten or twelve times."

"You had no right to do that."

"That's true. I had no right at all."

"What a disappointment for Roger! I'm surprised he would marry you knowing you had done that. You did tell him, didn't you? You wouldn't deceive him with a thing like that, would you?"

"Of course I wouldn't!" Aspen cried. "What kind of a monster do you think I am?"

"Roger is the salt of the earth," Hope said.

"Yes, he's a very forgiving man. You couldn't ask for anyone to be more understanding."

"As for telling Mother, that's out of the question now. So get rid of that idea this instant. I'm not exaggerating. It would kill her, old and frail as she is. No, really, you can't breathe a word of this to Mother."

The sisters hugged one another and wept. "I love you so much, Aspen. But this is so terribly sad."

"Yes, it's terribly sad," Aspen said.

8. Amending Aspen's Conscience

Near six, John left for Koosharem Canyon. Durfey said he'd wait for Elaine, who was likely to show up any minute. While he waited, he had a bowl of cooked cereal diluted with milk.

"I'm surprised she isn't here by now," Durfey kept saying.

At six-thirty Sharmane said, "Give her a call."

He thought of the little girls who would still be asleep in the motel room in Cedar City. He decided he could wait awhile. A little after seven it occurred to him that Elaine didn't intend to come. She didn't intend to phone him and let him know. She had washed her hands of this reunion.

That was just as well. One thing had become clear to him this morning. The veracity issue was settled. Aspen wasn't lying to him. Gerald Sheffield was his son. So he'd ride up to the reunion with Sharmane and Anne later in the day and see whether there was something more that needed to be said between him and Aspen. As for Elaine, she had a right to know. The question was just when to tell her. No matter when, it wouldn't make a pretty scene. It was likely to be the end of a marriage.

Despite all that, he wanted to see Gerald again. He wanted to talk to him, understand his prejudices, find out what big things had happened to him. He wanted to shake his hand, put an arm around his shoulders, kiss him on the cheek. He'd ask Aspen how he ought to proceed. Maybe Roger would help out. He couldn't believe Roger wasn't behind all this. Durfey had got over his disgust for the man. In fact, he admired Roger, who had struck him yesterday at the luncheon as kind and sensible. He had probably said to Aspen, "It's time to tell Durfey. Don't keep him in the dark any longer."

Luckily, John came back to the house about seven-thirty, having never got out of town. He had been called to the jail by radio to fill out more papers on the drunk he had arrested the night before. Also a calf had got loose from somebody's back yard on the west side of town, and he'd had to find one of his assistants to impound it.

John was passionate about keeping strays off the streets. "Tourists will think we're a bunch of hicks here if we don't keep the animals locked up," he said.

John and Durfey drove up the Fishlake highway in the patrol car, and in the tiny hamlet of Koosharem they turned onto a rough gravel road that led yet higher into the mountains. While John rambled on about the tribulations of keeping the peace, Durfey mused on the clear morning sky, the shadowy canyons, the wild flowers on the border of the road.

Dennis Gundersen's summer home in Koosharem Canyon was a rustic mansion of molded logs and a dozen Swiss gables. Behind the house were lawns, a tennis court, and a stable. Four saddled horses waited patiently at a hitching post. Presumably someone would want a ride later on. A group of men pitched horseshoes with wordless intent, and mixed teams of shouting men and women played volleyball. Two couples engaged in combat on the tennis court, and another foursome played croquet on the lawn. Dennis himself emerged from the house in a sequined Oriental robe and climbed into a swirling, steaming outdoor jacuzzi. Clusters of chairs, tables, and awnings were scattered about the lawns, ready to promote conversation. Reminiscence was the order of the day. Here, in these pleasant surroundings, the Class of '51 would resurrect itself for some few hours.

A breakfast of pancakes and sausages was served at a grill beneath an awning. Durfey selected a glass of orange juice and took a seat on a veranda overlooking the lawns and tennis court. The morning was cool, and he was glad for the sweater John had lent him.

Trelawny and Pamela Smith joined him on the veranda. Trelawny wore light blue jeans and brown and white lizardskin boots. Pamela, a reformed Texan, wore impeccably pressed slacks and a brocaded vest. Masses of tiny silver curls circled her head with perfect conformity. She was eating a bright red apple.

"It'll be a while before I can eat an apple," Durfey said gloomily.

"You could scrape an apple with a spoon," Trelawny said. "I recall my mother doing that for me when I was small."

"I'll scrape one for you," Pamela said. "You look like you need some mothering."

"Thank you," Durfey said. "The offer's as good as the deed. I'll not trouble you for the actual product."

Trelawny had met Pamela while in the navy. He was the first in four generations of Smiths to have married outside Mormonism. Though everyone back home in Richfield expected Pamela would eventually convert, she never had. However, as Durfey knew from his sister Mora, their children had been raised Mormons.

"I once kept an apple on my desk till it shriveled and went brown," Durfey said. "Finally it got to where I thought it could serve for what medieval monks used to call a *memento mori*—something like a skull to remind me of death and the foolishness of becoming too attached to this world when there's a better one awaiting."

"My God, you sound like a Baptist preacher," Pamela said. She gazed reproachfully at the half-eaten apple in her hand.

"It doesn't seem to me a shriveled apple could be considered in the same class as a human skull," Trelawny said.

"Apples would be more convenient," Pamela said, taking another bite.

"I've always wondered if there wouldn't be a financial opportunity here," Durfey said. "There ought to be a market in skulls and shriveled apples, don't you think? People would appreciate being reminded of death, damnation, and all that."

"A wonderful idea," Trelawny said. "When do you plan to start up?"

"I thought Mormons didn't believe in original sin," Pamela said.

"They don't," Trelawny said.

"Durfey does."

"Just a whim," Durfey said. "I wondered all night why I bit off Bradford Higley's ear. Innate depravity. There's no other explanation."

They saw that Aspen had arrived, apparently without her spouse. She was making her way slowly through several clusters of classmates and partners, laughing and gesturing with evident pleasure. There was no question that voices became louder and happier wherever Aspen went. Eventually she went through the breakfast line, acquiring a pancake and a cup of diced fruit. For a moment she looked around. Trelawny waved and she called something pleasant and made her way to the veranda. She took a seat facing Durfey. She wore white slacks, a blouse of light blue, and small gold earrings.

"No husband this morning?" Pamela asked.

Aspen explained that Roger had gone to Hanksville with their son Gerald to inspect an airplane that was for sale. Gerald had got a crazy notion that he wanted to become a pilot.

"He came by unexpectedly this morning and invited us to go along on the drive just for the fun of it. I said certainly we would go with him. Roger said we shouldn't miss the reunion. I said, 'What are a bunch of stuffy old friends compared to Gerald?' Gerald said, 'Way to go, Mom. Glad to see you've got your head on straight.' But Roger said no. If I'd come down to attend the reunion, by golly, that's what I had to do. So we decided to split up and here I am."

"Is Gerald your oldest?" Trelawny asked.

"That's right. Maybe you saw him and his boy Donnie at the rodeo last night. They took best time in the team roping."

"I'm sorry we didn't make it to the rodeo," Trelawny said.

"I was there," Durfey said.

Aspen examined a tiny cube of cantaloupe she had speared with a white plastic fork. She put it in her mouth and picked about in her fruit cup before deciding to spear a bit of pear. "I must say," she said to Durfey, "that bandage on your lip is a big improvement."

"I think I may survive now," he said. He touched the bandage lightly. "I apologize for being such a spectacle."

"I'm glad to see Durfey isn't boiling with rage over being knocked down," Pamela said. "Actually, we are all grateful to you and Bradford for giving us something to talk about. I've heard at least six versions of your fight. It's all anyone could discuss when we first got here."

"Tell me the most flattering version you've heard," Durfey said. "That'll be the official one."

"I'll tell you the least flattering. You provoked Bradford by calling him a name and that's why he knocked you down."

"I called him a name after he knocked me down."

Trelawny said, "According to Toby, Bradford is coming up from town this afternoon to beg your forgiveness."

"Oh, lord," Durfey said. "I've already forgiven him. If I have to look him in the face again, I might change my mind."

The sun had come over the eastward ridge and, though their immediate surroundings were still partially in shadow, much of the verdant, misty canyon below was splashed with gold.

"Isn't this glorious!" Pamela said.

"Paradise," Durfey agreed. "Summer in the mountains of Utah— that's all I want of heaven."

A tall aspen stood nearby, some of its boughs overhanging the veranda. On its trunk someone had recently carved a heart with initials in the center. Durfey was reminded he had once carved a heart on an aspen trunk in Fry Pan Canyon. In all times and ages, smooth white aspen trunks invite declarations of love.

"So where is Elaine?" Aspen asked. "I've been looking for her all over."

"Elaine and I divided our forces like you and Roger. She went back to Cedar City last night while I stayed with John and Sharmane. As you may have noticed, I haven't had a change of clothes this morning, so you should keep a respectful distance."

"So Elaine didn't take in the rodeo?"

"Rodeo isn't something she enjoys."

"And she didn't drive up this morning?"

"I haven't seen her. I scarcely expect her to come now. So I'm an orphan for the day."

"Too bad," Aspen said. "We'll miss her."

Someone at the horseshoe pits made a ringer and a horseshoe clamored like a bell in the crisp air. "It's funny people still play at horseshoes," Durfey said. "It's the game of an animal-powered society. Finding an old horseshoe is supposed to bring good luck. Actually a horseshoe is a solemn object. Its shape is a broken circle, the sign of failure and incompletion."

"You are absolutely in a morbid mood!" Pamela cried.

"He's a poet," Aspen said.

"Just a farmer," Durfey protested. "That's all I ever wanted to be."

"Durfey believes we were shortchanged by our education at Richfield High," Trelawny said. "Our general science course did teach the planetary model of the atom—a handy concept for the average person."

"I was a great disappointment to every teacher I ever had," Durfey said.

"Yes," Aspen agreed, "because you read everything except what they wanted you to read."

"I've been limited all my life by lack of technical knowledge," he lamented.

"That's nothing," Aspen said. "I've been limited all my life by male privileges. I know how to do a lot of things a woman isn't supposed to do."

The croquet players were now calling for Trelawny and Pamela, who had promised to engage in a round or two. "Drat it," Trelawny said. "I guess we've got to go." They went down the stairs, crossed the lawn, and took up their mallets.

"Awfully nice people," Durfey observed.

"Absolutely," Aspen said.

The advancing sun had cast new patterns of light and shade across a vast complex of ridges and ravines. The nearer slopes were densely forested with aspen and fir. High distant slopes appeared to be bald but were, as Durfey knew, covered by sagebrush and cliffrose.

"This reminds me of Fry Pan Canyon," Aspen said.

"Yes, it's very much like Fry Pan Canyon."

Durfey considered their present position on the veranda from the perspective of the lawn, where perhaps fifty people were engaged in conversation and play. A couple of classmates, known to have been intimate in former times and now about to engage in a long and earnest conversation, could scarcely fail to rouse curiosity.

"Do you think we ought to follow the example of Trelawny and Pamela and go mingle with the bunch?" he asked.

"That's certainly an idea."

Neither of them made a move to leave. They sat in the full sun now. A warm day was in the making, and Durfey regretted not having his sunglasses. He noticed two butterflies copulating on an overhanging aspen bough. The female clung to a stem devoid of its leaf, her antennae wavering rhythmically. The male clung to her abdomen, his abdomen pulsing. They were beautiful creatures with wings of white, brown, and gold. Durfey mused briefly on the fact that sexual union went on everywhere in the summer-blessed mountains. Plants, animals, insects, all living things went forthrightly about the crucial task of renewing the generations.

He said, "I was quite insincere yesterday in chiding you for having so many children."

"You old scrooge," she said contemptuously.

"I do love children," he insisted.

"So do I, especially tiny ones," she said. "I liked being pregnant. I felt important. There was some use for me in the world. I'm compatible with little children. I can tolerate their demands and antagonisms. When they get older, well, that's another matter. I had some hellish fights with some of my teenagers."

"With Gerald?"

"Especially with Gerald."

"And Roger—did he have fights with Gerald?"

"Roger doesn't fight. He just stands by wringing his hands. It's pathetic how badly Roger wants to please Gerald. That's why it's such a miracle for him to go to Hanksville today. They haven't gone somewhere alone together in twenty years."

"I envy him," Durfey said. "I'm jealous. Yes, that's the truth. I'm jealous of Roger going to Hanksville with Gerald today."

Aspen fidgeted with her engagement ring, twisting it from side to side so that at one moment it was misaligned from her wedding band and at another it resumed its proper position. Obviously she had never taken the trouble to have the rings soldered to one another.

The butterflies on the overhanging bough remained in Durfey's view. Durfey was thinking that only human beings were unseasonal in their mating. Only humans failed to have an instinctive grasp on when the female is in estrus. Among human beings both male and female were receptive to sexual intercourse at almost any time, the race having become addicted to orgasm as its chief pleasure.

An astonishing idea now came to Durfey. A sedate, aging couple from the Class of '51 had only to wander into the privacy of the surrounding trees and strip off their clothes and proceed with that most natural of acts, which could be accomplished in five minutes or less—romantic utterances, perfumes, dainty laces, fresh sheets, and a shower being mere accessories.

"I hope you're not making plans to see Gerald again," Aspen said.

"Well, yes, that's exactly what I'm doing. I'd like very much to see him again. I'd like to get to know him."

"Can't you just go home to Newport Beach? Can't you just leave Gerald alone?"

"I'm stunned by that," he said. "Why shouldn't I see him? What on earth was your reason for telling me about him if you didn't intend for me to get to know him?"

"There wasn't any reason. I had a throbbing headache. Your lip looked so bad. There just wasn't any reason." Sunshine struck tiny silver tracks on Aspen's cheeks.

"If you go to see him, he won't have anything to do with you," she said. "I know him too well. He'll come storming home to me and demand to know if what you said is true, and if I say it is, then that's the end for me and Roger too. He won't ever come back. He's always been wild. He ran away from home when he was fifteen. He smokes, he drinks, he lives with women he isn't married to. He doesn't care about anything. He won't ever come back. He won't belong to our family anymore."

Durfey saw tennis balls flashing back and forth on the courts. He heard horseshoe ringers. All his old comrades seemed extraordinarily happy. Certainly he envied them.

"I was convinced this morning that you had acted on Roger's advice when you told me about Gerald in the drugstore," he said. "But it appears you didn't."

"Good heavens, no," she blurted. "Roger didn't have anything to do with it."

"And he wouldn't have wanted it told to me?"

"He doesn't know about it himself."

"Doesn't know that you've told me?"

"He doesn't know Gerald is your son."

"My God, Aspen! Not that, surely!"

Some of the volleyball players shouted loudly, as if winning the game mattered a great deal. They were intent on symbolically killing one another, Durfey supposed.

"So you never told anybody about Gerald?" he said.

"Just you."

"You didn't go back to your bishop?"

"I never went to my bishop in the first place."

"I'm referring to that autumn, after our summer in Fry Pan Canyon, when you confessed to your bishop and I confessed to mine."

"I know what you're referring to. I didn't confess what happened in Fry Pan Canyon. You did, but I didn't."

He stared dumbly at the slats on the deck of the veranda. He rubbed his chin for a long time, slowly shaking his head.

"I can't confess to anybody, Durfey," she said. "It isn't in me."

"Except to me."

"Yes, except to you."

"I should feel honored," he said.

"Yes," she said, "you should feel honored."

He went into the house and took a pain pill. He went out the front door of the house and wandered down the road. He was fated, it seemed, to suffer shock after shock at this reunion. He couldn't explain the intensity of his feelings. He reasoned the whole matter was of no concern to him. He had done all that was required of him. If Aspen had told him forty years ago she was pregnant, he would have married her. That was for sure. As for Gerald, he had all the father he needed in Roger, who, it appeared, was one of the most gullible, unseeing men God had ever created.

Durfey got onto a horse path that circled Dennis's place. He found another path that angled upward across the side of the canyon. He climbed the trail through groves of aspens, sweating and puffing as it became steeper.

If there was any coherence in his mind, it was in the reformulation of the familiar idea that subterfuge and deceit had characterized

Aspen's behavior toward him from beginning to end. This idea helped him feel less angry and bereft. Scorn buoyed his spirits; contempt gave him new energy. Pusillanimity was the word that occurred to him now. It implied a rank, irretrievable pettiness of spirit. He felt obliged to be candid with himself. It was his duty to call a spade a spade. Morally speaking, Aspen was a quadriplegic. She had no fiber, no backbone.

The trail ended where the aspens gave way to a dark, impenetrable forest of firs. Durfey sat where a shaft of sunlight came down through a final canopy of aspens. His legs trembled and his throat was dry. The labor had done him good. He noticed now, with some pleasure, the wild grasses, forbs, and flowers that grew all about.

A mother woodpecker flew from a dead aspen trunk; two fledglings poked their fuzzy heads from the hole. These little creatures emitted forlorn squawks, reminding him of his own ludicrous penchant for grief over his failed relationship with Aspen Marooney.

He granted he had no grounds for feeling superior. He too had been a practitioner of deceit. Elaine believed herself well acquainted with his affection for Aspen. Nothing could be further from fact. Elaine had no ability to guess at the ubiquity, the perpetuity, the enormity of his addiction. Certainly he had made no moves in recent years to undeceive her.

The thought now came to him that a man capable of such candor with himself was actually well down the road to recovery from his addiction, and he began to feel more kindly toward Aspen. He decided to think of her as a beloved sister or an affectionate friend toward whom he bore neither animosity nor passion. He fancied the shocks he had suffered during the past twenty-four hours were proving therapeutic. He fancied a forty-year weight was lifting from his shoulders.

He returned along the downward trail to Dennis's place and joined a circle of comrades in the shade of an awning. He was surprised to find Evelyn Chancellor in a relaxed conversation with

146

Bruce and Linda Horrocks. On other occasions he'd heard Evelyn voice loud scorn for phlegmatic Mormon patriarchs and their downtrodden wives. Rosalyn Bailey, Durfey's obese cousin, was also present. Rosalyn wore a broad-brimmed gardening hat, which she removed from time to time while she ran her fingers through a head of unruly grey hair. A wooden lawn chair shivered and groaned under her comfortable bulk.

In time the conversation shifted to Rosalyn, who explained that she and her second husband, a retired Forest Service man, had moved near Redmond. They kept horses and raised flowers and vegetables. Also they had a pond with geese and ducks.

"Gad, that's exactly what I wish I had," Durfey said.

Rosalyn began to tell how one of her ducks came to have no phallus, as she delicately called it. Originally, it had become prolapsed, hanging so completely outside the duck's body that the poor creature stepped on it and other ducks pecked it. Rosalyn took the duck to a veterinarian in Nephi, who sutured the weakened sphincter that was supposed to keep the phallus in place. In time, the sutures failed, and the veterinarian determined upon amputation. Although there was no literature as to procedures for the removal of a duck phallus, the ingenious vet followed a description of a procedure for parrots.

"So he's just fine and dandy these days," said Rosalyn. "He swims and quacks and chases female ducks just like he had all his equipment."

Evelyn burst into laughter. Bruce and Linda Horrocks stared with wide solemn eyes.

"You shouldn't tell a story like that around a couple of impotent old men like Durfey and Bruce," Evelyn said.

"Agreed," Durfey said. "All men, if they live long enough, come to a symbolic amputation under the scalpel of a surgeon called Time."

"What a hoot!" Evelyn said.

John Izatt had set up a portable loudspeaker near the tennis court. Seated on a kitchen stool, John strummed his guitar and began to sing a western song about blue shadows on the trail. Though this was only a preparation for John's afternoon performance with Sharmane and Anne, Carrie Payne pulled her husband from a lawn chair and led him onto the tennis court and they began to dance cheek to cheek. Despite the heat of the late morning sun, another couple followed, and then another and another. Charmed by the fact that his classmates were dancing to his music, John went on strumming his guitar and singing his sad old western songs.

The group with whom Durfey sat was breaking up. Evelyn said, "Catch you later," and moved to another group.

"I believe I'll get a cup of ice water," Rosalyn said, heaving herself onto her feet.

The Horrockses settled into their chairs, apparently mellowed by the old songs. Bruce crossed one leg over the other and kept time with his hanging foot. Linda took a nail file from her purse and gave herself a manicure.

Durfey was astonished to see that Aspen and Trelawny were among the couples dancing on the tennis court. Pamela, engaged in animated conversation in a group, obviously didn't care. Durfey couldn't repress his old jealousy. Everybody had liked Trelawny, everybody had admired him. Small and agile, he had excelled in football, basketball, track, and debate.

Putting that aside, Durfey concentrated on his first dance with Aspen, the Harvest Ball of 1949. Outside there was a full moon, which Durfey had watched come up over the Fishlake mountains while he milked cows in a frosty corral. The walls of the gymnasium were decorated with drooping strands of brown and orange crepe paper. Shocks of corn and real pumpkins stood in the corners. Cider and doughnuts were served from a booth.

According to custom, boys and girls stood in separate groups. Even those who had come as dates tended to congregate with their own gender. One set each evening was specified as girl's choice. For all others, boys enjoyed the prerogative.

A boy wanting to dance with Aspen Marooney had to ask well in advance. On the strength of their acquaintance in typing class, Durfey wasn't entirely presumptuous in asking her to dance. For a while he brooded at the edge of the crowd, his heart beating fast and his tongue feeling thick and unwieldy. At last he asked. To his astonishment she accepted with pleasure.

Durfey danced in a stiff, mechanical style. In the sixth grade his teacher had instructed her students in the sliding steps of what she called a waltz: two steps forward, one to the side, two steps forward, one to the side. Durfey didn't do well. Having watched him and his unfortunate partner, his teacher shrugged her shoulders and said, "Go ahead. Do it your own way." Nonetheless, Aspen adapted to Durfey's movements with gracious ease. Later he recognized that she had taken the lead and he had somehow managed to follow.

After a half dozen songs John called to the dancers, "Had enough?"

"Nowhere near enough," Carrie Payne replied.

As John began to strum again, Aspen and Trelawny left the tennis court. They paused to chat with John, who had not begun to sing. Trelawny crossed the lawn and took a seat by his wife. Aspen spoke longer with John, looked around, saw Durfey, and walked toward him, smiling.

She said, "Will you dance with me? John says we have his permission." The Horrockses turned round, questioning eyes on Durfey.

"Sit down and let's talk it over," Durfey said. "Dancing at midday promotes indigestion."

"If you two are going to dance, you better get at it because I'm about ready to quit," John called. "This ain't the real program anyhow."

"Shall we?" Aspen said, standing. She walked toward the tennis court, her arms folded, her eyes lowered. Durfey followed, detesting

149

the spectacle they made for their schoolmates.

John began to sing that sad, sad song Aspen had sung in the sheep camp in Fry Pan Canyon:

> The sweetest hours belong to lovers in the gloaming.
> The sweetest days were the days that used to be.
> But the saddest words I ever heard were words of parting
> When you said, "Sweetheart, remember me."

Durfey and Aspen faced each other on the tennis court. Though he hadn't danced in years, the familiar old shuffle returned to him automatically. Aspen took control, and his feet began a mysterious syncopation. He found it better not to think about his feet. If he tried to figure out what they were doing, he'd stumble.

"I need you to tell me you aren't angry with me," she said.

"I'm not angry with you. Not at all."

"Good. That's really all I wanted to know."

"The mistake on my part," he said, "was to assume I had a stake in your integrity."

"So you are angry," she said.

Beads of sweat had appeared on her forehead. He supposed it was no pleasure for her to look up toward the bandage that only half concealed his swollen lip. As for her welt, it appeared more vivid than yesterday. He was thinking he had never regretted the illicit passion that had passed between them. He had regretted only its brevity.

"You've made it quite clear," he said, "that I'm to neither contact my son nor inform my wife about his existence."

"You'll be saving both of us a lot of trouble if you'll go along with me on that," she said.

"As for yourself—I suppose there's no reason to expect you'll ever get around to telling Roger or your bishop."

"Oh, I'll tell Roger someday. Yes, I'll do that."

"Not soon, I expect."

"Quite soon, I think. Roger is a good man, Durfey. He's almost a saint. I know he'll forgive me. He won't disown Gerald."

"I'd like to tell Elaine," he said. "It seems essential that I do so."

"If that's the way you feel, you'd better do it. Just wait till you get home."

"It'll be the end of my marriage."

"Oh, dear. Then don't tell her."

"It seems to me Gerald ought to know too."

"Don't frighten me, Durfey," she said. "Just go home to California. Just leave me alone. Let me handle my side of things in my own way."

"You've never thought of telling him?"

"Certainly I've thought of it. I've thought of telling everybody—my mother, Gerald, all my other children."

"I don't think your mother and your other children have a right to know."

"So you would tell Elaine but not your children?"

"Well, of course they'd find out. She'd have to tell them why she was leaving me."

"You really think she won't forgive you?"

"Elaine wants to be loved in an exclusive way. She can't stand the thought of sharing me with another person."

"But she hasn't shared you."

"Oh, but she has, Aspen, as she knows too well."

"You need to know I told my sister about our summer in Fry Pan Canyon last night. I thought it would be wonderful. I would feel so cleansed, so restored. But I lied to her, Durfey. She said, 'Surely you've told all this to Roger.' I said, 'Of course I told him, long ago. What kind of monster do you think I am?'"

"I'm sorry you told her. I won't be able to come back to Richfield again. I couldn't risk meeting her."

"That's not brave of you, Durfey."

"No," he said. "I'm astonished how the human creature loathes discovery, how almost any burden of guilt is preferable to confession."

They fell silent, and she leaned her forehead against his chest. She tried to pull him closer, and his strut-like arms said no. "Durfey, *dance* with me!" she cried.

He relented and pulled her tight. She pressed her cheek against his throat, and he leaned his ear down against her hair. He could feel her breasts pressing where his abdomen joined his ribs. He could feel her thumping heart and hear her quiet, resonant voice. He could hear his own alien voice, echoing as if from distant and unknown chambers.

Elaine had often insisted that no one is forced to choose evil. So why, Durfey had often asked, do so many people choose wrong? Because of bad influences, Elaine always replied. There were problems with that view. For one thing, it implied that the will had no moral presence of its own. It implied the will was simply a faculty for absorbing the moral radiation of its environment—like a heliotropic plant, opening by day, closing by night.

"If either of us left this reunion a little more honest, a little more squared with our conscience," he murmured into Aspen's ear, "that would be a great good, wouldn't it?"

"Oh, yes," she said.

"I think as a bare minimum you must tell Roger soon."

"It's no use promising you when I might tell him, Durfey. I'd be sure to break the promise."

"What if I go with you?" he said. "What if I stand by you?"

"In front of Roger!"

"Obviously that's a stupid idea. Maybe this idea would work. You can phone your bishop from here. He wouldn't have to know I'm with you."

"We can't use a phone in Dennis's house," she protested. "Somebody might listen in on an extension."

"We'll drive down to Koosharem. If there isn't a booth there, we'll keep driving till we find one." They pulled apart. He saw that goosebumps had returned to her arms.

"What if it all spills out?" she said. "What if everything becomes public?"

"I don't think it will. Bishops are very discreet."

She pulled him close again. He didn't resist, feeling suddenly secure. He thought how incredible it was that these two bodies had, like returning comets in the immensity of space, crossed paths again at this reunion. He felt wonderfully freed, wonderfully unburdened.

"Is it agreed?" he murmured. "Shall we go find a phone?"

"Yes, it's agreed," she said. "As soon as this song is over we'll go find a phone."

9. An Old, Restless Grave

Aspen went into the kitchen, where a half dozen women prepared platters of cold cuts and fruit for lunch. She put on an apron and began to slice melons. Durfey had suggested they meet in fifteen minutes. If she went out the front door and he came around from the back, they wouldn't attract attention.

She had mixed feelings about Durfey's plan for helping her confess. On the one hand, she admitted she needed help. On the other hand, she resented his zeal. She didn't need a moral consultant for her affairs of conscience. She didn't like to be forced. She didn't like being cheated out of self-approval for acting on her own.

Emily Forbisher was berating the women in the kitchen for the fact that it was they, rather than their male classmates, who labored there. Emily was a city desk writer for *The Salt Lake Tribune*.

She said, "There's a conspiracy among men to keep women in the kitchen. But we don't need men at all. Synthetic sperm is only a few years away. It will be superior to natural sperm in all respects, including the fact it can be programmed to produce only female babies."

"Do you really think so?" Joanne Gundersen said. "Well, I've always liked to cook. I don't mind putting on a nice meal."

Aspen knew that men lorded it over women. But she didn't know

154

what was to be done about it. Moreover, she didn't know what was to be done about the fact that both men and women lorded it over children. She pitied all the children who weren't treated with kindness and respect. If she ever took up a cause, that's what it would be—making the world nicer for little children.

In the meantime she had a more urgent matter to deal with. The biggest problem with allowing Durfey to help her confess was the illicit satisfaction she would take from it. Durfey's presence would turn the confession into a mutual act, creating a kind of connubial intimacy.

She rinsed her hands, took off her apron, and went down a hall to the master bedroom. As she expected, a telephone sat on the night stand by the bed. She locked the door and seated herself next to the telephone. The bedroom appeared to have been appointed for Saturnalias. It had a lush carpet, a shower and hot tub surrounded by see-through glass, and a gilded statuette of Cupid and Eros. There was a balcony with an open door off the bedroom. Loud, reproving voices came through the balcony door from the lawn below. Aspen couldn't imagine who might be feeling so passionate.

When Roger had first been made a bishop, she sat by the telephone every evening he was out of the house, trying to get up the courage to phone the stake president and tell him the new bishop's wife wasn't worthy. Her hands had seemed detached from her arms. They wouldn't pick up the receiver though she willed them to do so. Now, as she picked up the phone and dialed directory assistance in Salt Lake City, she perceived herself to be standing elsewhere in the room watching a stranger place a call. She had only a moment to reflect on this mystery before an operator came on. It turned out there were two men of her bishop's name in Cottonwood Heights. She took both numbers. She punched the digits for one of the numbers and entered her credit card code. She was thinking how straight-forward and simple things are nowadays for single girls who get pregnant and want to keep their babies.

The phone rang six or seven times. Angry voices continued to come from outside. She couldn't keep her thoughts straight. She hung up and went onto the balcony. On the patio directly beneath, John Izatt was arguing with Toby Jackson over the burial place of a gentile fornicator lynched by Mormons in frontier times. Others, including Durfey, had gathered around, adding their opinions from time to time. They appeared grateful for the distraction.

Aspen knew the story, as did anybody who had grown up in Sevier County. The fornicator, a miner named Hobart, had seduced a Mormon girl from Elsinore. Her bishop, accompanied by two of her brothers, ambushed the fellow near Otter Creek; after a pursuit, they captured him high in Koosharem Canyon and hanged him from a cottonwood limb. The sheriff of Sevier County, also a Mormon, cut Hobart down and buried him in a small tributary canyon. No charges were ever filed against the bishop of Elsinore or the girl's brothers, nor was there a record of a coroner's inquest.

The present dispute had to do with whether Hobart's grave was in Lamb's Canyon or Wentworth's Hollow. John favored the former while Toby argued for the latter. There was a small headstone bearing Hobart's name in Lamb's Canyon, said, ironically, to have been erected by the grandson of the seduced girl, who had eventually married another man and had a large family. Toby declared, however, that a rough natural stone without lettering marked the true grave in Wentworth's Hollow and that he himself had once dug in that grave and found bones and artifacts such as leather shoe soles and coins.

Dennis Gundersen, still in the robe and slippers he had worn since emerging from the jacuzzi, was among the listeners. "Hell almighty," Dennis said, "let's get some shovels and go settle this matter. It's got to be one or the other. It can't be both of them."

Slippers flopping, he strode to his tool shed and distributed a half dozen shovels, a pick, and a crowbar. Returning to the patio, he roared, "Gather round! Soon as I put on some pants, let's take off. John, you lead the way to Lamb's Canyon. Let's dig there first.

Climb into your cars, folks, and John'll show you where to go."

Aspen unlocked the bedroom door only moments before Dennis burst in, shouting, "Hey, there, Aspen, look the other way while I rip into some clothes. We're off to see where that gentile who got lynched is buried."

Aspen went onto the front porch and watched while people swarmed into the parking area and climbed into automobiles. John and Durfey came around the corner of the house, John conducting Durfey by a firm grip upon his arm.

"Gotta have you along," John insisted. "You're a man of sound opinions. That damned Toby—he'll dig up a root and claim it's a man's rib."

Durfey saw Aspen as they went by the porch. He rolled his eyes helplessly. Dennis emerged from the house, tucking in his shirt.

"Are you riding with me and Durfey?" John called to Dennis.

"You bet."

John opened the door on the passenger's side and motioned for Durfey to enter.

"I'd better stick around here," Durfey said. "You can't ever tell. Maybe Elaine will show up."

"This ain't going to take more than an hour," John said. "For crying out loud, Durfey, jump in there. It won't be no fun without you along."

"Durfey, get your ass into this car," Dennis ordered while he climbed into the back seat.

Durfey gave Aspen another helpless glance and got in. John backed out from his parking place and spun into forward motion. More than a dozen cars pulled in behind, and soon the parade of vehicles disappeared around a bend, leaving a pall of dust hanging in the late morning air.

Aspen remembered the phone numbers she had scribbled on a pad on the night stand. If Dennis found those numbers, it would be just like him to dial them from simple curiosity.

"What I want to know," Dennis would say to her bishop, "is what

157

your phone number is doing on my night stand."

She returned to the bedroom and found Joanne Gundersen and Emily Forbisher seated on the bed having a low-voiced conversation. "I was going to make a credit card call," Aspen explained as she tore a sheet from the pad and crumpled it in her hand.

"Don't bother with a credit card," Joanne protested. "Just dial direct."

"Thanks. I've changed my mind."

"Well, all right—but if you still want to make a call, there's a phone in the study."

Aspen returned to the front porch. With some relief she watched a squirrel in a small grove of firs that stood nearby. The squirrel went down one trunk and up another and out onto a limb, where it paused to scrutinize Aspen. It was small—almost miniature—and had reddish grey fur and tiny ears. It twitched and jerked, even when sitting, being, as Aspen supposed, of an irresolute mind like herself.

At Fishlake lodge she had learned that squirrels are furious in mating. The male chases the female for hours—up and down trunks, across rocks, in and out of hollow logs. If she outlasts him, his genes go unreplicated.

Her thoughts moved to the propensity of boys to get an erection when dancing body to body with a girl. She couldn't remember the first time she had discovered this. Her mother had always warned her not to dance cheek-to-cheek with boys. Her thoughts moved next to the fact that a couple can make love anywhere. They can do it while on a casual stroll through the trees. They do it on trampled grass, ignoring sticks, stones, ants, and flies. She and Durfey had done it that way once.

An unanswered question which had entered her mind was how to control Durfey after the reunion was over—how to make sure he wouldn't inform Roger or her bishop, how to make sure he wouldn't seek out Gerald. She considered what a new, freshly enacted guilt might do for Durfey, what might be the effect of his leaving the reunion in a state of total moral shock.

Adultery was a word she hated to pronounce. In the silent colloquies she held late at night, awake beside the sleeping Roger, she had always insisted, "In all these years since our wedding, at least I haven't done that."

The squirrel had disappeared without her noticing. She was of half a mind to go around back and see who had remained in the chairs on the lawn. Unfortunately Trelawny and Pamela had gone on the grave-digging expedition. She couldn't think of anyone else she cared to talk to just now.

She thought of Trelawny's offer of a stirrup made from his two hands yesterday at the parade. With that recollection came a dream from the night just past—totally forgotten until this moment. She met her father in her dream. She said brightly, "Oh, you're not dead after all." Her father said, "No, I've never been dead." They went out of the house and through the yard till they came to the neighbor's chain link fence. Her father knelt and made a stirrup of his clasped hands. She stepped in and leaped lightly over the fence, landing amidst the neighbor's roses. She turned and her father was gone.

If this dream had a message, it was this. Her dead father was saying, "Aspen, leave this reunion. Clear out and go home. Don't try to see Durfey Haslam again."

She left the porch and got into her car. She felt decisive. She was minding her father. She was on her way to Hope's house. She drove to the junction with the road in the bottom of Koosharem Canyon, which, at this point, though narrow, was graded and covered with gravel. She paused with a foot on the brake. Birds flitted in the dense underbrush of the canyon bottom, and Koosharem Creek dashed and frothed. Sunlight washed the dusty road. A scented balm wafted on the breeze. Long ago she had fancied heaven had such an immediacy. But no longer. Heaven was infinities away.

She didn't believe in dreams even if her mother did. Why would

God send her a dream? What had she ever done to deserve it?

She turned the car onto the upward canyon road. The motorcade had left a visible track upon the shower-dimpled texture of the dusty road. Within a couple of miles the track of the motorcade turned into a small tributary canyon. At last she came to a grassy grove where cars were parked helter-skelter. She parked her car and climbed a hillside shaded by aspens and carpeted by tall grass and flowers. Her leather-soled flats slipped, and she fell on one knee, soiling her white slacks. She went on, coming out soon on a ridge where the trees and grass gave way to scattered sagebrush.

Her classmates clustered around John Izatt, who, with shovel in hand, stood thigh deep in a grave. She pushed through the crowd and saw a small granite stone at the head of the grave. There was a solemn incongruity between this polished artifact and the otherwise wild environment. John labored with rhythmical energy, singing "Yo-oh, heave ho" and throwing out a shovelful of gravel each time he pronounced "ho."

She saw Durfey at the rear of the crowd on the other side of the grave. She stepped around beside him and said hello. He smiled with warm relief. "I'm so glad to see you," he said. "Now I can forgive myself."

She brushed her soiled knee. "I had a little fall. I think I've skinned my knee."

"Oh dear," he said. "We're not having good luck at keeping our bodies intact, are we?"

She asked whether he had any sympathy for the gentile fornicator whom John was digging up. He said the episode was too far in the past for him to have any feelings about it.

"On principle," Aspen said, "I'm for virginity before marriage. But not to the point of lynching those who lose it."

Durfey said, "I think the idea is to lynch a man who takes advantage of a defenseless girl."

"If the girl from Elsinore wanted a gentile to deflower her, that was her business, not her bishop's."

"Bishops still pay attention to such things, though not with such drastic results," Durfey said.

"Also, I don't approve of digging up the dead."

"Said like the daughter of an undertaker," he replied.

"Isn't it against the law?"

"I believe it is."

"Shouldn't someone point that out?"

"Yes, I suppose someone should."

She stepped forward a little and called, "Isn't it against the law to dig up graves?"

The thought apparently hadn't occurred to anyone else, least of all John, who paused and looked about in annoyance. He wore, as yesterday, brown pants and a tan shirt duly affixed with a gleaming brass star. Everyone awaited his pronouncement on this matter. John was not known for speedy mental calibrations and long seconds passed before his face brightened with comprehension and he said, "I *am* the law." He resumed digging and everyone appeared to feel better.

"So much for your attempts at reform," Durfey said.

"I've never been good at swaying public opinion," Aspen replied.

Soon John unearthed some small pieces of bone and thereafter with almost every shovelful he brought out a fragment or two of bone. Bruce Horrocks, who had once been a biology teacher, turned the fragments this way and that and finally declared them to be human. Their classmates pressed forward and formed a close circle around John and Bruce, leaving Aspen and Durfey apart.

"I've given up on confessing," she said. "I'm not going back to the reunion. I came out here to say goodbye."

Durfey had kicked at the root of a sagebrush till the toe of his shoe had become dusty. He stooped and wiped the toe with his handkerchief.

"So you won't call your bishop?" he said.

"Not today."

"When?"

"Someday."

"Not soon, I suppose."

"Maybe soon. Yes, maybe quite soon."

"This time it's my fault," he said. "I screwed up by letting John and Dennis pressure me into coming out here."

"If you want to feel guilty about it, go ahead," she said. "Then I can feel worse because you feel so bad."

He continued to kick at the root of sagebrush.

She said, "I used to daydream we had lost our spouses through death. After a proper mourning in my daydream, we got married. But in real life that would be hell, wouldn't it? One of our spouses would die and the other wouldn't, and it would be hell waiting and wishing, wouldn't it?"

"I've had that fantasy many times. I'm afraid I'll go on having it."

"It's just a daydream," she said. "In real life, you can't undo forty years."

"No, you shouldn't even want to."

"Will you please leave Gerald alone?"

"I'm sure he wouldn't welcome me."

"Thank you, then," she said. "That's everything I needed to know."

The crowd was quarreling over whether to go to Wentworth's Canyon and dig in the grave Toby claimed was there. It seemed they couldn't decide whether the bones in this grave in Lamb's Canyon belonged to the gentile seducer or not. Toby said there had once been a mine in Koosharem Canyon and a number of people had been buried in this general vicinity. At last someone decided they would go to the other canyon and most of them trooped down the hill and got into their cars and drove away. John and Jerome Payne stayed behind to fill the emptied grave. Durfey said he'd help too.

While Aspen watched with folded arms, John carefully replaced the small pile of bones in the bottom of the grave.

"I gotta do this right," John said. "Can't have the undertaker's daughter say I'm not respectful of these mortal remains."

Durfey said, "If these are Hobart's bones, they have been here about a hundred twenty years. Do you think bones would last that long?"

John said, "Sure they would in a high, well drained place like this ridge top. Now don't get no strange ideas, Durfey. These bones are Hobart's, all right. They couldn't belong to anybody else."

They began to fill in the grave. The earth thudded and a slight dust rose.

"Do you remember Buster Phillips?" Durfey asked. "He drowned in the Sevier during the summer of '50. He was from Glenwood and I helped dig his grave."

"This is a lonesome place for a grave," Aspen said. "But then, graves are lonesome by nature."

"That's sober talk for an undertaker's daughter," John said.

"Do you know why undertakers are so respectable?" Aspen said. "They see so much grief at work that they can't risk any exceptions in anything else they do. They become the most timid, proper citizens in town. They're desperate to be known as fine, wonderful fellows."

"Sounds reasonable to me," John said.

Durfey said, "Do you think that gentile would have married the girl from Elsinore if he had had the chance?"

"Not likely," John said.

"They didn't give him a chance," Aspen said. "They made an object lesson out of him."

"Speaking of an object lesson," John said, "do you remember the night we dumped that English teacher's garbage cans on his front porch? Or the night we took the planks off the bridge across his irrigation ditch and he drove home and dropped his front wheels into the ditch."

"I wasn't in on all that," Durfey said.

"We ruined his life," John said. "He quit teaching mid-year. Not

163

very funny now, is it? But it was then."

The men threw a final few shovels of earth on the grave. Oddly, there was not quite enough soil to bring the grave level with the surrounding ground.

"You'd think it would be just the opposite," John said. "You'd think stirring up the soil would make more of it."

They began a slow descent from the hill, picking their way through the grass and shrubs. Aspen slipped and Durfey took her arm. At the bottom, they placed the shovels in the trunk of the patrol car.

"Durfey will ride with me," Aspen said. "You two go on ahead."

John gave them a long, hard look.

Aspen said, "We're going out into the trees and commit adultery. So it'll be a little while before we catch up with you."

John hung onto her arm and laughed till tears came down his cheeks. "That Aspen! Isn't she something else!" he cried.

John and Jerome got into the patrol car and drove away. Aspen and Durfey stood by her car, watching till the patrol car had disappeared. They got into Aspen's car, but she didn't start the engine. A breeze sifted through the open windows. Leaves fluttered. The sun descended through boughs in shafts of hot light.

Durfey said, "Light dances on aspen leaves like on a choppy pond. You can't fix a position among them. They seem to come from nowhere in an instant and just as quickly disappear."

"That's beautiful," she said.

"It's my only excuse for what we did," he said. "I couldn't help loving you."

She started the engine and drove down the rutted road, stopping at the junction with the road in the bottom of Koosharem Canyon. The tracks of the motorcade turned down the canyon. Nodding toward the upward road, she asked where it went. Durfey said it eventually made its way over these mountains and came down near Richfield, though long before it reached the top, it would undoubt-

164

edly deteriorate into a path only vehicles with four-wheel drive could negotiate.

Sagebrush dotted the clearing near the road. The engine idled and songbirds twittered. A hawk floated in the high blue sky. Aspen waited for Durfey to decide whether they would take the lower or upper road. She had already assented to his decision, whatever it might be. She fidgeted with her engagement ring, twisting it from side to side. Durfey stared fixedly at the radio display on the dash or perhaps at a cassette lying in the recess beneath the display.

She considered the cost of adultery. For her the cost was indistinct. Guilt was the result of purchases on the deficit side of the moral ledger. The total of her debt was beyond calculation. She supposed God knew its sum. Any new debt seemed a modest increment to the principal she owed. For Durfey the cost appeared exorbitant. If he had existing debts, they had to be minor ones. He was an innocent. He could be ruined by a hard sell.

The putt of the engine and the singing of birds went on. The breeze came cool and sweet through the windows. She was thinking that emotion is a kind of combustion. It produces heat, it scorches. Her stomach was scorched just now.

Durfey threw her a helpless, agonizing glance. That seemed a decision. She turned onto the lower road. He put his hand on the wheel. She stopped and waited. Still no words passed between them. However, she understood their goodbye required a starker, more indelible statement. She reversed the car into the side road, shifted into forward, and turned onto the upper road. She sensed no policy or connivance among her motives. By now it was all a matter of desire. No more, no less.

Far up the canyon she turned off on a path that led to an old sheep corral. She parked the car, and they climbed a slope through the aspens till they found a level spot amidst tall luxuriant grass. Bees and flies buzzed in the noontime heat.

"We did this once before," Durfey said.

"Yes, long ago in Fry Pan Canyon."

165

He trampled a spot in the grass where a ragged bit of shade fell. Wild flowers of white, lavender, and blue bowed and nodded at the periphery of their bower. They faced each other with weary, questioning eyes. She approached, stroked his cheek, gazed sorrowfully upon his bandaged lip. She unbuttoned his shirt and helped him remove both his shirt and the top of his temple undergarment. His ribs curved like the slats of a barrel, and his belly fell into a bulging little pouch. She unbuttoned her blouse and unfastened her bra and slipped down her undergarment, and her long, pendulous breasts hung freely upon the folds of her belly. He stared morosely down upon her age-speckled skin, his hands caressing her naked shoulders.

He removed his pants and she her slacks, and he laid them on the grass with her blouse and his shirt and their underwear, forming a kind of composite blanket, and with a motion of his hand he invited her to lie, and in a moment they had assumed that ludicrous, vulnerable, face-to-face posture by which the human race attempts to transmogrify a carnal animal act into a gesture of affection and profound respect. The sun beat down with an incongruous heat and clarity upon his white, emaciated back and her stout spreading legs.

"I can't get inside," he said. "You'll have to help me."

"You look so afraid," she said. "You look so sad."

"My God, don't do this to me," he said in a grim, choked voice. "You'll never be happy again."

"Let me be the judge of that."

"It'll kill you. It'll just kill you."

He groaned and fell off. He sat with his elbows on his knees and his chin cupped in his hands till she had pulled on her slacks and handed him his pants. He rose and slowly dressed, latching his shirt buttons with silent, solemn care.

"The same old game," he muttered at last. "Get him heated up, then say no. That was the old pattern, Aspen, with certain notable moments to the contrary. Get him heated up, then say no."

"I'm so sorry, Durfey," she said over and over.

"Let's go," he said gruffly.

"Not yet," she pleaded. "Let's stay till you're not quite so angry."

They seated themselves with their backs against an aspen trunk, their shoulders touching and their faces pointing in different directions.

After a long, morose silence, he said, "I've been angry with you for forty years. I've resented you all this time."

"As you should have," she said.

"Yet it was a bit of heaven in Fry Pan Canyon that summer. I can't deny that."

"Yes, it was very much a bit of heaven," she agreed.

"At the end of our summer in Fry Pan Canyon, God paid us a visit and, hearing his voice, we hid and put on our fig leaves. And life has been more difficult ever since."

"It's just a matter of growing up," she said.

"Well, yes. That's what the Fall is all about—just a matter of growing up."

In time he relaxed and began to philosophize on the meaning of a class reunion. He said a class reunion is a ritual of self-assessment, because you always think of school as a time of preparation, and a reunion means you have gathered to measure what that preparation has come to.

"Where are the high achievements of the Class of '51?" he asked.

"Don't look for them," Aspen said. "We are all very ordinary people."

"But some of us at least seem to be happy. About half of us, I'd judge from the accounts given during the luncheon yesterday. And for the most part our happiness lies in our children and grandchildren. Now isn't that true?"

"That's very true," she said. "What other happiness is there?"

"Exactly!" he said. "Happiness and immortality always lie with the next generation. Nowhere else. As for you and me, leaving our children and grandchildren out of the equation, it seems we have

167

returned to our starting point, except that now we know there is nothing except our starting point because we've already had our future, and as we've just now seen, our future didn't amount to anything. All we have now is the past. Memories, you know. Fantasies, too."

"I can't say that I follow you," she said.

"You and I have just had a trial of sorts," he said. "We have been both the accused and the victim. We are the prosecution and defense, judge and jury, and we have been found guilty."

She saw how good intentions come to nothing. She had halted Durfey in the midst of passion, and now he was as stricken, as stunned, as if she had given him his pleasure. She had simply let things get too far along. There was no other judgment to be made.

They were shaded by leafy boughs. High above stood a ridge black with fir and pine. Puffy clouds drifted in the sky. All this beauty belonged to the world of weeds, she was thinking. Weeds aren't useful. They defy authority and grow to suit themselves. In God's eyes, nature in general is a weed; it takes undesirable shapes and expands in its own unwanted ways. She was thinking: Aspen Marooney is a weed whom God refuses to pull up just now. For the present, it suits his purpose to let her grow.

She took Durfey's hand and pressed it to her cheek. He went on talking in a morose, whimsical vein, and she went on caressing his hand. With love pulsing in her wrist, she recognized how, in a profound and irredeemable way, infidelity had been the daily quotient of her forty-year marriage to Roger Sheffield.

10. A Day with Roger's Son

Gerald and Roger left for Hanksville soon after breakfast. Gerald's van had power windows, velveteen seat covers, an ice box, and a small table with built-in holders for drinks. Gerald said this was where he entertained his friends. Roger knew he meant his female friends.

Gerald asked what was going on with his siblings. So, while they drove, Roger brought him up to date. Robin, who lived at home, had responded well to medication and was no longer suicidal. Julian, a senior in high school, spoke of a pre-med major at BYU. Elizabeth lived in New York City and had to make four bus changes to attend church each Sunday.

"Why doesn't Elizabeth stay in Utah if she can't think of anything better to do on Sunday?" Gerald said.

Continuing, Roger said that Kinley and his wife Constance, who lived in Spokane, had blessed and named their sixth child. Shelley and her husband Arthur, who lived in Ogden and had two children, were discouraged by Shelley's apparent inability to become pregnant. Debra was of course well along with her fifth pregnancy. Martin and his wife seemed bent on finishing their degrees before venturing upon a family.

"What's wrong with those two?" Gerald said. "Don't they know

169

you can't belong to this family if you don't breed like rabbits?"

Roger had said nothing about Loraine, his greatest worry. A married policeman had been coming to Loraine's apartment at midnight and leaving at dawn two or three times a week. This information came from Loraine's bishop whom Roger had asked to keep a tactful watch over his errant daughter.

Gerald made other derogatory remarks about the reproductive habits of his parents and siblings. "About the time I turned twelve or thirteen, it dawned on me you and Mom weren't going to quit having babies. I got where I hated to face my friends. They'd say, 'Your mom's pregnant? My God, she's an old lady!'"

"I trust you have a more tolerant view of it now," Roger said.

"Sure," he said. "Even old people like to screw."

Gerald stopped at the visitor's center in Capitol Reef National Monument and used the rest room. Returning to the van, he said the woman walking away from the car in the next parking stall looked something like his current girlfriend.

"Her name's Louise," Gerald said of his new girlfriend. "She's a waitress across the highway from my shop. She's forty-five, got a couple of grown kids who never call or write. Been knocked around by a lot of men. Women like her are all over the place. I can take you into any bar on Friday night and point out half a dozen. This poor critter has a uterus that hangs down into her vagina. It hurts her to have sex. She needs an operation. No way to pay for it. No insurance where she works, that's for damn sure. She could wear a pessary if she was willing to give up her sex life."

Gerald had been married three times. He had three children by his first marriage. He willingly paid alimony and child support for that failed marriage, but he couldn't understand why he had to contribute to two other women who had no children and were as capable of earning a living as he was.

Beside being a master of the unsavory word, Gerald possessed the dubious talent of candor. He was willing to discuss his girlfriends even in the presence of his mother. Roger believed he did

170

so from mixed motives. On the one hand, it was his way of carrying on the old contention between them. He flaunted sin, defied salvation. On the other hand, it was also a show of intimacy, a sharing of his life as it really was.

In Hanksville they found the man with the airplane for sale, a garrulous fellow named Homer of about Gerald's age. Homer immediately led them to his shop to show them an antique engine with radial pistons. While they discussed aeronautical matters, Homer cut off a large plug of chewing tobacco and put it into his mouth. Every few minutes he stepped outside to spit tobacco juice in a glistening arc.

On one of his spitting sorties, he managed to saturate a bee humming on a thistle. "Practice makes perfect," he muttered with satisfaction.

While the two younger men went on talking about airplanes, Roger wandered into the back yard, where an emaciated woman with clipped, mousy hair was fixing a shade over the corner of a pig pen. She said her name was Ronnie Jean and she and Homer were thinking about getting married. This was his place, not hers, though she'd been here for a couple of years. Homer had picked her up at a truck stop in Farmington, New Mexico, where she was waiting on tables. Before that, she had worked in the hospital in Durango, Colorado. She got fired for pilfering medication.

"I wasn't no addict," she said. "I just needed something for stress."

Roger recalled that his own daughter Loraine seemed bent on joining the ranks of aging, defeated women who serve uncaring men as mistresses. He didn't know what he could do to dissuade her. At thirty-two, Loraine esteemed herself to be a tough, worldly-wise woman for whom a father's advice was merely a provocation to do the opposite.

For the moment Ronnie Jean was worried about her garden, which was wilting under the heat. "We don't have anything but culinary water. Costs plenty to keep a garden."

She said she used to be a vegetarian. "But it's just as bad to kill a plant as an animal. So whatever I eat, I eat just as little as possible to get by." She stroked a corn plant. "Come on, feller," she said. "Straighten up."

"Plants can hear you," she said. "Don't think they can't."

Roger got into the van with Gerald and Homer, and they drove to a nearby airstrip. The airplane was a four-seated Cessna with a high wing and single propeller. Gerald examined a small tear in the fabric of the fuselage, which Homer claimed could be easily repaired.

The three men belted themselves into the airplane, and Homer taxied to the far end of the graveled strip. He revved the engine till the aircraft rattled and shook. He pulled a quart Mason jar from the footwell and spit tobacco juice and then released the brakes. The antiquated craft lumbered down the runway, gaining momentum yet refusing to lift off. The fence and power line at the end of the runway grew larger with each second. Roger imagined their charred bodies strapped in the smoldering cabin. So he said a silent prayer, and at the instant of his saying amen the rumbling of the tires ceased and the craft was airborne. A couple of seconds later it passed over the power line.

"I was keeping open the option of going under the power line," Homer explained. "I've done it before. Hot day today. Usually the old crate lifts off sooner."

Homer turned the controls over to Gerald, who steered the craft in wide, spiraling circles until it had climbed high in the sky. From the air the earth was another planet. The canyons of the Colorado and the Escalante were an intricate maze, and, along its narrow, twisting bed, Lake Powell traced the indentations of a jigsaw puzzle gone crazy. After a final circle, Gerald turned the craft north. The barren peaks of the Henry Mountains slid beneath them. The timbered bulwark of Boulder Mountain slipped away to the west. Soon the San Rafael Swell appeared, cut through by a serpentine gorge in whose bottom a tiny stream glistened.

Gerald spotted a landing field which Homer said was used by paleontologists engaged at the Cleveland dinosaur quarry. Gerald wanted to land and inspect the quarry. Roger objected, saying the airplane had barely made it off the ground at a much lower elevation than this airstrip.

"Oh, we can get her up again," Homer said with a cavalier toss of his head. He spit into his Mason jar, took the controls, and landed the craft, not without an alarming bounce that seemed likely to send them cartwheeling at eighty miles an hour through the nearby junipers.

"Jesus, but I get a kick out of flying," Homer said as he taxied to a parking area.

They made their way afoot to the visitors center, where a technician from the University of Utah informed them that the quarry was closed. There was no one there but himself, and he intended to depart for Salt Lake City as soon as he had tidied up his morning's work. Homer began to chat with the technician, and soon this man relented and said, "Well, what's the rush!" He unlocked a gate and led them to a small cliff where a multitude of giant fossilized bones had been half-excavated and left in relief as a display for visitors.

"Sixty-five million years old!" Gerald said. "Jeez, if that ain't something. This is my Bible right here. None of that Adam and Eve hocus-pocus for me. Dad here believes you can have it both ways. He believes in Adam and Eve on Sunday and evolution the rest of the week."

"Now that isn't quite true," Roger said. "I just happen to believe evolution is God's way of creating."

Gerald, Homer, and the technician took a seat on a shady bench near a pop machine. Roger remained at the display for a while, carefully reading each of the prepared captions. When he joined the others, he found their conversation had evolved into an exchange of war-time experiences.

The technician claimed that during World War II the Australians had furnished American soldiers with an unvarying diet of lamb's tongue, which had proved so onerous that one of his comrades wrestled a six-foot iguana into submission and butchered it for table fare. The technician conjectured that the Australians sold the choice lamb cuts to the Japanese.

Gerald, a veteran of Vietnam, told about a peasant woman whose breasts and ribs had been blown away in an air attack. Gerald helped load her into a helicopter for evacuation to a hospital, but when it became apparent there were more wounded than the helicopter would hold, he helped remove this woman and set her in the shade, where a medic gave her an injection and she soon died.

"I could see her lungs through the hole in her ribs," Gerald said, "and these little bloody bubbles formed along the seams of her lungs. When she quit breathing, the bubbles stopped."

"Yeah," said Homer, "that was Nam. All that killing and nothing came of it."

Soon Homer was congratulating himself for passing through the dives and fleshpots of Saigon without contracting a disease. Upon his return, riding a bus from San Francisco to Seattle, he met a redhead who induced him to pause on his homeward journey and spend a night in her Portland apartment. Relying on her youth, he dispensed with his former precautions and was astonished to discover he had contracted the clap.

"So young and pretty," he concluded with a sigh.

All this while Roger was considering Gerald's need to flaunt his atheism. It was a phenomenon that went back to the year Gerald turned sixteen, the year he ran away from home. For days Roger and Aspen worried that he had been kidnapped or murdered on some remote highway. Then the police of Redondo Beach phoned that they had picked him up hitchhiking along the ocean.

While Aspen stayed home with the other children, Roger drove to Redondo Beach. As they returned through Nevada, Gerald gave short, sullen answers to Roger's questions. He said he was tired of Aspen's carping at him night and day to clean up his room. He resented the fact that after he had gone to the trouble of getting a job as a grocery bagger, Roger had reduced his allowance. He noticed that Roger hadn't reduced Kinley's and Debra's allowance even though Kinley had a job delivering newspapers and Debra made good money from baby sitting. He also resented the fact that Kinley had been allowed to go on a church-sponsored outing to Provo while Gerald's plans to attend car races on the Bonneville salt flats had been vetoed. But the culminating indignity occurred on the Sunday he fled from home. Giving in to Aspen's nagging, he went to church for the first time in months. After priesthood meeting the instructor collared him in the hall and said he ought to come regularly or not at all. That night he took money from Roger's wallet and got a friend to drive him to south State Street, where he began hitchhiking toward California.

About the time they got to the Utah border, Roger asked Gerald if he'd like to stop in Richfield to see whether Hope and Dan would take him in for the remainder of the school year.

"You bet!" he said. "I'd like that a lot."

Roger routed the car through Zion National Park, and they got out at a viewpoint at the base of the Great White Throne. Roger was gratified by the interest Gerald showed in his discussion of sedimentation, faulting, and other geological processes. He was also surprised by how much Gerald already knew on the topic. While they drove on, Gerald seemed cheerful, and when he made his astonishing statement, it was in a casual voice, as if his statement was based upon the most obvious, everyday kind of a fact.

He said, "I know you and Mom aren't my natural parents. You adopted me, didn't you?"

He had to repeat the statement before Roger could properly grasp its meaning. Once he had understood, Roger protested loudly. "What a terrible thing to say! Of course you're not adopted."

175

"I figured it all out," Gerald insisted. "It explains everything. I'm not your kid."

He had learned in a biology class that the genes for brown irises are dominant over blue and that parents having the same color of irises never bear offspring of a different color.

"You and Mom have got blue eyes," he said. "My eyes are brown. None of the other kids have got brown eyes. They're all blue."

At first Roger stammered out denials that only reinforced Gerald's freakish notion. Soon, however, he regained his composure and assured Gerald that he had the most compelling evidence that he was indeed the true natural son of Roger and Aspen Sheffield.

Gerald said, "How do you know they didn't make a mistake in the hospital and change babies on you?"

"Because," Roger said, "I happened to be present in the delivery room. The infant I saw with an umbilical cord still attached was none other than the infant we took home from the hospital. No one could mistake your short, stubby legs. As for your conception, I happen to have been present at that too. I happen to know the exact night and the exact place of its occurrence."

Gerald seemed satisfied, and they dropped the matter. Following a brief visit with Hope and Dan, they drove home so Gerald could say a proper goodbye to his mother and siblings. Roger said nothing to Aspen about Gerald's conjecture about adoption.

A few days later, while they returned to Richfield, Roger informed Gerald that he had consulted a friend on the medical faculty at the University of Utah regarding the genetics of iris color and had been told it is not invariably true that parents having the same color of irises bear children of that color. The moment seemed ripe for reminding Gerald that a person could know certain things beyond the realm of evidence—things that might at the time seem contradictory to evidence but that ultimately would prove harmonious with it. Roger mentioned the seeming disparity between the Bible and the theory of organic evolution.

176

"In eternity we'll understand," he said. "Everything will be made plain."

Gerald startled his father by a precocious show of atheism. "That's just bullshit," he said. "Nobody made the world. It just happened. Do you think God was out there with a pick and shovel making all those formations we saw in Zion Canyon the other day? Erosion made them. Running water did it."

Neither Roger nor Aspen saw much of Gerald after that. Gerald lived with Hope and Dan until the following year, when he dropped out of school and took a job at the cattle auction in Salina.

When Gerald, Homer, and the technician had exhausted their interest in wartime stories, the flyers thanked their host and returned to the airplane. Homer cut another plug of tobacco, revved the engine, and let the craft roll down the runway. Once again it seemed they must perish in a fiery crash, for the airplane had barely got into the air by the time it reached the end of the runway. It skimmed a wide expanse of sagebrush without achieving further elevation. Suddenly a gorge opened before them, and to Roger's horror the craft swooped downward into the abyss. Once again Roger called on God to lift up their wings, and at the very instant he finished his silent prayer, the airplane began to rise with dramatic speed. Upward it spiraled out of the gorge, and soon they were high above the wrinkled, eroded land.

Homer explained their rescue in natural terms. "I knew there'd be an updraft in the canyon. I saw ravens circling above it before I decided to go ahead and land."

After they had landed at the Hanksville airstrip, Roger was not surprised to hear Gerald decline Homer's offer to sell his airplane. "It's too old," Gerald said bluntly. "I've got to have something in better condition. Thanks a whole lot for taking us up."

Gerald and Roger drove to the Hanksville mercantile and bought provisions for a late lunch. They proceeded to a tiny park at the edge of town and took a seat at a picnic table beneath an elm. Across the highway a man and a woman emerged from a trailer house carrying scope-sighted rifles, which they placed on a rack in the back window of a four-wheel-drive pickup and drove away.

"Going jackrabbit hunting," Gerald guessed.

"Likely," his father agreed.

"Seems like more women are into hunting now."

"I suppose so. It's a new era."

Across the highway a small flock of chickens scratched in the barren front yard of the trailer house. "Do you know what I'm thinking about?" Gerald said.

"I believe I do."

Gerald broke into guffaws. "I still can't believe Mom shot all those chickens."

"Yes, that was extraordinary."

"Where in hell did she learn to shoot?"

"Oh, out on Uncle Isaac's farm, I think. Also, she used to chum around with a boy named Durfey Haslam. They did some horseback riding and a little shooting, I believe."

During the early years of their marriage, Roger and Aspen had rented a house in West Jordan so Aspen could have a big garden. Their neighbor, Mr. Jacconi, was a former Italian prisoner of war who had returned to Utah following his incarceration there during World War II. Mr. Jacconi bred fighting fowl for sale in Mexico. One of his cocks and several hens escaped his coops and, proving more than a match for cats, skunks, and raccoons, multiplied over a period of three or four years into fifty or sixty freely wandering birds. They foraged like locusts, eradicating Aspen's sprouting vegetables.

"Make Jacconi pen them up," Aspen demanded of Roger.

"I've asked him a dozen times," Roger replied.

"Sue him," she said.

"Sweetheart," he said, "keeping the good will of our neighbors is worth more than a few plants."

One Saturday as they left on a shopping trip to Salt Lake, one of the cocks confronted their automobile in the driveway. He ruffled his feathers and thrust out his chest and prepared to do combat. Roger stopped the car.

"Run over him," Aspen commanded.

"Goodness no!" Roger protested.

Aspen got out of the car and tore a loose picket from the fence and chased the cock away.

"That does it!" she said, giving the picket a heave.

When Roger came home from work one evening during the following week, Gerald and Kinley met him in the driveway.

"Mom shot about a hundred chickens!" Gerald said. "They are lying around all over in the back yard."

Roger went into the house. The kitchen was in its normal state of hectic clamor—dinner yet to be put in the oven, children whining, Aspen losing her temper.

Gerald continued to tug at his arm. "Come on out and see. She killed a hundred of them!"

"I've been told something I can scarcely accredit," Roger said to Aspen.

"It's nowhere near a hundred," Aspen said. "Maybe fifteen."

A scene of carnage greeted Roger in the back yard. There were dead, bloodied cocks and hens everywhere—in the furrows of the garden, beneath the rose bushes, even on the platform of an old wagon that stood near Mr. Jacconi's fence.

When he spied Roger, Mr. Jacconi climbed through the fence and came forward, wringing his hands piteously. He said he had no right to complain, for he had proved a bad neighbor by not controlling his chickens. He said he had got to thinking of the free fowl as belonging to the Sheffields, since the latest generations of them had for the most part been brooded in nests along the brushy bank at the back of the property they rented.

"But your wife has gone too far," Mr. Jacconi said. "I stood in the door of the shed over there and saw it all with my own eyes. I could do nothing for the poor birds. I have read about such rage in novels

179

of war. She shot twenty-seven of them! I had to finish off some of them by wringing their necks after she went into the house. Poor things! She put the rifle to her shoulder and bam, bam, bam, one after the other, without mercy she shot them like an enemy sniper."

Roger returned to the kitchen. He seated himself gloomily on a stool. "Where did you get a gun?"

"I borrowed it," she said. "I went over to Thelma's this morning. It belongs to her husband. She gave me a ride into town, and I bought a box of bullets."

"How did you manage to hit so many?"

"Any idiot can shoot with a scope," she said scornfully.

Roger and Gerald went on with their lunch in the Hanksville park. There were cans of soda, a loaf of bread, a package of baloney, a small jar of mayonnaise. Both were sweating. It was close to a hundred degrees.

Gerald said, "There's something about Mom I've never been able to figure out. She's not like Aunt Hope. She keeps something back from you every time. She sees everything from a funny angle. The only time she ever relaxes is when she's holding a baby."

"That's perceptive," Roger said. "It's true your mother has a privacy that no one can violate. I don't know anyone like her."

After they finished eating, they drove north on an unpaved road through Goblin Valley, whose scenic erosions Gerald wanted his father to see. They were taking a long route around to Salina, where they would load the roping horses in a trailer and pull them to Richfield for the evening rodeo. About an hour from Hanksville, Gerald parked the van and led Roger afoot amidst a variety of strange hillocks and deformed pinnacles. These formations had been eroded not from stone but from a greenish-grey clay which had combined chemically with rainwater to form a surface only a little less durable than concrete. They climbed one of the hillocks and took in a panorama of grotesque erosions, distant mountains, and solemnly drifting clouds.

Drenched with sweat, Roger was thinking about that exceptional soul who had consented to be his eternal mate. He was remembering a summer's visit to Arches National Park, only a hundred miles or so to the east of Goblin Valley. The trails among the natural arches were faint and devious. They skirted cliffs, turned aside from sudden plunges, balanced along high rocky protrusions, sank between parallel walls of stone.

Roger asked Aspen to come back from a dimly traced trail where red Entrada sandstone radiated a fierce heat. Aspen went heedlessly on and disappeared. With unusual determination Roger kept the children from following. The car with open doors provided shade for the children, who were sweaty and quarrelsome. An hour later Aspen returned. She climbed into the car and Roger started the engine and turned on the air conditioner. Her return from the labyrinths reassured him. Thereafter his prayers in her behalf took on a new imagery. "Bless my sweet wife, who has such an obdurate will," he often said to God. "Guide her safely through the lost, rocky mazes of this world."

Gerald and Roger returned to the van and drove on. In a mile or two they came upon a small motor home, which listed in the barrow pit with a broken axle. Gerald passed the motor home, then changed his mind and stopped. A haggard woman and two frightened children came around from the shady side of the vehicle.

"Somebody coming to help you, ma'am?" Gerald asked.

"My husband," she said. "He should be back any time."

"Okay," Gerald said. "I just wanted to be sure."

He returned to the van, started the engine, then shut it off. "That doesn't make sense," he said. "They look like they've been here for a while."

He got out and the woman and children came from the shade again. "Why didn't you go with your husband?" Gerald said.

"He caught a ride with a man on a motorcycle. Except for you, he's the only one who has been by here since we broke down."

"When did he leave?"

"About this time yesterday."

Gerald whistled.

"Oh, he'll come," the woman insisted. "Any time now." They were on vacation, far from their home in Illinois. She supposed her husband had met difficulty in finding a replacement axle. It wouldn't make sense for him to bring a mechanic out if they didn't have a proper part. "So thank you very much," she said. "We'll just wait till he comes."

Gerald got into the van again and adjusted his seat belt. Then he said, "Like shit I'm going to leave that lady and those kids out here in this heat." He got out, and an emotional discussion ensued.

"You'll die of dehydration," he said.

"He won't know where to find us," the woman wailed.

"We'll leave him a note. We'll say you're at the motel in Hanksville."

"He has the credit cards," she said.

"You gotta come," Gerald insisted.

"Somebody will break into the motor home. He wanted us to stay and keep an eye on it."

"That's a risk you'll have to take."

With a rush of tears the woman conceded, and she went into the vehicle, prepared a note, and emerged with a couple of bags. Then she and her children climbed into the van, and they turned back toward Hanksville.

At the motel Gerald paid for a night's lodging for the woman and children. She wept again when he forced a couple of twenty dollar bills into her hand. He told her to notify the sheriff if her husband didn't show up by the next day.

In the van Gerald said, "Lord, I'm in trouble now! There isn't time to loop on around by Salina and pick up those horses. Maybe I can get hold of somebody on the phone who'll trailer them down to Richfield for me."

He found a phone at the service station and made a number of calls. Returning to the van, he said, "Couldn't locate Donnie, so I called Rich. He's one of my mechanics. But he wasn't home either,

182

so I had to depend on his wife. Kind of an outspoken woman. She said, 'For fuck sakes, Gerald, don't you trust me? I know how to load horses in a trailer. Just tell me which ones to put in.'"

As they drove, Roger ignored the speedometer and could only surmise that on the straightaways the van was doing ninety or a hundred miles per hour. Despite a voluble impatience, Gerald forced himself to drive at a sedate pace through the little towns of Wayne County, and once beyond them, he resumed his former speed. Roger wasn't worried. Renewed in respect and affection for this first son of his, he felt perfectly resigned to sharing Gerald's fate, whether good or evil.

Gerald spoke again about his girlfriend. "I don't want any more weddings. But, Dad, I swear I'm going to pay for her operation. She's so damned uncomfortable. No matter what, I'll pay for her operation. If I was going to marry her, I could view it as an investment, couldn't I? But, my God, I do hope I have sense enough not to marry her."

It occurred to Roger that Providence had shaped this day in each of its events with the intent that Gerald should exert an intervening hand in Loraine's life. Gerald had the special qualities required for the task: brute strength, a forward will, and an exceptional empathy for women in trouble.

"I have information, son," he boldly said to Gerald, "that Little Sis, as you have always called her, is experiencing serious problems. She has been taking in a sordid man two or three nights each week, a member of the American Fork police force reputed to exact sexual favors from women he has arrested."

"For Christ's sake, what's happened to that girl?" Gerald exclaimed. "Has she gone wack-o? She's the prettiest kid that ever was. She doesn't have to settle for shit like that. I'm going to drive up there and tell her to chop him off."

"I wish you would," Roger said. "She respects you enormously. You could do her a world of good. But you mustn't let her know I've told you."

183

The sun was ready to dip behind the western mountains, and the sprinklers in nearby alfalfa fields splashed with rainbow colors. For the first time in weeks Roger felt reassured about Loraine. Though she might resist Gerald's counsel, the knowledge that a hardy, no-nonsense brother watched over her could not fail to have a healthy effect upon that miscreant of a policeman.

Soon they went over the summit of the Fishlake highway and passed by the junction to Koosharem.

"I imagine Mom's reunion is over by now," Gerald said.

Roger supposed so too and hoped Aspen had had a wonderful day. Moved by a surge of appreciation for his wife, he rejoiced in the prospect of seeing her within a couple of hours.

At dusk they left the Fishlake highway and entered the freeway, from which they caught a glimpse of the brilliant lights of the rodeo arena at the north end of Richfield.

"Lord, I hope those horses are there," Gerald kept saying.

It was dark by the time they arrived. At the entrance Gerald leaped from the van and ran. After Roger had parked, he made his way to the staging area where ropers and riders awaited their cue. There sat Gerald and Donnie upon their mounts with lassoes looped and ready. Gerald had no Stetson and wore the same open-throated white shirt and dress boots he had worn throughout the day.

Waving to his son and grandson, Roger went on to the grandstand and leaned against a pillar, awaiting the moment of their appearance. When it came, his heart went as chill as steel, and he uttered a prayer for their success. Donnie's loop sailed out with utter perfection and settled on the steer's neck. Hard upon it flew Gerald's loop, entangling the animal's heels. In a second the steer lay stretched out upon the ground. The two horses faced about and put tension on the ropes, and the judge declared their feat accomplished.

The crowd roared. Everyone knew it was the best performance of the entire rodeo. Roger continued to lean on the pillar, feeling assured that God would not fail to assist him in bringing safely back

into his presence all those over whom he had been give steward-
ship—Gerald, Donnie, Loraine, Aspen, and many others he could
not at this instant remember.

11. Instructions from a Retarded Aunt

Durfey and Aspen agreed she would drive him to Cedar City in time for the greenshow. In the meantime, they'd go back to the reunion. By the time they got there, the crowd had returned from Wentsworth's Hollow, where they had found more bones. Toby believed the seduced girl's grandson had dug up some of Hobart's bones in Wentworth's Hollow and reburied them in Lamb's Canyon. If this were the case, the contention between him and John would be an even draw.

Durfey contemplated the advantage of spreading a man's bones between two graves. Perhaps the process could be viewed as a seeding from which identical twins would arise on resurrection morning. Durfey was standing alone at this moment, carefully masticating a sandwich, and he had no one with whom to share his whimsy.

Strolling toward a chair, he was intercepted by Bradford Higley. Bradford extended a hand and asked Durfey's forgiveness for smashing his lip. "I was under the influence yesterday," he said. "I wasn't myself."

Durfey grasped Bradford's hand and asked forgiveness for biting off his ear. "I was under the influence too," he said. "Not of liquor. Just plain old malice."

They stood arm in arm awhile, reminiscing about their famous fight. It had started with Bradford picking a quarrel with a frightened boy from Junction and with Durfey, among the onlookers, directing sarcastic remarks toward Bradford. When Bradford and Durfey began to fight, the boy from Junction slipped away.

"You didn't have any business butting in on that kid's side," Bradford said. "That kid called me a pig fucker. Nobody calls me a pig fucker and gets off with it."

"I certainly shouldn't have butted in," Durfey agreed. "It doesn't pay to get involved in other people's disputes." He had by no means got over his loathing for this short, bald, muscular fellow, who truly would have been handsomer if his remaining ear had been taken off.

By now, counting partners as well as classmates, there were sixty or seventy people at the reunion, mostly clustered on lawn chairs and benches in shady places. Wandering about, Durfey heard confusing bits of conversation. Jim Foreman claimed God had touched Mikhail Gorbachev's heart with the spirit of *glasnost* so that Mormons could proselytize Russia. Shirley Sue reported that her grandson had kicked a hole in his dormitory wall. She hoped he'd settle down now and justify the expense of sending him to college.

At a bank of microphones under a canopy, Henry Ross announced John, Sharmane, and Anne. When the applause died down, these three began a soft, haunting western song, "Blue Shadows on the Trail." Durfey took a chair next to Pamela and Trelawny beneath a large umbrella. He slumped in his chair and pulled his blue golfing cap down over his eyes so an onlooker might have thought he was asleep. His half closed eyes rested on Aspen, who sat in a group across the lawn. For the moment it was a pleasure simply to watch her.

John, Sharmane, and Anne next sang "Oh, Bury Me Not on the Lone Prairie" and then "The Streets of Laredo." There was a soothing melancholy in the harmony of guitar, violin, and electronic keyboard. Sometimes John missed the center of his note, then found it and stuck. Anne's alto voice underlay his baritone with a sweet, bearable grief. Just now the past struck Durfey as having a living beauty, its losses cleansed, even burnished, by the solvents of time and distance.

He began to muse on the latest episode in the lost, fated love of Durfey Haslam and Aspen Marooney, namely, their fervent, sweaty near-copulation among the trees and grasses high in Koosharem Canyon. Already that remarkable, aberrant deed belonged to the distant past, his memory of it seeming hallucinatory and unreal.

He thought of an incident that had occurred, or, rather, that could have occurred and hadn't, in Antwerp in 1953, while he served with the U.S. Army in Europe. He was waiting in Antwerp for a packetboat to carry him on furlough to Dover. He had arrived by train from Frankfurt and had half a night to spend. He bought a supper of steamed mussels, crusty bread, and wine and then wandered the streets of Antwerp. Circling by the railroad station he saw a prostitute sitting, as they do in Belgium, inside a well lighted window. She reposed in a stuffed chair, her legs crossed demurely, her hands folded in her lap, her plump arms bare nearly to the shoulder. He stared because, despite differences in body and stature, she was, in her facial features, not unlike Aspen.

He walked rapidly away into dark cobblestone streets. When he came to the grand cathedral of Antwerp, he tried the door and found it open. He sat in unfamiliar awe amidst the shadowy columns, darkened arches, and immense black spaces of the nave. A spot of brilliant light fell upon the altar at the front of the church, and in an aisle innumerable small candles burned before a shrine for the dead. Though in a church, he lusted for the harlot who looked like Aspen Marooney. Yet he determined he wouldn't return to the street where she waited. It wasn't precisely for God's sake, and certainly it wasn't for Aspen's. It was for the sake of his future wife, whom he hadn't yet encountered. He was, as he saw clearly that night in the cathedral of Antwerp, a monogamous man.

He now contemplated the ruin of that monogamous man, weighing whether it was, as Aspen claimed, something short of total. He was willing to assert that when a respectable man and woman, nearing sixty and virtual strangers to one another, disrobe in a sundrenched grove, undeterred by their own ridiculous nudity, it is not for erotic pleasure. Rather it is for the perfection of their guilt, which is self-initiated punishment, a mode of self-replicating pain.

He heard the clatter of a lawn chair and saw that Pamela had positioned herself closer beside him.

"Are you asleep under that hat?" she asked.

"Yes. Soundly asleep."

"How's your lip feeling? Better, I hope."

"Yes, much better, thank you. I've been able to eat a sandwich."

"Tell me what you've been thinking about sitting here by yourself. You must have been thinking about something."

He pushed up his cap and looked directly at his visitor. Her smile was refreshing, engaging, and slightly ironic. At something close to sixty, she had managed to retain a girlish figure.

"As is proper at a reunion," he said, "I've been ruminating further on the now achieved destiny of the Class of '51. I've been particularly thinking that the ruling passion of our class has been greed. We were born in the midst of the Great Depression. Even as we graduated, the affluent society dawned. No other generation ever learned more quickly how to waste irreplaceable natural resources."

"Your children know how to much better than you."

"Well, of course, " he agreed, "we have trained our children to follow our example. However, we are self-taught, we invented the procedures."

"So have you truly got rich? Are you a man of wealth and leisure?"

"Oh, no," he said. "Wealth is an invidious thing. No matter how much you have, if someone else has more, you are an indigent."

He said that on the way to the reunion he and Elaine had passed a couple of casinos on the Nevada border. From a distance the casinos floated in a watery mirage. "Those casinos," he said to

189

Pamela, "tempt jaded Californians on their way home from Las Vegas into one last fling with Lady Luck. You have to understand that campfollowers from California's mines created Nevada. Nevada's gambling industry exists chiefly to service California's continuing fantasy of bonanza."

Going on, he said when he had moved to California, he ardently believed he would get rich. He smelled bonanza on the ocean breeze. He wouldn't have to game or gamble. Simple, honest toil would do the trick. But it hadn't. Now that his future had become his past, he could ruefully appreciate how much less than grand his material destiny had been.

He said, "Raisins on my cereal; asters in the bedding plots outside my condo; a Buick with leather-covered seats: these are the magnets that pull me along the track of daily life. By my parents' standards I'm rich. By the standards of my neighborhood, I'm merely comfortable—no, actually, I'm less than comfortable. In Newport Beach, a $30,000 Buick is a poor man's car."

"What a pity," Pamela said. "You are absolutely deprived."

"To bring this discussion of the destiny of the Class of '51 to its natural conclusion," Durfey went on, "I'll point out that after forty more years we will be represented by a handful of living cadavers in nursing homes. I hope I'm not among them."

"You're certainly in a fit of melancholy," Pamela said. "It's lucky I'm here to cheer you up."

John, Sharmane, and Anne sang a final song and put away their instruments. Durfey looked at his watch and said, "Gotta go. Gotta make Cedar City in time for the greenshow. I phoned the motel a while ago and left a message. Said I'd be there."

"Do you need a ride?"

"I've got a ride, thank you. Aspen says she'll take me."

"I might have known. Now the tongues will wag even more furiously. It's hard to judge which has provoked more interest among your classmates—your unfortunate incident with Bradford or the time you've spent with Aspen."

190

"Damn 'em all. Why don't they entertain themselves with more edifying topics?"

"May I say, even though it certainly is none of my business, it appears after all this time you and Aspen are still in love."

He looked away toward the vast stretches of aspens on the lower slopes and, above them, the firs bristling in the high steep canyon heads.

"I suppose," Pamela went on, "you and Aspen considered getting married while you were dating in high school."

"Certainly. That was totally on our minds."

"What kept you from it?"

"Aspen's parents, of course. They weren't going to have her marry a Haslam from Glenwood. I won't pretend to say whether Aspen is still in love with me. As for myself, past experience tells me I can expect to think about her fifteen or twenty times a day."

"Every day?"

"No exceptions. Day in and day out. No time off. No vacations."

Pamela now brooded wordlessly, as he supposed, over the imminent unknitting of two marriages of forty years' duration.

"There'll be no divorces," he reassured her. "We have come here and had a few words with each other, and now it's over. We've agreed to attend no more reunions."

Aspen led Durfey from cluster to cluster of their classmates, saying goodbye without pretenses. Amidst the hugging, hand shaking, kissing, and protestations, she told them all, "We've got to go. We've got to get Durfey back to Cedar City where his family is waiting."

"This is hostile behavior," John said, grasping Aspen by the arm. "You're busting up a good party."

"Nonsense," she said. "You'll get by just fine without us."

"That's the problem with a reunion," John said. "Sooner or later it's gotta end. Then you're right back where you started from with the big, long Lonely."

Evelyn responded to their goodbye with a suspicious stare. "Come on, you two!" she burst out. "Give us your real reason for leaving early."

"Ah, yes, our real reason," Durfey said. "The real reason is this. This reunion is Lotus Land. If we stay too long, if we accede to its anachronisms, we'll never escape to the present. I for one want to get on my way toward home. For all that I detest in it, California is my proper geography."

"You're so full of horseshit," Evelyn said.

"Thank you," Durfey said. "You couldn't honor me more."

He was surprised how many of the men hugged him with a frank embrace. When they were young and full of testosterone, they despised the thought of hugging another man. It occurred to Durfey that men were less and less masculine and more and more human as they got older. The world was better for that fact. It was too bad men didn't age sooner.

As they got into the car, Aspen was seething over what Evelyn had said. "What a bitch!" she exclaimed.

"Will she make trouble for you with Roger?"

"She'll try."

"We haven't been exactly discreet."

"We can start being discreet tomorrow," Aspen said. "In the meantime, Evelyn had better watch her wicked tongue."

Recovering her composure while she drove, Aspen began to talk about trivial things. She said she and Roger were fans of BYU athletics. Every year they bought season passes for football and basketball, driving from Salt Lake to Provo on weekends throughout fall and winter.

She began to tell Durfey about a tour of the Continent she and Roger had taken years ago. In the Prado museum in Madrid she remembered having noticed small ventilators open to the street. There were screens in the ventilators to keep out rats and mice but no glass to prevent the free air of heaven from circulating inside the museum.

"I thought, 'How quaint, how primitive!' And this shows you the nature of my mind. Instead of remembering the great works of art, I remember ventilators with screens in them."

They passed through Koosharem, turned onto the Fishlake highway, descended from the mountains, and got onto the freeway on the valley floor. Here, while Aspen accelerated to speeds of seventy-five and eighty miles an hour, Durfey asked her to talk about Gerald. "Give me something to visualize him by," he pleaded.

She said Gerald was a babbler till age four, not catching on till then that sounds were meant to signify something. He learned to walk earlier than many children, and once in possession of his legs had proved a renegade in church, breaking free and dashing up one aisle and down another.

The freeway skirted Richfield on high ground that allowed a pleasant perspective on the town and surrounding fields and pastures. Soon they saw exit signs for Elsinore, and Aspen informed Durfey that she had a great aunt—a younger sister to Adelia's mother—in Elsinore whom she hadn't seen in a long time. Since the old woman's house was close to the exit, she wondered whether there was time for a brief, ten-minute hello.

"I'm just thinking I might find it useful for future reference if you and I stop to see Aunt Brenda."

"Well, of course, then," he agreed. "Ten or fifteen minutes won't make much difference."

Aspen exited the freeway and parked by a cobblestone house with a wispy lawn and borders of hollyhocks. She and Durfey crossed over a gurgling ditch swept by a weeping willow. They knocked, and an old woman shuffled to the door and let them in. She was attired in a clean white sweat suit, much too baggy for her tiny frame. Her grey hair was neatly bobbed; her olive face was marked by liver spots.

At first Aunt Brenda seemed ill at ease. She sat in a rocking chair and responded to Aspen's questions with a vague misdirection. She stared at Durfey's bandaged lip, repeatedly rubbing her own upper lip.

"You don't have to sit in that chair," she said to Durfey. "You could sit in that one over there."

He dutifully took the other chair, and she shifted her rocking chair so that she faced Durfey rather than Aspen. She appeared to feel better now.

"Did you know Balis Haslam?" he asked her. "He was my father."

"Yes, I knew Balis Haslam."

"And who was your father?"

"Oh, dear, that's the problem," she said. "Did I have a father?"

"Of course you did," Aspen said. "And a mother too. Their names were Eugene and Hortensia. Don't you remember?"

"Oh, thank you! Yes, I remember them very well." She became wistful and added, "There were these important people doing a very fine thing up there. I was very much in the middle of all that."

"Where was this fine thing they were doing?" he asked.

"Who were we talking about?"

"Eugene and Hortensia," Aspen said. "Your father and mother. Do you remember them?"

"Oh, thank you!" she said with a wave of her hand. "I was very much in the middle of all that. They said, 'We've got to have Brenda along. Can't do without Brenda.'"

Durfey reconsidered Aspen's motive for stopping. He was starting to believe Aspen wanted this aged, debilitated woman to mitigate the impetuous grief of their goodbye. She wanted him to take consolation from the fact that neither of them would know the other in this condition. Neither of them would have to see the death of the other. They had had their dying, had become widow and widower, long ago while they had youth and strength for making the adjustment.

The old woman said other things that seemed close to rational. She mentioned Aspen's daughter Elizabeth and asked when she would be getting married.

"Not soon," Aspen said. "She's in New York working for a publishing firm."

"Well, I hope she doesn't get married outside the temple."

"Oh, no, not Elizabeth," Aspen said. "She'll insist on a temple wedding; you can count on that."

Brenda directed their attention to a large color print of General Schwartzkopf, hero of the Gulf War, which hung on her wall. "I love that man," she said.

Aspen said she loved him too.

"He's not a Mormon," the old woman said, "but I'd convert him so we could get married in the temple."

She paused to fidget with a bit of yarn she had found in her lap. She sang a couple of lines from an old hymn. Finally she said she couldn't enter a temple. For a time she had worked as a cook's assistant in the cafeteria of the St. George temple. It was her duty to arrive early and open an outside door to the kitchen. One morning when she tried the key, the door wouldn't open.

"God froze the lock. He didn't want me inside the temple that day. He froze the lock. So I quit working there. I never went back."

Aspen asked why God had frozen the lock. Brenda said she had something on her conscience. Aspen asked what it was. Brenda said she couldn't remember.

"Maybe it's all right now to go back," Aspen said. "People say God doesn't hold things against you forever."

"No, he doesn't want me inside. Never again." Brenda crossed her hands over her breast.

Aspen said they had to go. She helped the old woman to her feet and hugged her at great length. Brenda turned to Durfey with feeble, outstretched arms. He was startled by the tiny, bony bundle she made within his embrace.

Outside he waited beside the car while Aspen crossed the street and knocked at the door of the cousin who kept an eye on Brenda. The cousin, a large women in a calico apron, followed Aspen to the gate and smiled and waved while Aspen and Durfey got into the car and drove away.

"What was your Aunt Brenda's sin?" Durfey asked.

"Who knows?" Aspen said. "All she remembers is that she did sin."

Durfey asked himself how he could avoid attending the temple next time Elaine might want to go. People in his stake made a social event of going to the temple. They attended together and afterward repaired to someone's home for a potluck supper.

"It seems God has not locked you out of the temple," he said. "As I understand it, you have gone to the temple from time to time."

"As necessary," Aspen said.

"And you will continue to go?"

"I don't go because I want to. I go so I won't disappoint those who expect me to go."

"What do you think I should do?"

"The simplest way is to keep doing whatever you've done in the past."

"What if I can't?"

"Are you quite burning with guilt?"

"Yes."

"Then so am I," she said.

"Have we or have we not committed adultery?" he asked.

"If you think we have, then we have."

"The woman thou gavest me gave me of the tree, and I did eat."

"I stopped you in time," she protested.

"Your stopping was a mere technicality," he said. "The Russian winter drove Napoleon's troops from Moscow in 1812. There was no merit in that for the Russians, who retreated steadily without giving battle."

"So besides being Eve, I'm a Russian winter?" she said.

"Well, yes, and I'm a Russian soldier, saved through no valor of my own, and what kind of salvation is that?"

They returned to the freeway, which quickly turned westward into a gently rising canyon. Durfey watched over his shoulder as Sevier County, with its wide, fertile fields and rugged rim of mountains, disappeared—perhaps forever, he was thinking, given his present reluctance to return to a scene of repeated defeats. Soon the freeway made a junction with Interstate-15, and they sped southward on this twin concrete artery linking Mexico and Canada. To the east loomed another wall of mountains, black with timber. To the west opened the vast hazy valleys of the Great Basin.

They began to pass accumulations of Mormon crickets on the shoulder of the road. "We owe a great debt to these crickets," Durfey said. "Their invasion of pioneer farms provoked a feeding frenzy among the sea gulls nesting on the Great Salt Lake. That is why the California gull is the state bird of Utah."

"Thank goodness for obliging crickets."

"I must say, however, that crickets are among the ugliest creatures I know of—wavering antennae and bulging eyes and tiny buck-toothed mandibles. All in all, they remind me of Hans Wofford."

"Is he the one with the amputated finger?"

"Yes. He lost it to a jointer while I looked on."

"I didn't know him very well. Wasn't he the one who always wore stained yellow T-shirts?"

"He wore other colors, I believe. Always stained, of course."

"I heard Hans say today that you sometimes used to whistle at school assemblies. I didn't know that you whistled. How did I miss it?"

"There were a lot of things you didn't know about me."

"That's what we haven't had," she said bitterly. "We've never got to know each other."

"That's true," he said. "However, there are advantages to that fact."

People who fall in love, he pointed out, project enormous hopes on one another. If they marry or otherwise live together, they find out how vain those hopes are, and then, as likely as not, they don't

197

live together anymore. "You and I had our divorce, so to speak, before we became hateful toward one another."

She said, "I don't think I would have ever found you hateful."

Soon they had passed Beaver, Paragonah, and Parowan and began to see freeway signs declaring the approach of the Cedar City exits. During these final silent miles, he mulled the last sentence she had pronounced: "I don't think I would have ever found you hateful." These words grew on him with warmth and with some degree of consolation for the general debacle that this reunion had proved to be. He found himself feeling neither acrimony nor spite—feeling instead a simple resignation to the fated necessity of her temptations, deceits, confusions, and mistakes.

They left the interstate at the midtown exit. Aspen turned off the air conditioner, and they rolled down their windows and took in the fresh scent of lawns, flowers, and trees. She parked the car beneath overhanging boughs across the street from the college campus. He thanked her for the ride and climbed out.

"Durfey!" she called in that old inimitable tone of affection and command.

He got into the car again and she pulled his face against hers, saying, "Remember me."

"I will," he said. "I always will."

He crossed the street and entered the campus, where he was greeted by a pleasant building, manicured lawns, a gushing fountain, and bravely flapping banners. He strolled toward the building, an auditorium where Shakespearean plays were held on rainy nights. He paused at the entrance and turned for a final look. As he expected, she waited in her car beneath the overhanging boughs across the street. She waved, and he waved and then went into the building.

It was greenshow time and people were streaming toward the outdoor theater. He went into a rest room and carefully lifted the bandage and inspected the gash in his lip, which was patterned by sutures and a line of black blood. He reapplied the bandage and went out to the greenshow. A crowd milled in all directions. Elizabethan entertainers buttonholed passersby and played to them on the mandolin and krummhorn. Wenches vended tarts, fruit, and horehound candy.

He spotted his family seated upon the grassy mound beyond the greenshow stage—Elaine, Sally, Steve, and the two little girls. He fancied Elaine's face lighted with affection and relief when she saw him. He sat beside Elaine on the grass, and she stretched an arm across his shoulders.

"Daddy, where on earth have you been!" Sally scolded.

"I've been surveying the earth from the perspective of the Class of '51," he said. "It's a strange angle to see things from."

"Look at your bandage! No wonder Mama was so worried about you."

"It's the expiation of an old crime," he said. "Evil deeds have a way of returning to afflict you."

Elaine said very quietly, "You're back."

"It's been a hard experience," he said. "I'm glad it's over."

Almost immediately he was approached by the same apple vendor from whom he had made a purchase during his earlier attendance at the greenshow. Again this woman made a low curtsy, offering her basket of red apples and the same generous view of her bosom. On this occasion he bought apples for all his party, and the aging vendor thanked him with a buss on the bald pate. "There's a good 'un," she said with evident satisfaction. She went away, calling in her imitation English accent, "Apples 'ere, red apples 'ere."

"I sure as heck can't eat this apple," Durfey said.

"You poor dear," Elaine said. "You haven't had any dinner, have you?"

"A couple of lemon tarts will do," he suggested, "and maybe a carton of milk."

Just then he saw the three-legged dog hobbling his way down the slope. Unluckily Durfey was again seated near the sapling favored by the dog. It entered Durfey's mind to sit fast and see whether the animal wouldn't piss on him again. If ever in his life he deserved being pissed on, it was now.

Then it came to him he owed Elaine a seemly behavior. He was determined to be a sufficient husband or none at all. So he got up and shooed the dog away. For a moment this sturdy cripple stood in astonishment. He couldn't believe someone would object to his marking off his territory. Durfey shook a fist at him and the dog decided to go elsewhere. Durfey was thinking he'd simply continue going to the temple when there was no help for it.

"What was that all about?" Sally asked in reference to the three-legged dog.

"That dog and I have done business before," Durfey said. "As far as I'm concerned, he's ruined his credibility. You can't trust him." He sat again beside Elaine, and she leaned her cheek against his shoulder and he was greatly comforted.

12. The Neighbor's Peacocks

At dusk Aspen pulled into the Flying-J truck stop at the north Richfield exit. She filled the tank and washed insects from the windshield. Giant semis with whining gears rolled slowly by on their way to the diesel pumps in back.

The noisy semis seemed very close and real, as did the balmy dusk and fluttering moths beneath bright lamps. Durfey Haslam did not seem close or real. He was gone from the world of textures, depths, and presences.

Durfey would appear in the insubstantial vision of her mind almost any time of day or night. She'd see the ripple of his Adam's apple or the flex of his knuckles. She'd see his narrow hips and slanted shoulders and shiny bald head, or maybe sometimes the thick curly hair he used to have.

Was there any consolation in that? Not for the moment, certainly. Still, it wasn't time for tears. Tears comforted in cases of stress and frustration. They didn't help in cases of irretrievable loss. They made a person feel worse.

As she finished the windshield, a horn honked. It was Trelawny and Pamela Smith, pulling up to a pump. Aspen crossed the bay separating their cars.

"Heading home?" asked Trelawny, who had begun to fill his

tank.

"Tomorrow. We'll stay one more night with my sister Hope."

"We're outta here right now," Trelawny said. "Enough is enough. We'll make Brigham City by one-thirty or two."

Pamela got out of the car and said she'd had a marvelous time. She said she liked seeing Trelawny in a former environment.

"I wouldn't call it a former environment," Trelawny said. "I'd call it a new environment. This is forty years later."

"Wrong!" Pamela said. "A big tree may have a lot of rings in it but underneath is still the little tree it used to be."

"Now there's a non-sequiter for you."

"Oh, no," she said. "All those memories were pumping the whole bunch of you. You were reinventing 1951 like mad."

Aspen went inside to pay for her gas, followed by Pamela, who wanted a cola. "When we get together with Tyler and Mora," Pamela said while they stood in line, "they tell legends about Durfey. There's the story that when he was a boy, Durfey had a burro that'd drink beer and afterward Durfey would ride the burro staggering around town. Did you ever hear that one?"

"I heard it from Durfey."

"Do you suppose it's true?"

"If Mora said it happened," Aspen said, "it probably did. You couldn't rely on Durfey's stories. He used to practice a lot of cosmetic surgery on reality."

"I think I saw some of that in him at this reunion," Pamela said.

"Oh, not much. Not now. It's gone. He's into things like original sin and the Fall. That's what interests him now."

"Yes, I saw some of that too. He'd make a good Baptist!" They paid the cashier and strolled toward the door. "For whatever it's worth," Pamela went on, "you and Durfey added a great deal to the interest of this reunion. Everyone watched you with envy."

"Maybe disapproval is a better word."

"No, everyone recognizes you are sweethearts of the classic kind."

202

"Not sweethearts," Aspen protested. "Things were much too complicated for that."

Outside they found Trelawny replacing the dipstick under the hood of his car. "It's the engineer in him," Pamela said. "He checks the oil every time he gets a tank of gas. It's always up. He wouldn't keep a car that burned oil."

"Gotta follow procedures," Trelawny said.

Aspen said, "Trelawny is my true sweetheart. When we were barely fifteen, he and I went to a church dance in Gunnison with my parents. On the way back we cuddled in the back seat while Mother and Father had a conversation up front."

"I remember the dance," Trelawny said. "I don't remember the cuddling."

"You kissed me thirty or forty times."

"You fiend," Pamela said.

Trelawny went inside to pay for his gas. Aspen and Pamela leaned against a fender. A mile or so away the rodeo arena glittered in the gathering night. The voice of the rodeo announcer had a distant edge. Gerald and Donnie would be at the arena. They'd be saddling their horses, looping out their lassos, looking around with nervous glances. Last night Durfey had seen them. Only last night? How could things so recent seem so far away?

"Did you know Mora well?" Pamela asked.

"Better than any of the others in Durfey's family," Aspen replied. "She was a year behind me in school. Sometimes we chatted in the halls."

"She seems to know a good deal about what went on between you and Durfey."

"She probably knew more than anybody else. Sometimes she was our messenger."

Trelawny emerged from the convenience store. "Well, honey-bunch," he said, "let's climb in our flivver and roll."

"We've been talking about Tyler and Mora," Aspen said.

"Is there some news I ought to know about?"

"No news," Aspen said. "Just a bit of commentary. The sky didn't fall when they got married."

"Well, of course not."

"You must have attended their wedding reception."

"Sure," he said. "That was a couple of years after we graduated from high school."

"My sister Hope was there. She said it was comic to see the Haslams trying to make do in the society of the Smiths."

"Comic? I don't remember anything comic about it."

"Maybe it was only the Marooney family who found it comic," Aspen said.

"I wouldn't know."

Aspen went on. "I asked my mother once whether she disapproved of Tyler marrying Mora. She said certainly not. She said neither one of them was careful about grooming and dress."

"That's true," Trelawny admitted. "They're rather messy—both of them."

"Mora was okay for your brother," Aspen said bitterly. "But Durfey wasn't okay for me."

"I understand how things were between you and Durfey," Trelawny said. "I'm sure with the wisdom of hindsight, if you had things to do over, you'd both want to do them differently. But don't dig up all that old stuff, Aspen. That was a long time ago. It can't be helped now."

Pamela said, "Maybe it ought to be dug up. You can't blame her for feeling resentful."

"Of course not," Trelawny said. "But her life hasn't been ruined."

"Mora thinks Durfey's life was ruined," Pamela said.

"I wouldn't bring that up just now," Trelawny said. "Mora exaggerates things anyhow."

"My grandmother, Caroline Lorimer, didn't want to marry my grandfather, Thomas Chokling," Aspen said. "On the way to the wedding, my grandmother tried to run away. Her father, Cyrus

Lorimer, threw her bodily into a buggy, and they went on to Manti to the temple."

"So that's how it is," Pamela said to Trelawny. "Bondage runs in the family."

"Don't add fuel to the fire," Trelawny said impatiently.

"There's no reason for Aspen to hold it all in. She's with friends."

"I'd rather not make a scene," Aspen said.

Pamela took her hands. Pamela's hands were cool and dry. Aspen's hands were hot and sweaty.

"Go ahead and cry," Pamela said. She opened her arms and took her in, and she began to sob. "It's too bad you came to the reunion," Pamela said in the kindest voice. "You should have stayed home."

Aspen remained outside awhile in the dark, watching children bounce on the trampoline on Hope's front lawn. One of the little girls leaned against her legs. Aspen found a momentary comfort in placing a hand on the girl's sweet, sweaty hair. She was again feeling that families have mass and substance while individuals are petty and uncemented.

She went inside and found Hope and Cindy canning peaches in the kitchen. Hope had acquired three bushels of early windfall peaches which threatened to spoil before Monday. They had to be canned tonight, Sunday being a day of relentless rest in this house.

Aspen helped herself to remnants of dinner on the table and began recounting the day's events. Soon they heard Roger come in the front door. He paused to chat with Dan and Adelia, who had been watching TV in the family room. The TV went silent, and the three came into the kitchen.

"Ah, food!" Roger said cheerfully. He gave Aspen a kiss, got a plate, and joined her at the table.

"You're in fine fettle," Aspen said. "You must have had a successful day."

"We've had a great triumph as a family," he said. "Gerald and Donnie took first money in the team roping."

"A tribe of champions—that's the Sheffields!" Hope said.

"We got Gerald a part-time job out at Thatcher's ranch that winter he lived with us," Dan said. "That's where he learned to rope."

"You were awfully kind to take him in," Aspen said.

"He was restless," Hope said. "He just had to move on."

"You can lead a horse to water," Adelia muttered, "but you can't make him drink."

"Did he decide to buy an airplane?" Aspen asked.

"Not that particular airplane, thank goodness," Roger replied. "It was an antediluvian relic. Only by the grace of God have I come home safe and sound. We flew to the Cleveland dinosaur quarry. On both take-offs we got off the ground only at the last possible moment. In fact, on the second take-off we plunged over the end of the runway into a canyon where an updraft took us up."

"Oh, dear!" Adelia said. "That simply makes me tremble! Gerald has no business exposing you to such risks. I won't be able to put it out of my mind for a week."

"Now, Mother, please," Roger pleaded, "the danger is over. I won't get into an airplane of that sort ever again, I assure you."

"Well, do let me deliver these papers I've dug out into your hands," Adelia said, rising unsteadily. She went with a shuffling gait into the living room, where she said in an irritable voice, "What on earth would Aspen do if he had been killed? She'd be in a pretty fix, now wouldn't she?"

"Who got killed?" one of the grandchildren asked.

"Nobody, nobody at all."

In a moment she returned with packets of letters, legal documents, and unpublished poems for Roger's use in writing her life. "I don't know what weakness of character prompts me to turn these papers over to you. I feel more strongly than ever that you ought to do the life of Caroline Lorimer. There's somebody the young people of the family need to remember."

"We'll certainly write the life of our dear great-grandmother Caroline," Roger said. "That's a solemn pledge. But first, your life needs to be in print while the grandchildren and great-grandchildren still have the privilege of knowing you in person."

Aspen washed her hands, tied on an apron, and began peeling peaches, falling into a rhythm with Hope and Cindy. The three women sliced the rosy fruit in half, removed the pits, and dropped the halves into jars that stood steaming on the counter. As jars became full, they added water, capped them, and placed them with other jars awaiting two giant kettles that hissed and sizzled on the stove.

Roger came to the sink to watch their work. He slipped an arm around Aspen's waist. "I met John Izatt as I left the rodeo," he said. "John says the class had a memorable time in Koosharem Canyon talking and eating and playing volleyball and tossing horseshoes all day long. He says you all went on an excursion to dig up the grave of a gentile who was lynched in the canyon back in pioneer times."

"Yes, they dug in two places and found bones in both," Aspen said.

"John didn't tell me you dug in two places."

"No, he wouldn't have told you. He was pretty insistent that the fellow had been buried in Lamb's Canyon."

"If they found bones, somebody must be buried out there," Hope said. "As for a gentile supposedly lynched by the bishop of Elsinore, that old story is all a fabrication."

"It certainly is," Adelia agreed. "Who ever heard of a Mormon bishop who would take part in a lynching?"

"Be that as it may," Roger went on, "John says Aspen had a nice visit with Durfey Haslam and did the good deed of giving him a ride to Cedar City."

"Yes," Aspen said. "Elaine decided not to come today. Durfey wanted to make it back in time for the greenshow. Their daughter and family came along, and they've been taking in Shakespeare every evening in Cedar City."

"I wonder if somebody would slice me a bowl of those peaches," Roger said.

"Well, of course, you poor man!" Hope said, immediately pulling a bowl from a shelf. In a moment Roger was seated again at the table with a bowl of peaches and cream, liberally sprinkled with sugar.

"Roger is a naturally delicate eater," Adelia said, observing her son-in-law's manner of cutting each slice into small morsels with his spoon.

"Thank you for that vote of confidence, Mother," Roger replied. "Pleasure is greatest when taken in small portions."

"Proper eating is a form of elocution," Adelia continued. "The best that can be said about most men is that they get so much satisfaction from food that you can almost forgive their rude way of eating."

Aspen locked her eyes on her fingers, busy pulling skin from steaming peaches with a paring knife. She imagined the dark knitting of her sister's brows, the consternation of her slightly pursed lips. She knew Hope's thoughts as well as if she herself were thinking them. In fact, she *was* thinking them, if not in the same phrasing, at least with the same intent:

"You've spent hours and hours alone with Durfey Haslam, with whom long ago, so you have confessed, you had illicit sex on many occasions. At the very least, it seems you care nothing about appearances, nothing about discretion. At the very worst—well, God forbid, but I can't help having this thought! Aspen, dear sister, what in the name of heaven have you done today?"

"While I was driving Durfey to Cedar City this afternoon," Aspen said in a calm, casual voice, "I left the freeway at Elsinore and paid a visit to Aunt Brenda. Durfey was in a hurry, and I promised I'd not take long. I was afraid it'd be too late when I came back up the road and she might already be in bed. I also stuck my head into Cousin Betty's house for a second or two. Betty is cheerful and in good health. Aunt Brenda is much more feeble than the last time I visited her. I feel so guilty not seeing her more often."

"I'm glad you stopped," Hope said. "That was nice to do."

Who could accuse a woman of illicit deeds who stops to visit a senile aunt? Certainly not Hope, whose last statement was, as Aspen had expected, scarcely more than a weary, reassured murmur.

Roger was still awake when Aspen slipped into bed beside him. Snuggling against her shoulder, he told her more about his happy day. He found pleasure in the farms in Wayne County, the fanciful erosions of Capitol Reef, and the wide plains beyond the San Rafael. He had found even greater pleasure in Gerald's congenial behavior. Gerald had in fact seemed to make a point of treating him with respect.

"No father could be more flattered than I was today."

"I'm so truly glad," Aspen said.

Roger described in detail Gerald's good deed in behalf of the woman and children stranded on the road through Goblin Valley. "He insisted on paying her lodging at the motel in Hanksville," he told Aspen. "The poor thing was totally grateful. And I was deeply touched by his generosity. I have never lost faith in that boy. All will be well with him yet. You'll see it happen!"

Satisfied by this communication, Roger rolled onto his back, thrust his feet about as if loosening the tightly bound sheet, and soon breathed in the deep, comfortable cadences of sleep. Aspen now felt the old tug of penitence, the old desire that her half love for this good man be made whole. She saw again, as she had so many times before, that innocence is an attractive force, and in the absence of a counter force, a tired, yielding will slides toward it.

She fell into a fitful sleep, so disturbed that she had the sensation of waking over and over, yet later, when she became truly awake, she realized she had only dreamed of waking. She also dreamed other dreams, so vague and incoherent that it was, again, only upon truly waking that she realized these other dreams were fragments of a single dream, which gradually became incarnate in the image of two incredibly muscular men, unclothed, who stood in a retreating chariot pulled by champing horses. She had never before seen such rippling, well-muscled backs, such bulging, sensuous buttocks, and she knew they belonged to the Father and the Son, who drove away from her, their glory intended for others.

She awoke with a start and perhaps a cry—she wasn't certain. Then she heard the shrill crow of one of the cockerels and knew her sleep was ended. She put on her robe and went to the bathroom. Examining her face in the mirror, she was irritated to find her welt still faintly visible. She went to the kitchen and poured a glass of chilled water from the refrigerator. She drank half the water and swirled the rest around in the glass, looking down into it under the glow of the open refrigerator. Water splashed on the floor, and she thought of the pool on the Sevier where girls with little breasts and scant pubic hair launched themselves off a rope from an overhanging cottonwood bough.

"Have we or have we not committed adultery?" Durfey asked a dozen times during their stay in the grove high in Koosharem Canyon.

Intentions count, as he had pointed out. "If there's been any virtue in our last-moment forbearance, it's all been on your part, though, as you've admitted, you did lay a snare for me."

"Yes, I laid a snare for you."

He had brooded darkly and persuasively on the inevitability of sin. "The only hope for anyone," he concluded, "is in the dim possibility that God will surprise us with salvation, that he'll give it to us despite our unworthiness."

There was no use thinking about that. She cherished her unworthiness too much. All these years she had indulged in fantasies of confession. No more of that. As Durfey said, reunions give a new view on old situations. If she had learned anything at this reunion, it was that her secret had long ago become as indispensable as breathing. She had confessed nothing by sharing her secret with Durfey, informing him as one informs an accomplice. Down some dark Fallopian conduit of her spirit swam a seminal power. Each

210

year her secret doubled and redoubled its cells. It fed, it stirred, it exerted weight within her abdomen—vital, reassuring, beloved. Without it there was no such person as Aspen Marooney.

Hope put on a simple breakfast of cold cereal because it was Sunday. People lined up for showers, combed their hair, pressed Sunday dresses. Although Roger wanted to go to church in Richfield, Aspen reminded him Evelyn expected to go home in good time. Missing church made him gloomy.

"Cheer up," she said. "You can go twice next Sunday."

He gave her a perplexed glance. Why did she make silly jokes? Yes, why indeed, Aspen asked herself.

When it was time to say goodbye, Aspen lingered in the feeble embrace of her mother. "God bless you, dear Mamma," she said with a sudden, bitter grief.

Each time she said goodbye to her mother, she wondered whether it would be the last. Time after time it hadn't been. One day it would be, and then with astonishing speed this beloved, perplexing, iron-willed woman would become no more than a shadowy ripple in the currents of the past.

Aspen and Roger drove to Shirley Sue's house and Aspen went in to get Evelyn. She sat a minute while Evelyn finished her coffee.

"It was a good reunion, thanks to you and Evelyn," Aspen said to Shirley Sue.

"A damned good reunion," Shirley Sue agreed.

"Next time, they can get somebody beside me to do the publicity," Evelyn said. "You can't locate all of them. People move around too much. I missed Josh Pringle. At the last minute he wrote me and said he'd found out about the reunion from Janie Schuster, but if we didn't want him that was sure fine with him, and though he had time off he wasn't about to come. So I wrote back and said, 'Good, we didn't want you at this one, and please stay away next time too.'"

"You never wrote any such thing," Shirley Sue said.

Evelyn drained her cup and went into the bathroom. "Don't you think Durfey Haslam's nose has got bigger than it used to be?" she called through the open door.

"Like your butt," Aspen called back.

"Look who's talking," Evelyn retorted.

"Hey, lay off!" Shirley Sue said.

"It wasn't me grabbing every opportunity to hit on an old flame!" Evelyn said.

"For Christ's sake, Evelyn," Shirley Sue objected, "we're not Victorians. It's not as if a man and woman have sex every time they go somewhere together."

"Who said anything about sex?" she called through the open door.

Evelyn got her bags and they kissed Shirley Sue goodbye and went out. Roger opened the trunk and pulled out some of his and Aspen's bags and began to rearrange the load. Evelyn and Aspen got in the car, and Evelyn said, "I'm not going to mention Durfey in front of Roger."

"I don't care if you do."

"Of course you do. I can't breathe his name without you sticking your fist down my throat."

Roger got into the car and the two women fell silent. They zoomed along the freeway to Salina, exited near Gerald's shop, which was closed for Sunday, and headed up Highway 89 toward Gunnison. Evelyn and Roger got into a discussion on meglomarts, as Evelyn called them, giant stores that house groceries, drugs, bakery, pharmacy, and delicatessen under a single roof. Evelyn returned two or three times to the point that a meglomart was the opposite extreme of the neighborhood shop that sold only one thing, like bakery products or meat.

From almost the beginning of the discussion, Aspen let her mind wander to other topics. As they approached Gunnison, she could see a chalky white cone on the crest of the eastern mountains. Once, long ago, from this same highway, Durfey had pointed out this high chalky cone.

"It's called Molly's Nipple," he said.

"It's also called Bishop's Prick," Aspen replied.

"Holy mackerel! What a terrible word for a woman to use!"

"I didn't learn it at home," she said.

It was a summer Sunday and the sky was broken by patches of blue and clots of brooding clouds. Durfey's brother Curtis tended the sheep in Fry Pan Canyon, and Aspen had the day off from the lodge without her parents' knowing. Aspen and Durfey were on the loose in his old pickup; nobody knew where they were but themselves. They left Highway 89 at Fairview and for the rest of the day followed unpaved roads. They took the Skyline Drive south to the Fremont River and finally, late in the day, crossed the ridge north of Thousand Lakes Mountain in a rainstorm. They got stuck and Aspen had to drive while Durfey pushed from the rear. When they were out of the mire, she got out to let him into the driver's seat and they kissed passionately while standing in the mud. Still holding her, he lapsed into moodiness.

"My dad and mom haven't got around to having my little brother Gilbert baptized," he said.

"I'm sorry to hear that," she said. "They should do it."

"When we're married," he said, "we'll go to church on Sunday."

"Yes," she agreed. "Every Sunday without fail."

"Shall we make love in the mud?" he said, brightening.

"Not if I've got to be on the bottom."

"I've heard of it being done," he said.

They got into the pickup and drove on, and she saw, from the moody, uncharacteristic silence into which he lapsed, that his lust and daring and relish for the quaint and unconventional had been displaced by grief and a longing for serenity and regeneration.

Remembering that, here in the presence of Roger and Evelyn, whose discussion now centered on the margin of profits in the retail industry, Aspen returned to the unspeakable event that had occurred yesterday in Koosharem Canyon. She and Durfey had removed their clothes methodically, laying each piece upon the

213

trampled herbage as yet another offering to candor, and at last she lay back upon this makeshift blanket and raised her arms, beckoning him to come, and as he came down gently upon her she saw on his face a reticence and weariness and, yes, she also saw that old grief, that old longing for serenity and regeneration.

While the car sped between Gunnison and Levan, she saw rising in the north the high pale peaks of Nebo. Clouds floated in a blue sky, their billowy sunward side brilliant with promise and hope. How could it have been adultery when she had felt so cheated of a final solace? How could it have been adultery when she had forfeited Durfey to hope?

Watching the clouds over Nebo, she was bold to pray for Durfey. She asked God, in view of Durfey's reticence and weariness and longing for regeneration, to surprise him someday with salvation.

Aspen and Roger got home mid-afternoon. Robin and Julian were gone, doing the Sunday routine with their friends, and the big house was empty. Roger toted their bags into their bedroom and unpacked. He carefully sorted the clothes they had worn from those they hadn't got around to putting on. No indiscriminate washing of clean clothes for Roger. Efficiency was his middle name.

When she saw him next, he had put on a white shirt and tie and was reading in the Book of Mormon—his way of salvaging a bit of the Sabbath. Aspen, however, put on jeans and went outside to do a little work in the enclosed vegetable garden. She was shocked with what she saw. Somebody, Julian probably, had left the gate open, and Ted's peacocks were inside foraging on her plants. As far as she could tell from a distance, they had demolished the green tomatoes and Brussels sprouts.

She returned to the house and sat awhile across from Roger. At last he noticed she was there and asked what was the matter. He flushed red when she told him. He went out to have a look for himself and came back to his recliner, muttering, "This is outrageous."

By then she had begun to get control of herself and no longer thought about going to some shopping center and buying a scope-sighted rifle. The situation had begun to seem funny. Destiny was involved. They had gone to a lot of trouble to build an enclosure for her garden. She had hired the metal poles set in concrete and had a gate built, and she herself had attached the sections of wire netting to the sides and top. Cosmic forces didn't want her to have a garden during this particular summer. Or maybe they had offered a trade-off she had failed to recognize, which was that the price of having a garden was staying home from the forty-year reunion of the Class of '51.

"This is the last straw!" Roger said.

"I'd better go chase them home and see what's left of my plants," Aspen said. "I think I can be trusted now not to do anything drastic."

"Drastic measures are called for," Roger said grimly. "I have asked Ted to keep up his peafowl dozens of times. Will he heed the earnest plea of a kindly neighbor? Apparently not. Then let him heed a neighbor's wrath!"

He got up and took her high-gauntleted gloves from the coffee table where she had set them and went outside. She followed as far as the rear deck.

"Don't do something crazy," she called.

He walked down the path, entered the enclosure, and closed the gate behind him. The half dozen peafowl, two of them cocks with lush, iridescent plumage, moved to the opposite side of the enclosure. Roger held the gloves by the tops of the gauntlets like heavy leather flails. Suddenly he charged with smashing, spanking blows. Birds exploded in all directions, crying, shrieking, bouncing repeatedly off the wire netting in a vain attempt to escape. Heedless of the vegetables beneath his feet, he whirled and chased and smashed, and when he saw bent, crumpled tail feathers shedding off the cocks he went after them even more furiously. At last, when he opened the gate and let them all go, the cocks were strange, unbalanced things without a shred of a tail.

215

He came back to the deck and sat in a redwood chair. He was white and trembling. His sweat looked cold. "There," he said, "I have instructed Ted in matters of neighborliness."

Soon he bent his face into his hands and wept.

"It's all right," Aspen said, "absolutely all right. Ted had it coming."

She sat on an arm of the redwood chair and put her arm around his shoulders, leaving it for others to judge whether a director of counseling for Deseret Industries should beat peacocks trapped in a pen.